FOR A. R. TORRE

A Fatal Affair

"Nothing is remotely routine in Torre's heady brew of serial murder spiced with fraud, torture, impersonation, and assorted celebrity hijinks . . . you won't put it down till every last drop of blood has been shed."
— *Kirkus Reviews*

"A thriller with surprises aplenty and a breezy pace that includes well-written characters and the singular challenge of looking for truth 'in a sea of professional liars and seducers,' this novel is sure to have wide appeal."
— *Library Journal*

A Familiar Stranger

"A whiplash suspenser that's a model of its kind."
— *Kirkus Reviews*

"The author skillfully reveals the characters' many lies and secrets. Torre knows how to keep the reader guessing."
— *Publishers Weekly*

The Good Lie

"Ambitious and twisty . . . Great bedtime reading for insomniacs and people willing to act like insomniacs just this once."
— *Kirkus Reviews*

"This kinky tale is compulsively readable."
— *Publishers Weekly*

"A blend of serial-killer story, court cases, and even romance, this is a tricky story that will keep readers going."

—*Parkersburg News and Sentinel*

Every Last Secret

"Deliciously, sublimely nasty: *Mean Girls* for grown-ups."

—*Kirkus Reviews*

"Torre keeps the suspense high . . . Readers will be riveted from page one."

—*Publishers Weekly*

"A glamorous and seductive novel that will suck you in and knock you sideways. I love this story, these characters, and the raw emotion they generated in me. I devoured every word. Exceptional."

—Tarryn Fisher, *New York Times* bestselling author

"Raw and riveting. A clever ride that will make you question everyone and everything."

—Meredith Wild, #1 *New York Times* bestselling author

THE
LAST
PARTY

OTHER TITLES BY A. R. TORRE

THE LAST PARTY

A. R. TORRE

THOMAS & MERCER

Text copyright © 2024 by Select Publishing LLC
All rights reserved.

Published by Thomas & Mercer, Seattle

www.apub.com

Amazon, the Amazon logo, and Thomas & Mercer are trademarks of Amazon.com, Inc., or its affiliates.

ISBN-13: 9781662519574 (paperback)
ISBN-13: 9781662519581 (digital)

Cover design by Shasti O'Leary Soudant
Cover image: © Lukasz Szwaj / Shutterstock; © Nattapol_Sritongcom / Shutterstock; © Manuela Rohwetter / ArcAngel

Printed in the United States of America

Mortui vivos docent.
The dead teach the living.

CHAPTER 1

PERLA

That family stuck out right from the start. We were all looking at them, even before it happened.

—*Cheryl Higgins, waitress (Tony's Truck Stop)*

The woman's face changed right before she fell. She was chewing, her eyes glazed, bored with the conversation at her table, her mind on other things. I watched her because I *felt* her. I felt that disconnect. Also, watching her was more interesting than listening to Grant talk about birds.

"... What's crazy is that their migratory patterns aren't based on ..."

I swear my husband intentionally set out to pick a hobby that would bore me to death. The other night, he stopped mid-thrust, head raised, ear cocked to one side, because he thought he heard a bearded woodpecker.

The woman could use some fillers in the deep crevices that ran from her nose to the corners of her mouth. It'd make her look ten years younger. I glanced at Grant, making eye contact long enough to prove that I was taking studious mental notes on the fascinating increase in swallows this time of year; then I flicked my gaze down to my plate—a sad display of rubbery grilled chicken, wilted spinach, and a few blue-berries—and back to the woman, two booths over, facing me.

She would never be able to afford fillers, so I kept that insight to myself, despite its potential impact on her face. No one in this diner was stepping anywhere near a plastic surgeon's scalpel unless it was for a boob job. The parking lot was a crowded mess of bumper-stickered, cheap vehicles with bald tires and dented fenders. In the midst of them, my Range Rover gleamed, a visual reminder that we were in the wrong place. We should have waited until we got back into town to eat. Instead, we were wedged into a sticky booth with three plates of food that would give us all diarrhea.

The woman's eyes locked with mine. I started to look away but then noticed her fingers clawing at the neck of her Ozzy Osbourne T-shirt, her mouth gaping open. I watched, fascinated, as her eyes rolled toward the ceiling and she tilted to her left, a chubby bowling pin slowly tipping over.

Her arms didn't move, her body was limp, and she fell to the tile without trying to catch herself.

It was a quick, hard hit, and she didn't bounce or roll; she stayed stuck on her side, one arm pinned underneath her, the other suspended in the air like a bicycle kickstand.

A hush fell in a tight knot around her body; then it spread, like a growing pool of blood, infecting each table in an outward circle until everyone in the diner was craning toward the sight, their faces alarmed, reactions ricocheting around the room. I pierced a charred chunk of chicken with my fork and placed it in my mouth, chewing quietly.

A delayed scream came from the woman's tattooed seatmate, who launched her rail-thin body out of the booth and onto her knees beside her friend. Looking frantically around the restaurant, she shrieked, "Someone call 9-1-1! Is anyone here a doctor?"

The room fell silent as heads swiveled—right, left, right. I sighed and set down my fork, then raised my hand.

"Perla," Grant warned, and I shot him a hard look before scooting out of the booth and standing.

A wave of murmurs swelled at my reveal. I snagged a napkin from a dispenser on the next table and wiped my hands clean as I approached the prone woman.

"You're a doctor?" her friend asked as she fisted the woman's shirt.

"Step back," I snapped. "Does she have any food allergies?"

"I—I don't know." The woman looked to the couple beside her for help. "Maggie? Frank? Do you know if Bev has any allergies?"

Bev. She looked like a Bev. I knelt on the sticky tile and rolled the woman onto her back. Running my fingers quickly over the back of her head, I could feel that there was a knot where she had collided with the floor, but no blood or split skin. I bent forward and put my ear close to her mouth, waiting for any sign of breathing.

"She's not breathing," I announced. The room hummed in response, and everyone's attention was on me. Waiting to see if I saved this woman or killed her.

I pulled open her lips and checked her mouth for any food. I worked my fingers down her tongue, trying to see if there was anything there. The thin canal was slimy and warm and I quickly withdrew my hand. "Has someone called 9-1-1?" I asked, sneaking a glance in the direction of our booth. My husband stood at the head of it, our daughter in front of him, both watching my every move.

I bet a burrowing owl could have landed on Grant's shoulder right then and he wouldn't have even turned his head.

"Yes," the waitress said. "They're on their way. They said to begin—"

"CPR," I interrupted, my arms locked and hands linked on the center of Bev's chest, one on top of the other. I started the compressions, counting them in my head as I went. Bev had a thin gold chain with a cross on it, the necklace tangled and bunched in her dingy yellow curls. She looked to be my age—but a much harder thirty-five than me. Her face was a sea of sun damage, with a layer of extra fat that underlined her round chin. I hadn't gotten much from my mother, but I had inherited her expressive brown eyes, slightly upturned nose, and oval face. The crooked smile and emotional damage, I got from my father.

Twenty-seven, twenty-eight, twenty-nine, thirty. I stopped and pinched the woman's nostrils shut, noting the chip in my forefinger's polish. *I should call first thing in the morning and make an appointment at the salon.* I placed my lips on hers and tried not to recoil at the contact. I inhaled and pushed my breath into her mouth, then repeated the action. Thirty compressions, two breaths. Easy, yet everyone was gawking at me as if I were performing miracles.

I loved it.

I pulled off and returned my hands to her chest, resuming the compressions. I was on the seventeenth of the second set when her body shuddered beneath my palms.

"What was that?" Bev's friend still knelt beside me, and I glanced over at her while I continued, annoyed at her proximity. I shifted away from her, my pale-gray slacks rubbing against the floor. I'd have to throw them away after all this.

Bev was coming back to life. I could feel it, and the power rush was intoxicating. I smiled and continued my work. *Twenty-five . . . twenty-eight . . . thirty.* I pinched her nose and repeated the breaths, no longer fixating on the fleshy feel of her lips or the emerging zit staring at me from the center of her forehead.

"Come on," I muttered, restarting the compressions, my own heart seeming to sync with the counts as I forced the life back into her.

She coughed, and something flew from her mouth and hit my shoulder. I cursed and stopped the work, rolling her away from me as she coughed again, spittle spraying out.

"Bev!" the friend yelped. "Oh my God, Bev!"

Faint sirens sounded, and I raised my gaze from the woman to my family. My daughter bounced on her toes, grinning at me with pride as the entire restaurant broke into conversation and applause. Someone offered me their hand and I took it, heaving to my feet. Smiling at the room, I raised a hand in acknowledgment of their recognition. Everyone was beaming—everyone except for my husband, who glared at me, his face dark with anger.

CHAPTER 2

JOURNAL OF SOPHIE WULTZ

Hi. I'm Sophie Wultz. I'm eleven, almost twelve. This is the first entry for my summer writing project. We're supposed to write every day for at least fifteen minutes. On the first day of school, we're going to turn in our entries, and this really seems like an attempt for Mr. Alford to spy on the inner thoughts of his sixth-grade students. Bridget says Mr. Alford is a pervert, and I'm withholding judgment for now, but this assignment seems to support her opinion.

For that reason, I won't be turning in these pages. I'll be writing different, boring entries that will seem like they took fifteen minutes, but actually I'll whip through them in five. I'm a very fast writer. Or typer. Both. We took typing tests in class, and I was one of the fastest in the class. 67 WPM, that's how fast I was. At that speed, I could be a stenographer. Those are the people in court that type while people talk. I'd like that job, though I'd be tempted to make up things as I typed. Sometimes people say the stupidest things. When I watch Court TV, I can immediately spot the liars. Sometimes the lawyers can too, and they trip them up with questions, but a lot of the time, they don't. They just finish their questions and walk back to their seat, even though the person is clearly hiding something.

Dad says I'd be a good lawyer, but I don't know if that's what I want in life. Sitting in a courtroom all day long seems boring. I'd rather be an actress. Flying all over the world to act in movies with famous stars . . . that seems way better. Plus, you get training in things like martial arts and accents and horseback riding.

Dad said I can be anything I want to be, but Mom hates the idea of me being an actress. She wants all of the attention for herself, and I want all of the attention for myself. The only difference is that I'm a kid—and an only child—so I'm supposed to get all of the attention, and she's supposed to fix my lunches and buy me the right clothes, and take me and my friends to the mall, and if she doesn't like that—too bad. That was the deal she signed up for when she had a kid.

Plus, if she didn't want me to act, she shouldn't put on a show so much. I can see how much she enjoys acting—but it's not really acting. Like Dad says, it's lying. She lies and I like to lie too, so why not get paid for it and become famous and marry a movie star while you're at it?

I'm never going to have kids. No stretch marks, or baby vomit on my clothes, or packs of diapers in my purse. I'm going to be tall and gorgeous and sip champagne in dark bars while hot guys whisper in my ear and tell me that I'm beautiful.

I'm not beautiful now. Or tall. Or anything other than a decent soccer player with above-average typing skills and a flat chest.

That's me. Sophie Wultz. Normal with a capital N. But not for long. One day, I'll be famous.

CHAPTER 3

PERLA

I flipped down the passenger-side visor and opened the mirror, studying my makeup and reviewing the damage. My lipstick was shot to hell, so I opened my purse and withdrew the spare tube I kept there for emergencies.

Grant, who hadn't said a word since we left the diner, gunned my SUV up the highway's on-ramp.

I glanced at his handsome profile. "Okay, what? You just going to punish me with silence? You clearly have something you want to say."

"I can't believe you did that."

"Saved someone's life? I know, terrible of me." I twisted the bottom of the tube, pushing out the pale-mauve color.

"I thought it was supercool," Sophie chimed in from the back seat. "I'm going to tell all my friends and put it in my journal."

"You are *not* going to tell all of your friends," Grant instructed. "What your mother did was wrong."

"Oh, please." I rolled the color onto my lips. "It was a necessary evil."

"It wasn't. You could have done all of that without telling anyone you were a doctor."

"I didn't tell them that. They assumed."

"You raised your hand when they asked if anyone was a doctor. And then, when the ambulance arrived, you were giving them instructions! You told them you were a neurosurgeon from Green Bay."

"Whatever. I was having some fun. She was in the clear by then. Why does it matter if I fibbed a little?"

"'A little'? Perla, you don't know jack about medicine outside of that medical drama you watch."

I pressed my lips together, setting the color.

"If you want to pretend to be a lawyer and argue with a stranger about constitutional rights, fine—but this is taking your games too far. What if she had died, Perla? Or what if there had been a real health professional there? Someone who had called you on your bullcrap?"

"There wasn't a complete set of teeth in that building," I said dryly. "You think there were doctors eating at that shithole?"

"Swear jar!" Sophie sang out. "Mom, you owe me a dollar."

I ignored her. "You're just mad because they all clapped."

"I'm mad that you preened. And you let them buy our lunch. We should have bought their lunch—hell, the whole restaurant's lunch—for having to be pawns in your stupid little game."

"Swear jar!" Sophie clapped. "Dad, you too!"

"This is ridiculous." I capped the lipstick and tossed it back into my purse. "I did something nice for someone. I don't deserve to be treated like a criminal for it."

Grant's jaw worked as he changed lanes to pass a slow car. He stayed silent for a minute, and when that one minute stretched into two, I reached down and fished my wallet out of my purse. After unzipping the white leather satchel, I withdrew a five-dollar bill and passed it back to Sophie. "Give us a credit for the next few, will you?"

"You got it." She beamed at me and folded the bill in half, then quarters, and stuck it in her journal.

"So . . ." I checked my watch and did a quick calculation of how long it would take us to get home. "What do you guys think about dessert at Café Perla and then a movie night in the theater?"

Sophie let out a whoop of approval, and I glanced over at Grant. If there was a key to my husband's heart, it was carved out of labors of love and family time. He had spent an insane amount of money on the theater room in the basement, and movie nights were an easy shortcut around his anger. His fury would weaken with a few hours of quality time with Sophie, capped off by a steamy session between the sheets. I'd pay that penance. It was worth it for the moment when the diner had burst into cheers, everyone's eyes on me.

Saving a life had been thrilling. Too bad it couldn't compare with the inverse.

CHAPTER 4

Perla's home always looked like a magazine shoot. Even in the crime scene photos that were leaked online, you could see how meticulous and beautiful it was, despite all the blood.

—Kennedy Wells, neighbor and interior designer

Eight years ago, we built our home, using an architect to create a custom floor plan that took our dreams and brought them to life. We analyzed the school districts and picked a private gated community in Pasadena that offered estate-size lots. We picked one of the bigger ones on a cul-de-sac that backed up to conservation land.

I had thrown any budget out the window and used my inheritance to fund the project. The result was a nine-thousand-square-foot home that paired twenty-two-foot ceilings with an all-cream interior, eight fireplaces, walls of bookshelves, fine art, and bold wallpaper prints.

We designed an expansive first floor with double living areas, a massive kitchen and pantry, dining halls, and his-and-her workshops and craft rooms. On the second floor was our giant primary suite, complete with a steam shower, spa, and three walk-in closets. Both our offices and a laundry room bisected that level, with two guest rooms and Sophie's room on the other side of the floor. The basement level held the theater, a gym, an extra guest suite, a wine cellar, and storage.

I kept the home in order—a place where dreams could come true. The problem was that some of our dreams were the stuff of nightmares. I set one oven to 350 degrees and the other to Warm. Sliding open one of the island's wide double drawers, I surveyed the perfectly organized grid of long-stemmed silverware. After selecting a beverage whisk and coffee spoon, I placed them on the counter, then turned to Sophie. "Is your phone in the box?"

"Yep." She nodded toward the small wooden box where she surrendered her cell each evening after dinner. It was a halfhearted attempt to protect her from social media, predators, and the vacant soul suck created by an addiction to constant entertainment—but also provided a level of control that I relished.

"Have you gotten your father's order?"

"Oh yes." She pressed her palms together like she was praying. "He wants brownies and milk with a . . ." Her forehead crinkled as she tried to remember. "With a . . ."

I waited, already certain of what Grant would want. My husband was a man of order, precision, and consistency, which was how I knew that at that moment he was putting on his dark-navy pajama pants, gray socks, and a soft white T-shirt. Then he'd take a heartburn pill and brush and floss his teeth, despite the fact that he'd eat dessert and popcorn and have to do it again before bed. After sex—which would occur on top of the blankets, missionary position, followed by me on top—he'd shower, then dress in silk-blend boxer briefs and a fresh white T-shirt. No socks, because he enjoyed the feel of our mattress's heated footer function, which he set for two hours each night, on medium. He'd place his phone on the charger at least six feet away from his pillow before getting under the covers.

The predictability had annoyed me early on. Now I appreciated it. The ultimate power in a marriage is the manipulation ability of knowing how and when your spouse will act and react.

"Crap. Be right back." Sophie spun on her heel and darted toward the stairs. I got to work on the brownies, my preparations quick and efficient as I mixed the batter and poured it into a mini pan that would produce four brownies. The rest of the batter, I scraped into the trash. That was the last thing I needed—an extra plate of sugar and calories, tempting us all. Tonight would be bad enough on our diets. I pulled a tub of vanilla bean ice cream from the freezer and placed it on the counter to thaw.

Sophie, whose dessert order was also predictable, would want s'mores and a Coke. Grant would gripe at her over the negative effects of caffeine, all while sipping his own heart attack in a cup.

With the brownie pan in the oven, I created Sophie's s'mores, using the microwave to melt her marshmallow-and-chocolate sandwiches. By the time she returned, I was arranging the first one on a white china plate.

"Okay, he said he wanted brownies and milk and an Irish coffee."

"Got it," I said. "Do me a favor and whip his cream." I opened one of the island's lower fridge drawers and pulled out the whipping cream with one hand and a jug of milk with the other.

"He's pissed about what you did at dinner." Sophie took the items, her movements quick, the chore one she had done dozens of times. "Told me it was inexcusable."

I unscrewed the cap to the whiskey and poured an ounce into a glass. "And what do you think?"

"I don't know. I think it was pretty cool. Everyone clapped for you."

"Dad just doesn't want you to start lying."

"Yeah, but you did." She peered into the bowl, focusing on her task.

"Well, sometimes lies don't matter. I told them I was a doctor because I felt confident that I could help that woman and that the risk of side effects was low." I returned the liquor to its cabinet. "If you told people you hated math—"

"But I like math." She licked the end of the whisk, then stuck it back in the bowl.

"Okay, but let's say you told me you didn't. What's the potential side effect?" I scooped out a spoonful of sugar and added it to the cup, then placed the glass under the Miele spout and held down the button, releasing a stream of hot espresso.

"I don't know. I guess people wouldn't ask me math questions."

"Do people ask you math questions now?"

"No."

"See?" I pulled the steaming glass away from the machine. "So why does it matter if you lied?"

"Okay, so you won't be mad if I lie?" She was so opportunistic, this daughter of mine. Always looking for an inch, a shortcut, a permission. She shouldn't be asking; she should be taking. She'd learn that soon enough. If you waited for life to give you something, you'd never get half of what you deserved. If I had waited around, I wouldn't be married to Grant. I wouldn't have become George and Janice's daughter and eventual heir. I wouldn't have a life that looked anything like this.

Of course, you couldn't take everything. Sometimes there was interference, which was why Sophie was standing next to me when she should have never been born.

I used the spoon to move a dollop of fresh cream onto the top of Grant's coffee and tried to remember where our conversation had ended. Oh, right. Would I be mad if she lied? I cleared my throat. "Well, that's why your dad is worried. Because he's worried that you'll see me lie without repercussions and it will cause you to lie about things. Some things which might be really important and might have serious side effects. And I agree with your dad on that."

"Agree with me on what?" Grant entered the room with a warm smile. Maybe he'd forgive me quickly this time. Joining us at the island, he took the coffee from me. "The brownies smell good."

"They're almost ready. I was just saying that I agree with you, that lying is bad and something that Sophie shouldn't do."

She arched an eyebrow at me, and I winked at her.

"Well, that's something I can drink to." Grant took a small sip of his coffee, then did the loud lip smack that he always did when he really enjoyed something.

I hated that lip smack. I hated the sound of it, the tight pucker of his lips that preceded it, and I really, truly hated that I waited and looked for that smack of approval.

I had been the same way with my father, so desperate for his blessing. I learned back then how dangerous that trap was. I had held on to him so tightly, I'd lost him forever.

Sophie wrapped her arms around Grant's waist and smiled up at him.

Anger flared in my gut, and I turned away, unable to stomach the view.

CHAPTER 5

JOURNAL OF SOPHIE WULTZ

They worry that I don't understand when lying is acceptable, but I know more than they think. I'm smarter than both of them, and I'm smart enough to realize that I should keep that knowledge to myself.

CHAPTER 6

LEEWOOD FOLCRUM

Inmate 82145

I was here the day they brought him in. It was a big deal because the child killers always had to be kept out of general pop, otherwise they get roughed up too much. And everyone already knew who he was, even on the inside. So, uh, yeah. Twenty-three years I've known the guy. He ain't bad. Wasn't doing too well, this last year.

—*Carlos Zurate, Lancaster Prison corrections officer*

Prison loves rules. It's like the fucking walls were built from them. Nest inside those walls long enough, the rules started to feel like they mattered. Like they were the bones of this place, keeping everything standing. Like without them, your organs wouldn't stay where they should. You'd try to step forward and just fall apart. I'd gotten so used to the rules, it was like I needed them. Not just the big house's, but my own. The longer I was in here, the more rules I created for myself.

Don't let nobody in my cell.

Don't make friends. Period.

Finish a fight if it's brought to you, but don't bring that shit to anyone else.

Don't appeal. I'm in here, so I'm in here.

Don't talk about what happened on December 6. Ever.

Only read and write letters on Sundays.

I had a bunch more rules, pages of them, but that's the major ones. The ones I reminded myself of the most, especially if I was tempted to break them. The Sunday one, that's the one I came closest to breaking, because who really gave a shit if I opened up a piece of mail on Wednesday instead of waiting around till the end of the week?

I cared. I cared because I didn't have much to look forward to, and I learned a while ago that anticipation and hope were half of the enjoyment of life.

Maybe this was the week that she'd write to me.

Maybe that letter I was just handed was from her.

Maybe I was just a couple of days away from having some of my questions answered.

In here, the *maybes* could kill you, but they could also keep you alive.

By the time Sunday hit, four letters waited in a neat stack at the top-left corner of my desk. When I got back from lunch—fried rice, beans, and corn bread—I went to my desk.

Everything in my cell was designed to keep me safe, including the hard plastic stool that matched the wall-mounted desk. They both looked like something out of a kid's playroom. I sat on the stool and flipped through the envelopes, taking my time and savoring the handwriting on the outside of each one.

I always took the letters face down, letting my hope get a chance to live until this time each week.

Back when I was free, I used to buy a lotto ticket every Thursday and wouldn't check it until three days after the drawing for the same reason. In the anticipation, anything was possible.

The hope was what got you through the agony.

Three of the four letters were from regulars. I glanced over those, recognizing the familiar items in the top-left corner. Some of my pen pals used a discreet address and didn't put their names on the bottom of their letters. Others vomited out all their personal details and locations, like they hoped I escaped and showed up at their door, either to screw them or kill them. Maybe both.

I held the third envelope for a moment. No sender name and only a PO box for their address. Anonymous in one way, but I knew exactly who this neat handwriting belonged to, and I knew this box number by heart.

It was close by. Within an hour or two's drive, which was interesting but not surprising.

I placed it to one side and opened up the envelope from Tiffany.

> Hi babe.
> Sit down, because you aren't going to believe what happened to me at work this week. We had a contest to see who could sell the most of the egg roll appetizer and no, I didn't win BUT this one guy came in and ordered nine of them. Nine! It was Deb's table, of course. Whore.
> I have been thinking about what you said, about me taking some community college classes, but I just don't know. I mean, I feel like only losers go to community college. It's not like back when you were young. Like, if I put on my socials that I was a student there, my followers would freak. Plus, I'm really gaining traction on my videos. I wish you could see them. It's so stupid that they won't let you online. You would be so popular. Keep thinking about my visit, okay?
> Oh, and here's a riddle for you. What can you put in a bucket to make it weigh less?

Got it? I bet you do. You're so smart.

Big hugs from your girl,

Tiffany

PS Last week's riddle answer was: You don't have to worry about it, concrete floors are very hard to crack! < Ha! I thought that one was really funny.

Tiffany was one of the ones hoping for a screw. She was an idiot, but an entertaining one who had stuck around for more than a year. I put her letter to the side. I'd write her back later that afternoon, after I figured out her riddle, which she had probably found on the internet. I didn't give a shit. The questions kept me entertained, at least for a few minutes, sometimes longer. Hell, one I had thought about for days.

The second envelope was from Darby, another regular. Her letters were always full of detailed descriptions of what she wanted to do to me sexually and what she wanted me to do to her. I squeezed the envelope, gauging the thickness, and was pleased to feel that it contained a photo. Darby wasn't my body type—too hard and muscular—but at this point in my life, anything looked good.

Darby was all talk. She'd never come to visit, and if I ever got out of this place, she'd likely run in the opposite direction. It didn't matter. I wasn't getting out, and she enjoyed her fantasies. I'd gotten pretty good at writing stuff back, so I'd write something after my afternoon tug.

I pushed it to the side, unopened, and picked up the third envelope. A small smile crossed my lips. It'd been over a month since he last wrote, and while this was likely just like all his others, it still always gave me a jolt of energy—some adrenaline before the battle.

To the man who took away my world,

Today would be Lucy's 35th birthday. I should be driving to her house, where we would gather in the backyard and I'd cook ribs on her grill and we'd sip mojitos and spiked lemonade while her kids ran across the lawn and crawled into her lap. Instead, she is rotting in the ground while I sit alone and write to you. I have no nieces and nephews, no extended family to spend holidays with, no sister to ask advice of.

Like you, I have long stretches of time to think about what happened 23 years ago. Unlike you, I did nothing to deserve this.

Speaking of birthdays, I'll be 40 this year. Six years older than you when you did it. I've been looking into psychological breaks and it seems that the same kaleidoscope of events that cause midlife crises can also manifest new inclinations in someone's psyche. At this point, I know you better than just about anyone else in the world. I believe that what you share with me is sincere. You and I, we made a contract a long time ago. A contract written in blood, and while you are a despicable human in many facets, you are an honorable man in others.

In a letter that you wrote to me six years ago, you said that your first true Valentine was a girl named Kendra. Remember her? Of course you do. I've gone through your high school yearbook and there are no Kendras, not in the three years beneath you. There is, however, a Kendra Platt who was nine years underneath you. It took a while for me to find her, and then to track down through the records that her sister was a girl two years beneath you. There's a photo of you and Courtney, her sister, your arm around her at a football game when you were a senior at Longville High. You were a fall baby, so you were seventeen when you hung out with Courtney. Was it all under the guise of getting close to her eight-year-old sister?

As I've said before, I'm not here to judge you—though I certainly do. I just need to understand what recipe led to the death of my sister. I need to know what happened in those hours of the party. Did she suffer or if it was quick? Did she die first or last?

I don't understand why you won't share these things with me. I am a man in pain, and time isn't healing anything.

Please help me. Please. I'm begging you.

While you may have been cruel one night two decades ago, I don't think you're a cruel man at heart. Am I wrong?

He never signed the letters or put a name in the return portion of the envelope. It didn't matter. I'd figured out from the start who he was. The brother of the blonde one.

I spent some time with the letter. I read it a couple of times, weighing some words more than others and trying to hear his voice in my head. He's not anything special—just an ordinary man trying to understand an unordinary thing. I can relate to that. But I don't get the soft spot I have for him. Maybe it's because I never had a son, and when he first started writing me letters, he was still a teenager, trying to figure himself out. The two of us have carried on a twenty-three-year-long relationship, courtesy of the US Postal Service.

In the beginning, his letters were all hate and cussing. Sometimes the ink was blurred, like he'd cried while writing. He'd called me just about every name in the book and talked about killing himself, which was why I wrote him back instead of just throwing them away.

I didn't mind people hating me. Part of me enjoyed the venom in those letters. I deserved it all and could relate to their emotion. I hated myself a lot more than any of them, and if this were a state with the death penalty, I'd have volunteered to get the needle two decades ago.

An honorable man would tell him what really happened that night, but I kinda saw it as mercy, keeping it to myself. Nobody should know the gory details of their sister's death.

And . . . maybe I didn't tell him 'cause I was worried he'd stop writing me once he got what he was looking for.

But while those were both good reasons for keeping my trap shut, there was only one real reason I didn't confess every horrible and beautiful moment of that night.

Because of her. It all was because of her.

CHAPTER 7

PERLA

I was on my fifth mile when the podcast hosts paused their conversation on a rural murder-suicide and gave a brief teaser of their next episode.

"What happens when a birthday party goes horribly wrong? You won't believe what happened to twelve-year-old Jenny Folcrum and her two best friends. We'll be telling that story on next week's episode of *Murder Unplugged.*"

I pressed the "Incline +" button four times, ignoring the cry of my muscles as the treadmill rose higher. I already knew what had happened to Jenny Folcrum and her two best friends. The events of that night were the main reason I had a long-term and unfulfilled love-fear relationship with Leewood Folcrum.

Not that Leewood knew I existed. If he ever escaped prison and passed me on the street—my designer sunglasses on, hair and makeup perfect—he wouldn't look twice. Maybe he would if Sophie were with me.

It was a perfectly orchestrated murder spree that had ended poorly. Leewood had been an idiot, staying at the house long enough to get arrested. If he had just left, it could have gone down as one of the greatest events of our time. Instead, he was serving a life sentence for the crimes.

I eyed the treadmill's distance display as a bead of sweat ran down my cheek: 5.72 miles.

The podcast hosts were back to their discussion of the rural crime scene and picking apart the evidence. In their opinion, the scene pointed to a third person, but they were wrong. Sometimes the scene is exactly what it initially appears to be. The husband shot the wife, then himself. End of story.

My hamstrings screamed for help as I shortened my strides, getting in more steps as I increased the incline two more clicks. It was a good sign, *Murder Unplugged* covering the Folcrum Party. It was about time they focused on something interesting, and I was curious to see their take on Leewood's guilt.

I was an outlier in my stance that Leewood was innocent. It was one of the things that made our connection real. I *knew* he was telling the truth when he told the police, judge, and jury that he hadn't killed those girls. While no one else believed in him, I did.

I spoke to an attorney a couple of years ago, right after I saw a special on the Folcrum Party, one that dissected the forensic evidence and blood splatter. I told him that I would pay the bill for an appeal. I thought that would give us a reason for our paths to cross, for a relationship to form . . . but the attorney said Leewood refused to meet with him.

I have money, lots of it. I could get him out. Buy him a house and help him start a new life, and be a part of it. We could have a real relationship, as adults.

At six miles, I stabbed the "End Session" button, and the treadmill immediately slowed as it hummed its way down to the flat position.

The truth of the matter was, a future with Leewood was a fantasy that couldn't happen—not with Grant and Sophie in the picture.

I stepped off the machine and grabbed my towel from the hook, my heart racing as I wiped down my face and neck.

Too bad I couldn't get rid of them both. Clear the deck and start fresh with just two cards: Leewood Folcrum and me.

I set an alert on the app to remind me when the next podcast episode came out. In the back of my head, an idea sparked.

CHAPTER 8

People act all surprised now, like there were no clues of the insanity inside that house, but I could tell you within *minutes* of meeting that family that it was a messed-up dynamic. It's why I never let my daughter play with Sophie. I knew right away something was off with them.

—*Lydia Lee, Brighton Estates mom*

The Pasadena farmers' market was packed by the time we arrived at ten after ten. Grant eased the nose of my Range Rover into a tight space between a Tesla and a Porsche SUV.

"Watch the doors," I said sharply to Sophie, who had already unbuckled and was grabbing her bag from the floorboard.

"Money?" she asked, holding out her hand.

Grant shifted in his seat, pulling out his billfold and opening it up. After looking through the contents, he withdrew a crisp fifty-dollar bill, then handed it to her.

"Thanks," she said cheerfully, folding it into thirds and then tucking it into her bag.

"Try and stay close to us," Grant reminded her. "You got your phone?"

"Yep." She held it up.

I checked my watch. "Let's meet at eleven thirty at the food tent and eat."

"Sure. I got to go, Jordan and Bridget are already here." She cracked open the door, gauged the distance to the adjacent vehicle, then squeezed out.

I looked at Grant. "Fifty dollars is way too much. At her age, my dad would have given me five."

"And George would have given you a hundred," he said dismissively, unfolding the reflective sun shield and positioning it against the interior of the windshield. "Different circumstances allow for different things. She isn't spoiled. We're strict enough with her to prevent that."

Maybe. Still.

Grant locked the doors, double-checked that our parking pass was displayed, and then fastened the key chain's carabiner clip to his khaki's belt loop. He reached for my hand, and we wandered toward the entrance, our fingers loosely linked. It was a beautiful Los Angeles day, sunny and with a slight breeze.

We caught up with Sophie by the pet-adoption tent, where she turned to us, a big brown rabbit in her arms. "Look!" she called out. "It's Piketo!"

Grant's hand stiffened and I released it, scraping my nails gently on the top of the rabbit's head, then placing a kiss on that spot. "And what a beautiful bunny you are!" I cooed.

"Put it back," Grant called out, and I pretended it was due to his allergies and not our age-old argument over the story of Piketo and its role in our child's upbringing.

"Put Piketo back," I whispered to Sophie and gave her a conspiratorial grin. "You know your father hates that reference."

She tucked her lips in and nodded, her dimple peeking out as she tried not to smile. Twisting back toward the pen, she bent forward and dropped the floppy-eared bunny onto the straw.

I returned to Grant, grabbing his hand. I went in for a kiss but he pulled away.

"My allergies," he protested.

"Don't be a wimp." I grabbed him by the shoulders and rose onto my toes, kissing him square on the mouth. He allowed it and I grinned against his lips, then withdrew. "Fruit stand?" I suggested.

"Lead the way."

Piketo the bunny was a story my father had told me. I had waited until Sophie's sixth birthday to tell her the tale, because that's when he had told it to me.

As Grant had cleared away the wrapping paper and started unpackaging her new Barbie doll, I'd held her tiny hand in mine and told her the story.

"Piketo the bunny lived with her family in a big green field with lots of flowers and areas of shade."

Sophie had been staring at the Barbie, and I'd squeezed her hand to keep her attention. "Piketo knew a special secret, one that only she and her family knew. It was a juicy secret—the location of a hidden garden of carrots." I'd widened my eyes and raised the octave of my voice, amplifying the tale. "Because Piketo and her family knew about the garden, they could enjoy the carrots all they wanted, and as a result, Piketo's family was always happy."

"Happy." Sophie had beamed and swung her legs under the table, accidentally hitting my knee with her shoe. "Mommy, can I have some carrots?"

"*May* you have," I'd corrected automatically. "I'll have to see if we have any. But listen, Sophie, because the story is just getting good.

"Piketo was bursting to tell someone about the garden. Every time a bunny would brag about a carrot he found, or whenever there would be discussions and arguments about where to find the best carrots, her secret would bubble up in her little bunny chest, and she would have to pin her whiskered lips together to keep from telling the secret."

I'd held my hands together in front of my chest, my fingers pointing down like bunny paws, and pinned my mouth closed, then puffed out my cheeks. Sophie had burst out laughing as Grant chuckled from his place by the trash can.

"One day, Piketo couldn't keep the secret any longer and broke the rule. She told just one friend. A safe friend. Her closest friend. A friend that would never, ever, *ever* tell anyone." I had dropped my voice, making it sound serious and dark.

Sophie's eyes had narrowed as her little brain worked through what story possibilities would come next.

"A week went by, and her family continued their life of happiness and bliss. Another week passed, and all was well. In the third week, do you know what happened?" I'd placed my palms on the table and looked solemnly into Sophie's eyes, just as my father had when he'd reached this part of the story.

She had shaken her head quickly, making her little blonde curls bounce.

"Piketo's family was all asleep in their little rabbit beds, dreaming about green fields and sunshine, when the town came for them, furious that they had hidden the secret carrot garden from the others."

I had glanced at Grant, then continued. "Rabbits have extraordinarily long front teeth, and they used them to rip open the bellies of Piketo's sisters and mom. They tore out the eyes of Piketo's father and brothers. Within minutes, everyone in Piketo's family was bloody and dead."

"Jesus." Grant had sworn. "She's six, Perla. You're going to give her nightmares."

I had held up my hand to silence him and watched Sophie, making sure she was listening. Her eyes had been huge, her mouth a little O of surprise, and I'd known how she felt because I remembered my own reaction when I'd first heard the story. The twist of my belly. The fear it introduced in my heart. It had cemented this idea, this lesson, in my head—and in hers.

"Piketo didn't realize what she was doing, but her actions caused the death of everything that she knew and everyone that she loved. When we are told to keep secrets, Sophie, you must take that responsibility seriously. Especially the secrets of your family. Do you understand?"

I had reached out and grabbed her hands, squeezing them hard. "Sometimes something might not seem serious to you, but then you wake up and everyone you love is ripped open and dead."

"Okay, I think that's enough." Grant had picked Sophie up under her arms and swirled her through the air. "Who wants to go swimming?"

"Me!" Sophie had shrieked and smiled, but there was a moment when her eyes connected with mine, and there, for just that moment, I saw the confirmation. She had heard. She had understood.

I didn't need to do what my father had done. I wouldn't give her a baby rabbit for Christmas, one that would later end up gutted. I understand why my father bought the rabbit, why he brought the story's main character to life. The psychological impact of Piketo's tale was instrumental in creating a relationship of ironclad confidentiality and trust.

Grant had thought I was being too graphic, but I'd needed to give Sophie a small dose of the awareness I had received as a child, and if that could be done with vivid words instead of actual blood—less mess to clean up. Fewer questions to answer.

CHAPTER 9

I lay in the bathtub and stared at the ceiling, *Murder Unplugged* playing through my earbuds. The lights in the massive bathroom were off, the only illumination coming from the candles, which lined the upper windows of the room and cast the all-white marble tile in a flickering pale-yellow hue. The tub was situated on the far end of the room, with entrances to the steam shower on one side, the closets on the other, and his-and-her sinks and vanities stretching down the back side.

I had special ordered the tub and waited almost two months for its arrival. It was solid copper, a focal point in the room, and matched the sink and cabinet hardware.

Grant would say my water was unbearably hot, but I liked it at that temperature. I enjoyed the painful contraction of skin cells as they panicked, recoiling in a way that rarely occurred from any other stimulus. What did it say about my husband that he was too weak of a man to stand a dip in hot water?

What did it say about me that I had chosen a man like that to marry?

Grant didn't used to be so weak. When I was in middle school, he was like a god to me. The bad-boy older brother who swore and snuck beers and had a car and ignored us, except for every once in a while, when his eyes would meet mine and the corner of his mouth would tug up and I would swoon inside. No male had ever made me feel the way Grant had, except for my father—and his love had come with conditions and boundaries and, always in the back of my head, the understanding that being a parent wasn't a choice but often a chore.

Sophie was often a chore and had never been my choice. The older she got, the more I was reminded of that fact.

I inhaled deeply and then blew out slowly, watching as the air shuddered over the top of the water. The podcast hosts were discussing Leewood's refusal to talk about the crime and reading out comments from listeners who were weighing in with their opinions.

"Here's the thing," Rachel said. "And listen up, because this is important."

I paid attention despite myself.

"I combed through all the homicides in a five-hundred-mile radius, and do you know how many similar crimes like this occurred in the twenty years surrounding 2002?"

Of course we don't, Rachel. What a stupid question to ask.

"Zero. So you either have a killer who swooped in, pulled off a three-girl slash attack without leaving any DNA or fingerprints behind while framing the father for the murder . . . *or* . . ." She drawled out the conjunction, then paused.

"Or Leewood was the killer," Gabrielle said in a hushed tone, as if she'd just broken the case wide open. It was hard for me to decide which one of these two airheads I liked the least, but Gabrielle was holding her own as a contender.

"Right," Rachel said grimly. "I mean, otherwise, there'd be more murders. This isn't a one-and-done sort of guy."

"Or girl," Gabrielle chirped. Of course *she* was a champion of female equality. I unhooked the loofah from its hook by the hand sprayer and poured a generous amount of rosemary oil onto it.

The podcast hosts had a point. In every murder, there needs to be a motive, unless the motive is the enjoyment of the crime itself. If Leewood was ever going to get off, we needed a caricature of a different suspect. There wasn't one with a motive—who would have the motive to kill three preteen girls?—so instead, it would need to be a psychopath. Someone who enjoyed killing for the sake of killing; someone who had committed the Folcrum Party crime, then retreated into hiding, content to let Leewood take the fall.

I reached over and pressed Pause on the audio, letting the idea soak in. After running the loofah slowly over my arms and shoulders, I dipped it into the hot water once more to refresh it.

This killer would need to have a fresh event to put him on the police's radar. Something that tied him to the original crime. Something that would cast enough doubt on Leewood's guilt to trigger an appeal.

A recreation of the crime would do it. Three new preteen girls. A twelve-year-old's birthday party. A dozen or so details that matched the old crime to the new.

I had some great details. I had Sophie and her piles of preteen friends. I even had her birthday, coming up in a few months. Her twelfth.

Too many conveniences for it not to be fate.

It could work. It could more than work. It could, if done right, kill multiple birds with one stone.

I moved the loofah over my breasts and imagined Leewood's eyes warm with appreciation, his voice husky as he thanked me for everything I'd done to set him free.

I beamed at the thought.

CHAPTER 10

Finally, the house was quiet, save for the faint hum of the vacuum as Madeline worked in the rear of the home. Dipping my spoon into a bowl of granola and lactose-free yogurt, I stared at my phone's screen, watching an old Leewood Folcrum interview. The segment was titled "The Worst Father in America," but I would disagree with that.

It was filmed more than twenty years ago, when he'd been on trial for the murders. At the time, he was thirty-four, with dark-brown hair, intense features, and a presence you couldn't help but be drawn to. The interviewer, a voluptuous blonde with bright-red lipstick, was clearly attracted to him. Her lust was telegraphed in every flip of her hair, every forward lean.

"At the time of the event, you were a single father, raising a young girl. Can you tell me what happened with your wife?"

I didn't blame the interviewer for wanting Leewood. There was something incredibly magnetic about him, and it wasn't hampered by the prison jumpsuit or the deep lines of stress on his face. If anything, the effect was enhanced by the elements of danger. The annoyed looks . . . the strained, raspy voice . . . it all worked together in a beautiful way.

I readjusted my seat on the upholstered chair and rested my elbow on the round kitchen table, pausing the video at a rare moment when Leewood looked directly into the camera. It felt like he was looking into my soul—a tie between us—and I could imagine him nodding at me, encouraging my line of thinking.

He wasn't that far away. From my house to his prison, it was less than seventy miles. I could hop in my Range Rover and, by lunchtime, be sitting across from him and staring into that handsome face. Reaching out and touching it, assuming we didn't have a wall of protective glass between us.

What did he look like now? I hovered my finger above the screen, tracing it over the lines of his face. Probably even more handsome. Salt-and-pepper hair. A beard, maybe?

I needed to know but was terrified at the idea of visiting him. He might not even accept the visitor request. Or worse, he would, but he would dismiss me. Turn away at the sight of me and leave me sitting at the table, like a loser without a prom date.

I swallowed at the thought. The fear of rejection was one of the reasons why I hadn't initiated contact. There were certain things I didn't handle well, and rejection was one of them.

"My wife . . . she left us two years ago."

"'Left'?"

"She—she took her own life. I was at work. I found her when I got home."

"Given the recent events, many are saying that you killed her. Did you kill your wife, Mr. Folcrum?"

I watched, fascinated, as he glared at the interviewer. His hand, which had been loosely curled on one knee, tightened into a fist. "You know I didn't."

"How would I know that?" she asked innocently. This woman was lucky she was in such a protected environment, the camera rolling, prison guards at the ready.

He didn't respond, and she waited, sitting back in her chair and crossing her long, skinny legs. She was wearing a short skirt, and the red fabric rose up on her thighs. Completely inappropriate for an interview with a supposed killer.

I got up to refill my water because I already knew how this was going to go, and not just because this was the third time I'd seen the interview. You couldn't outwait this man. He had all the time in the world, while she had only sixty minutes, with almost half of those dedicated to commercials.

As I pulled the glass carafe out of the fridge, her voice sounded from my iPad's speaker.

"You're referring to the time of death? That was determined to be between two and four o'clock, which was when you were at work?"

Silence.

She sighed. *"Lee, can you walk us through how your wife died?"*

"I'd rather not. You have it all written down there, on your little pad. Why don't you tell them?"

"It's not common, a woman killing herself with her morning coffee."

"Please get to your point. It's not a day I like to relive."

I sat back down at the table, glancing at his face as I poured the ice-cold water into my glass. He always looked grim during this part of the video, as if in pain.

The police had never looked at him as a suspect in his wife's death. His alibi had been ironclad. He'd been at a construction site forty-five minutes away, with a half dozen witnesses. He'd also been distraught over her death—a stark contrast to the Folcrum Party aftermath. Some pointed to this as a sign of his guilt in the party murders. Others said there was no such thing as coincidences and that the latter pointed to his guilt in the former. They said that maybe Leewood wasn't the one who dropped a lethal amount of pain meds into his wife's morning coffee, but he either drove her to do it or he hired someone else to commit the deadly act.

My cell phone rang, and I glanced at the display, then sighed. Pausing the video, I answered the call. "Hey."

As Grant spoke, I closed the window, then went into the browser settings and deleted all the history associated with my search and the videos.

No one needed to know what I watched. Especially not Grant.

CHAPTER 11

LEEWOOD FOLCRUM

Inmate 82145

My daughter's wanting to go into criminology, but Leewood Folcrum is one of the number-one reasons I'm trying to dissuade her. Years ago, he was in my pod at the prison. You'd look in his eyes, and it was like there was a human there, like he was just a normal guy. I mean, I *liked* him, as weird as that sounds. I feel like our inner gut should be able to recognize someone that sick, but I didn't. Out in the real world, I would've been friends with him, and it probably would have been my little girl he carved up.

—*William Smith, Lancaster Prison corrections officer*

Dear Lee,
Can I call you Lee? It's interesting how it never seems to be shortened, but I would guess that those close to you don't use the full *Leewood* moniker.

I'd like to be close to you.

You and I are alike in more ways than one.

Like you once were, I'm married with a young daughter.

Like you, I don't have a problem doing the things that need to be done.

Like you, I might even enjoy it.

I think you enjoyed it, Lee, and there's nothing wrong with that. The chase of pleasure is the fuel that drives our world.

I have just one question for you, Lee.

Do you regret it?

You shouldn't. You should just regret that you didn't finish the job.

Your biggest fan

I met Timothy Valden my last summer at Lancaster. They had given me three more months there, and the countdown was dragging on, each day more painful and uncomfortable than the prior.

He came on a Tuesday, during my yard time. I was sitting in the sun, enjoying its warmth, when Thompson, the CO who whistled the *Andy Griffith* theme song too much, tapped me on the shoulder and told me I had a visitor.

I didn't like to be tapped on the shoulder. Or touched. Or have anyone within ten feet of me, and I let him know it with my glare.

The scrawny officer snapped his gum, which was bullshit. Decades ago, when my prison uniform was still stiff and new, I woulda punched him. Or spit at him. Or done something to wipe that stupid smirk off his face. But I was old now. Old and almost out of there, so I stood and followed him into the building. I didn't say a thing, not as we walked through the halls and rode up the elevator and then down another elevator until we came to one of the private visitor rooms.

And there, sitting at a metal table that was right up to the glass, was Tim.

I first noticed the way he smelled. There were thin strips cut into the glass, enough to let air and sound through, and I took a seat and inhaled deeply. He was wearing a cologne I used to wear, and my eyes closed, my mind ticking with a memory of how my life used to be.

The scuffed wooden dresser in the bedroom, the cologne bottle on top. A fresh shirt, hanging on a hanger off the drawer pull. The steam floating in from the open bathroom door. The sound of little girls screaming in the other room.

"Hi." He cleared his throat, and I opened my eyes, meeting his through the thick plexiglass. There was a briefcase and a pad of yellow paper in front of him. He wasn't thin but wasn't fat—not as tall as me— and he looked like a man who would lose in a bar fight.

Our rooms were mirror images of each other, my table the same as his, and as the CO left the room and locked me in, I tried to figure what kind of visitor he was.

Right after it had happened . . . I was Mr. Popular. But as time went on, the visitors dropped off, unless a podcast or TV show covered the case. Right about then, I'd get a slew of 'em. Then it was quiet again.

People loved to hear about little girls dying. They said they didn't. They made all sorts of sad faces and winced and waxed on about how horrible it was—but every one of them wanted a front-row seat. They wanted the details, and there were a few times, in the last twenty-plus years, when I'd shared pieces of it with them. Not all of them, but a select few. The ones who would give me something in return, even if that something was just them taking an interest in me. Them listening without interrupting. Currency comes in new forms in a place like this.

"My name is Dr. Timothy Valden. I have a card, if you'd like to see it." He half rose, reaching back to his pants pocket. I waved him off, then let my cuffed wrists rest on the table.

"And you're Leewood Folcrum," he said, as if I didn't know who the fuck I was.

I didn't let it bother me. I raised my hands, showing my palms. "Guilty as charged." Though I wasn't guilty—as least, not for the crimes for which I'd been convicted.

"I am a doctoral student from the local college. I'm doing my dissertation on—"

"I thought you said you were a doctor."

"Well, yes. I am a doctor already; I have a PhD in international affairs, but I'm getting a second doctorate in psychology."

"And you're doing your thing on what?" I shifted in my seat and tried to inhale a full breath.

"Confessions and deceptions."

Well, that was one I hadn't heard before. "And which side of that do I fall on?"

"Well, that's what I was hoping to talk to you about. I'd like to talk about what happened the night of the . . ." He hesitated. "The night of December 6."

"Do ya, now?" I yawned and then sniffed deeply, trying to clear my airway.

"I do. I'm studying the mental triggers of—"

I stopped him with a raise of my palm. "You got a pen?" I nodded to his pad of paper.

"Uh, yes. I can record the conversation, though, if that would be eas—"

"Just a pen."

He patted the front pocket of his white dress shirt, then his khakis. Twisting in his seat, he popped open his briefcase and withdrew a silver pen. "Here. Got one." He quickly clicked it into action and then posed it over the page.

"Arby's Roast Beef 'N Cheddar, upsized, with curly fries and a root beer."

He looked up. "Excuse me?"

"Arby's Roast Beef 'N Cheddar, upsized, with curly fries and a root beer. You'll need to get the warden to sign off on the outside food. There's a form you have to fill out."

"I don't understand. This is something you ate the night of the murder?"

"That's what you're going to bring me the next time we talk. Write it down."

He digested the statement. "I'm not sure there is an Arby's in Lancaster."

"Then figure out where to find one." I stood, and my wrist shackles clanked.

"Wait, could I just ask you a few questions?"

I moved over to the door and nodded through the window at Thompson, who swung open the metal door.

"You want him approved for the visitor list?" he asked.

"Yeah." I glanced at the clock above the door, anxious to get the handcuffs off and return to the yard while I still had a few minutes left.

It was sad how my relationship with Tim began. Had I known where it would lead, I would have asked for more, and he would've given it to me.

He'd have given me anything.

CHAPTER 12

PERLA

Perla and I immediately clicked. We're both private-school girls, you know. She went to Rochester, which is a few rungs up from Blaketon, where I went, but you know . . . we're cut from the same cloth. When she brought Sophie in for her interview, I was really impressed by their family. Grant clearly doted on both of them, and Sophie was so well mannered—and already one heck of a soccer player, even without our program. I was devastated when I heard what happened to her. I organized a little memorial for her in our break room. I tried to send something to her funeral but . . . obviously, I couldn't. Not once I found out everything.

—*Tina Anthow, Tom Pullic Soccer Academy*

My home office was on the second floor and overlooked the side yard and Sophie's tree house. The tree house had intentionally been built on the side—out of view of the pool area and hidden from the wall of windows that stretched across the back of the house. In addition to the tree house, the expanse between us and the neighboring estate held the vegetable gardens, the fruit-tree orchard, and a sandbox.

Sophie had outgrown the sandbox years ago. I looked down on it and made a mental note to have it removed before I listed the home for sale. That, and the tree house. The rest could stay. I'd spent years on the gardens, and someone would appreciate them. Maybe a woman like me. Someone fastidiously detailed.

Turning away from the floor-to-ceiling windows, I settled into my cream ergonomic desk chair and pulled open the middle drawer. Looking over the perfectly organized interior gave me a sense of calm, and I took a moment to line up all the white gloss pens before removing one and placing it on the clean surface of my desk. Everything in the drawer matched the wardrobe in my closet—all whites, blacks, and grays. I selected a fresh pad of paper and placed it beside the pen, then straightened a stack of Post-it notes and white mints before closing the drawer. I rolled forward until I was snug against the desk. There.

If I was going to do this, I needed to make sure it was worth the effort, and that I had a plan of attack for before, during, and after the event.

I wrote down section titles to outline my thoughts.

WHO:
WHAT:
WHEN:
WHERE:
WHY:

I put the pen tip beside the first title, then stopped, frowning. I drew a line down the center of the page, then repeated the list of queries and put headings above the columns.

Truth above the left. *Fake* above the right.

	TRUTH	FAKE
WHO:		
WHAT:		
WHEN:		
WHERE:		
WHY:		

Then I got to work filling each in.

Under the Truth column, I put the details of the potential crime.

WHO: Me.

In order for this to work, I couldn't use any accomplices. No loose ends. No potential snitches. I would have to pull off the murders myself.

WHAT: A recreation of the Folcrum Party event

I grinned as I wrote it down and resisted the urge to put a smiley face at the end.

WHEN: Sophie's 12th birthday party (August 13th)

WHERE: In her bedroom

WHY: To cast doubt on Leewood's guilt and trigger an appeal/mistrial. To justify me stepping forward and becoming involved in his defense.

Right now, if I pushed harder with an attorney or reached out to Leewood directly . . . my motives would be called into question. Grant would likely divorce me. It would be a disaster from the start.

But if my daughter were killed by the "true" Folcrum Party murderer . . . a grieving mother's quest for justice wouldn't be questioned—it would be applauded. Leewood would certainly accept my visitor request. And then, once he saw me . . . once our eyes met . . . My heart beat faster at the idea.

But the goodwill wouldn't come only from him. I'd watched the media footage from after the Folcrum Party murders. The candlelit vigils; the crowds of people sobbing, surrounding the dead girls' parents. So many shots of the teary-eyed mothers. Interviews. Cover stories.

I would be getting all that. A double helping of it. My story was too good to miss: torn from her father at a young age . . . forced to live with strangers . . . my hardworking climb to prosperity, only to suffer this tragedy.

I added it to the list as a *why*.

The aftermath.

I placed the pen down and rolled back in my chair, over to the long credenza that spanned the left wall of my office. Pulling on the wooden cabinet door, I opened the enclosed mini fridge and selected a sparkling Evian from the rows of bottles.

"Good morning."

I swiveled the chair around, surprised to see Grant in the doorway. He wore a cornflower-blue button-up and dark-charcoal slacks. His glasses were on, and he had a small piece of toilet paper stuck to his jaw where he must have cut himself shaving. "Hey," I said warmly, making sure my gaze didn't travel over to the desk, where my neatly written list was in plain sight. All Grant would need to spot was the word *Folcrum* and he'd read every word on that page.

"Whatcha doing?"

I laughed. "What are *you* doing? Shouldn't you be at work?" That was the problem with a house this big. People lost each other in it.

"I'm going to work from home today." His attention strayed toward my desk. "You in the middle of something?"

I let out a sharp gasp, grabbing my side, and his head snapped toward me, his eyes widening in concern.

He rushed forward and crouched beside my chair. "What's wrong? Is it—"

I gripped his shoulder, grimacing as I pressed into the imaginary pain. "I—oh my God. I'm . . . It's a bad cramp."

He looked up at me, alarmed. "But your period isn't for another ten days."

"Sometimes people get cramps," I snapped at him, both annoyed and pleased that he knew my ovulation calendar so well.

"Of course, of course." He patted my leg awkwardly. "What can I get you? Some magnesium? A Gatorade? Do you think you're dehydrated?"

"No, I just . . . I think it's passing." I kicked out my legs and leaned back in the chair, stretching out my abs. The act caused my blouse to rise, exposing a glimpse of my stomach, but my husband didn't even notice. Instead, his gaze had turned vacant. I had lost him to some sort of mathematical equation or line of database code.

I grabbed his face with both hands, forcing him to look into my eyes. "Go and work," I ordered. "I can just feel you thinking."

He smiled and I returned the gesture, an automatic motion set to On. "Okay."

When he was out of the room, I locked the door, then returned to my desk, my own ideas churning.

I moved to the second column, still crudely labeled as *Fake*. I needed a better moniker, but for now—for this mental exercise, which I would destroy at completion—it was fine.

This section was for the story I would create with evidence, misdirection, and testimonials for the press and the police.

WHO: The original Folcrum Party killer, who wants his rightful place in the limelight and another round in his cat and mouse game.

I read the line and liked it. Rachel and Gabrielle and their million-plus *Murder Unplugged* listeners would love it.

I quickly filled in the same details as before in the *What*, *When*, and *Where* sections. Then, the *Why*.

WHY: Because he's bored, wants the chance to kill again, and to pin this crime on a new scapegoat.

I laughed out loud, reading that over, because someone, somewhere, would try to poke holes in that and say it wasn't a valid motive, but I was proof positive that it was. This entire *event* would be proof positive that it was. Even if I was the only one who understood the true irony of it.

I sat back and twisted right, then left, in my seat, thinking. It took a while to put the various pieces together in my mind, but then I sat straight up, buoyed with clarity.

I leaned forward, scanning the faux scenario I would be creating, then printed neatly in the space beside the *Who* section: *Grant*.

Grant. He could be the killer, both then and now. But what would his motive be? I frowned as the legitimacy of the idea started to crumble. I crossed out his name and moved my pen down to the *Why* section, rereading my note.

Because he's bored, wants the chance to kill again, and to pin this crime on a new scapegoat.

Beside *scapegoat*, I wrote Grant's name.

Why not? If the first Folcrum Party pinned the crime on the father, wouldn't the recreation do the same?

Excitement thrummed through me, and I set down my pen and let out a silent shriek of happiness at the sheer genius of it all.

It would be difficult, the most complicated thing I'd ever set up. Brutal, given that the main victim would be my daughter. Tricky, because if they didn't see the setup, Grant would be convicted of the crime.

But I could do it, and if I did it right . . . Leewood would be free. We'd be connected, and then who knew what would happen. With my money and his freedom . . . anything was possible.

I underlined Grant's name, cementing his fate in my mind. It didn't really matter whether he'd be convicted of the crime. Most marriages didn't survive the loss of a child. Grant and I would part ways, due to his incarceration or our divorce. I'd been toying with the idea of an exit for a while, and this would give me an opportunity to take care of a bunch of to-do items at once.

Closing my eyes, I quickly went through the execution and then took my time with the aftermath. The attention. The sympathy. A warm glow traveled through my chest at the vision of the crowds that would line our street, the media vans, the pile of flowers and mementos, the front-page articles, the trending hashtags, the soft voices and concerned faces of the interviewers. I would only do one, maybe two. Very high-profile sit-downs, with perfect lighting and a line in the contract that would grant me control over the final edit.

A small smile tugged at my lips, and I allowed it to come. After all, this would be the cherry on top of all this. I would be wrapped in a warm embrace of the entire nation. How many people were lucky enough to experience that? Only a handful, and I would be one of them.

Of course, I would need to get rid of my mole before then. I opened my eyes and swiveled in the chair, looking in the dark reflections of the dual computer screens mounted above my second desk. The mole, which sat on the far end of my right cheek, just beside my ear, was my biggest flaw. That, and the hard bridge of my nose. I had considered fixing both in the past, but the surgeries had always been pushed aside for this reason or that.

But now, looking at my face in the dark glass, it was all I could see. I couldn't go on prime-time TV looking like this. People were cruel. They became easily fixated on things. I'd be spilling my guts on camera while a fat Kansas housewife laughed at my big nose.

Forget the crime planning. Top priority was surgery. If I couldn't complete that in time, I would need to pick someone else's birthday, which would mess everything up in terms of Grant's setup and Sophie's elimination. Hmm. I turned away from my reflection before I began to obsess over it.

I tapped the screen of my phone and checked the date, then counted off the weeks until Sophie's birthday. Nine weeks away. Was it enough time?

Nine weeks. I wrote down the timeline, then added a question mark beside it.

I started a to-do list, these tasks just as important as the first.

Nose job.

Mole removal.

I ran a hand over my once-flat stomach, then added *Liposuction* as a third item.

I looked over my list of *who*s, *what*s, *when*, *where*s, and *why*s, committing it all to memory. Once it was completed, I tore off the page and carried it over to the shredder. Feeding it through, I smiled as I watched the crosscut blades easily chew through the page.

For the first time in a long while, I was no longer bored.

CHAPTER 13

The thing is, I'd *just* listened to that podcast—the one on the Folcrum Party. And I told Todd—that's my husband. I told him that was the great thing about living in a place like this, that nothing like that will ever happen here. And he said I was going to jinx us. And look, well, maybe I did.

—*Kelly Schwartz, Brighton Estates homeowner*

In our protected bubble of the world, I was a cookie-cutter version of the other wives. It was a classification I both embraced and detested.

You could recognize us by our cars—Range Rovers were preferred, but any luxury SUV or six-figure sedan was accepted. Our husbands worked long hours; our kids attended the same elite schools; and if the wife worked, it was in a job like mine, something flexible enough to allow for long lunches at the club, afternoons at the spa, and vacations in Italy or Paris.

The outliers in the neighborhood—the female execs, the single moms, the internet models . . . they never made it into the inner circle, and it was important to me, from the beginning, to have a place there. Not just a place—a throne. I didn't come to play unless I could win, and I'd won inside these gates a long time ago.

Which mattered because these women would be vital in confirming my character and situation. In the aftermath of the party, they'd be questioned by the police about our family. When that day arrived, they needed to give the right answers about Grant, and about me.

While I was still figuring out those answers, I had no doubt they would deliver on whatever I needed from them. Everyone would. I'd spent years building my reputation, and it was impenetrable in its perfection. Still, a qualified expert would be nice. Someone trustworthy, who could speak to the media and be sworn in on the stand. Someone the jury and public would trust in and believe.

I needed a manipulatable pawn, preferably one with a lot of initials after their name.

I had a need, so I found a solution.

Dr. Leslie Maddox.

After pulling into the Stony Brook Medical Center, I parked in front of a small bungalow with window boxes full of hot-pink roses. I checked my phone. Twenty minutes early. Not wanting to look too eager, I waited in the vehicle's cool interior, listening to one of Grant's playlists as I watched the building's front door. I flipped past a Gin Blossoms song and started "Glycerine" by Bush. My husband had a nostalgic love of nineties alternative rock.

Dr. Leslie Maddox had been recommended by Laura, who had used her for marriage counseling, and Tracy, who had raved about her willingness to prescribe Ambien. I'd asked enough questions to arouse their interest, written down the woman's name and number in front of them, and then abruptly changed the subject.

Breadcrumbs. Lay enough of them down on the ground, and even the stupidest of animals will find their way. I needed a trail of breadcrumbs that would create doubt and suspicion around my husband, for the women in my neighborhood to gobble up like Vicodin.

We'd see how easily Dr. Maddox took the bait. I almost hoped she was savvy. It'd be nice to have some sort of a challenge in this game.

When the clock on the dash ticked to five minutes prior to my appointment, I turned off the engine and opened the heavy vehicle door.

———

"So . . ." Dr. Maddox tucked one blue-bottomed ballet flat under her thigh. "You're married, right? You said you were married?"

"Yes." I tried not to bite out the word.

"Oh, that's right, I wrote it here. 'Married to Grant.' Oh whillikers, married thirteen years." There was a twang of Midwest in her voice, and that, paired with the mousy-brown curls that reached her shoulders, the tiny gold hoop earrings in her ears, and the floral Apple watchband that bisected her chubby wrist, completed the caricature.

No one had mentioned she was a hick, and while I liked the low-hanging fruit, I wasn't sure how much confidence she'd invoke on the stand.

"I do marriage counseling also, just in case you ever have need of that."

"Yes, I saw that on your website. Your expertise is one of the reasons I picked you." That, and her immediate availability. Her calendar had more spots than a teenage boy's face, and I had been able to book a session for the following day.

"No pressure, of course—and that's not why you're here, right?" She didn't wait for me to respond. "Now, let's talk about *you*." She adjusted her red plastic eyeglasses with one hand and beamed at me. "What is there to know about Perla Wultz?"

"Well, I work from home, managing our family's apartment complexes. I have a daughter, Sophie." I delivered that idiotic smile parents revert to when they speak of their children. "She's, um—well, she's the light of my life. I'm sure every parent says that."

"Oh, you'd be surprised." She had her pen out, writing in a yellow spiral-bound notebook. I looked past her to her bookshelf, where there was a long line of these notebooks, organized by color, and wondered what yellow meant.

"What kind of a girl is Sophie? How old?"

"She's eleven. Very smart. She should be, especially with Grant as a parent. Creative. Funny."

"Do you consider Grant to be smarter than you?" She tilted her head and blinked at me in an uncanny impression of an owl.

I weighed the possible answers, taking my time and knowing that the longer I stalled, the more unsure and insecure I would seem. Good. I needed those pieces of the picture to compete with the arrogance I knew could potentially seep out.

That would be my downfall, if any. My cockiness. Of course, I was already ahead of that train. My confidence in my ability to handle that risk . . . the irony wasn't lost on me, and I stifled a smirk at the thought. Smirks didn't belong here. No smirks, no eye rolls. I needed to be a concerned mother and wife, just waiting for this professional to unlock "all" my secrets.

It was laughable, the idea that Dr. Maddox would scrape anything out of me. For her efforts, I had manufactured two juicy tidbits, ones I would place close to the surface and release easily once prodded.

The first would be that my husband had a growing obsession with the Folcrum Party murders.

The second would be that he was displaying increasingly odd and erratic behavior.

Both had little to no potential blowback for me, but would serve well in complicating the investigation into Sophie's birthday-party events. And that's really all I needed. To keep the cops juggling enough balls that they wouldn't have the time—or desire—to look for another one. I would go unnoticed as a potential suspect while reaping all the rewards of a grieving mother.

Out of all the roles I had ever played, it would be the most important, and I had no doubt of my ability to perform it.

"Perla?" Dr. Maddox prodded.

"Is Grant smarter than me?" I straightened in my seat. "Well, in some areas." I let my voice warm with pride. "Grant is a genius when it comes to math and computers. Sophie certainly got his aptitude for learning."

"In your intake application, you said that your husband was one of the things you wanted to talk about." She hooked her pen through the notepad's circular spine and lifted her chin, meeting my eyes. She did have pretty eyes. Bright green—like Kitty, God rest her soul. "What's going on there?"

"What's going on?" I shifted uncomfortably in my seat and realized we might reach the finish line of this to-do item quicker than I had anticipated. Talk about a sledgehammer versus a surgical knife. "That's a deep well to drop down. I just . . . I have some concerns. Probably silly stuff, really. I guess it finally feels like the right time to talk to someone and see if I'm crazy."

"Why are you worried about him?" The pen was staying in place and I had her full attention, which was good. She didn't realize it now, but I was going to make her famous. She'd end up writing a book about Grant and me, once I gave her permission to share the story. It would become a *New York Times* bestseller, with copies in every bookstore window.

"Well, I'm not even sure I should say." I looked helplessly toward her door, then at the clock on the wall beside us. Not even fifteen minutes into the half-hour session. "I mean, it's probably just me being paranoid."

"Well now, sometimes being paranoid is a good thing. It causes us to keep our eyes open. To see more." She smiled encouragingly. "So go on. That's why you're here, right? To see if your concerns have validation?"

Like leading a lamb to the slaughter.

I cleared my throat and knotted my hands in my lap, my mind flip-flopping over how far to push the envelope in this initial session. "There's a side of my husband," I said carefully, "that scares me."

From: tfk@hotmail.com
To: info@murderunplugged.com

Date: June 15 at 10:34 AM

Subject: hello

Thirty days has September

April June and November

I framed a Folcrum in December

The next event all will remember

CHAPTER 14

LEEWOOD FOLCRUM

Inmate 82145

I was Jenny Folcrum's friend in middle school. I came over to her house one day after school and her dad was home, working out in the yard. He had this motorcycle, and he offered to take me around the block. Said we could go down to the gas station at the corner and he'd buy me some candy. I did it and he held me really tight the entire time, like pressing me against his body. Jenny didn't invite me over again after that, which was fine because he had kind of creeped me out. There was definitely something wrong with him. I never told anyone about that, and maybe it's not important. I just thought that maybe it was.

—*Christina Shutter, orthodontist*

Hi, Leewood,
Last night I watched my wife sleep and thought of you. I thought of all of the ways that your actions,

now over twenty years ago, are still affecting me today. I guess, in some sort of way, you brought her and me together. We have both been through traumatic loss. Bonded over it. Looked into each other's soul and recognized the sadness there.

Grief does strange things to people. For some, it weakens them. For others, it makes them stronger. Harder. That's what my sister's death did to me. It fortified me with a potent combination of grief and rage.

I thought it would get easier with time, but the wound has only festered. Because of you, I look for evil everywhere. I doubt the words out of my wife's mouth, the motivations of a stranger, the supposedly innocent offers of a friend.

You spent over thirty years on this earth before you killed someone. Thirty years existing without feeling the need to destroy someone's world.

Maybe we're all just psychopaths waiting for our trigger.

Or maybe you killed earlier in life and no one ever caught you.

Which is it, Leewood?

The Arby's Roast Beef 'N Cheddar sandwich wasn't hot, but it still tasted like heaven on a bun. I ate it slowly, and when a drop of sauce hit the table, I wiped it up with my finger and sucked on the digit. Dr. Timothy Valden watched, his mouth turning down on one side.

I didn't care. I'm not sure my manners prior to getting incarcerated were anything to brag about, but shitting in front of strangers for two decades could make any man lose his inclination to give a damn about manners.

"So, I thought we'd start with what your life was like that spring. The spring of Jenny's birthday party."

I ignored the statement, holding the sandwich with one hand while I stuffed a curly fry into my mouth. It was limp but salty, and I closed my eyes as I chewed, savoring the flavor.

"Mr. Folcrum?" he prodded.

I opened one eye. "I haven't had one of these in over two decades. Shut up and let me enjoy it."

"And then we'll talk?"

I took another bite of the sandwich in response. As I chewed, I studied him. Today, he was in a collared cotton shirt, the kind with two buttons at the top. White. I raised up and tilted to one side until I could see the rest of his outfit. Blue-striped pants with loafers. Guy was probably born into money and planned to sit in classrooms until he was fifty, then move to the front of them.

He seemed old to be in college. Forty, probably. I took a sip of the root beer and swallowed. "You got a job, Timmy? Or do you just go to school full-time?"

He stiffens. "I'm in finance. Well, I was. I took a break to go back to school. Why?"

"Just asking. I was an electrician. You probably knew that already."

He nodded. "Oh yes. I can confidently say that I know just about everything there is to know about you, Mr. Folcrum."

"Lots of people think that." I took another bite of the sandwich and set it on the foil wrapper, sitting back in the seat as I chewed. "If you knew everything, you wouldn't be here wanting to know about December 6."

"Okay," he allowed. "I guess I know everything there is to know about you *prior* to that date."

"What's my momma's name?"

"Your mother's name was Blaine. She passed away ten years ago." He matched my position, leaning back in his own chair and resting his hands on his thighs.

"Okay. Who was my best friend?"

"Wally Nall."

"You talked to him?"

He smiled the sort of smug, annoying smile that would get a man punched in these halls. "No," he admitted.

"So you *don't* know everything. Betcha don't know that I was sleeping with his wife."

He frowned. "Were you sleeping with his wife?"

"Well, you don't know, do you? You should talk to him and see."

"He testified on your behalf at trial. If a man was sleeping with my wife, I wouldn't do that."

"You wouldn't?" I hunched forward and picked up a ketchup package, then tore it open with my teeth. "Well, that says something about you, Timmy."

He didn't like the nickname. His mouth went flat and tight, pinching together like a new intake, worried someone was gonna try to put something between their lips. It was either the nickname or he was pissed that he'd just shown me some of his cards. He came here to get the dirt on me, but I was more interested in him. I knew about myself. I'd read that damn book front to back a hundred times.

"Serious question." I flattened the ketchup package, emptying it out onto a napkin. "If you could help prove a man's innocence and keep him from going to jail for life, would you? If the guy was banging your wife?"

He held up his hands, showing off his lack of a wedding ring. "No wife, Lee."

"Just because you don't wear a ring don't mean you don't have a wife. Maybe you're worried I'll break out of here and kill her."

He scoffed. "I'm absolutely not worried about that."

"Don't think I can break out or don't think I'd kill her?"

"I don't think you'd kill her. If"—he corrected himself—"there *was* a wife. But there isn't. I'm divorced. Recently divorced. If you want to kill my ex-wife, please. Have at her."

"Why don't you think I'd kill her? Haven't you heard? I'm a killer, Timmy."

"Of little girls," he clarified. "Not anyone who can defend themselves."

There was something in the way he said the first part, a crack in his voice. A clue. I moved my chair closer to the table and peered at him through the cloudy glass. "You got a little girl, Timmy? A daughter? Some cute brown-haired preteen? Or maybe younger? Maybe—"

"Stop."

"Ah, so you *do* have a daughter. Or a niece? Maybe your own little girlfriend?" I grinned at him. "Maybe you do know everything there is to know about me, Timmy. Maybe you and I are more alike than I thought."

"Are you saying you did more than kill those girls? Is that what you're saying?"

"Oh, you know what happens to 'Chesters' in these walls." I used my tongue to dislodge a piece of food from between my right-front teeth. "I'd fess up to murder before I admitted to that."

He rose abruptly, and the chair squeaked as it scraped against the floor. "I think we're done here."

"Bring me a Big Mac next time, Timmy. Big Mac with cheese and all the fixings. Root beer and fries. Upsized." I grabbed the last fry and dragged it through the ketchup, then popped it into my mouth. "Don't forget it. I won't talk to you without it."

He stopped just before the door, and I knew what he was doing: considering telling me to fuck off, which was fine. But he wouldn't. And even if he did, he'd still show back up, paper bag in hand, begging for whatever he could get.

There was only one Leewood Folcrum. Even if I wasn't the monster they thought I was.

CHAPTER 15

PERLA

I loved when Perla came to the office because she always brought me something. Something small, like a box of chocolates or a candle. Once, she brought me a pot of tulips. No one ever even notices me at the desk, so that tells you something about her right there, and how nice she was.

—*Gloria Richards, receptionist to Dr. Maddox*

"Scares you?" Dr. Maddox moved to the edge of her seat, a dumb fish on the hook, and I pinned my lips together to keep from smiling. "In what way?"

Yes, Perla, in what way? I had to be careful here. Once I said something, it would instantly be set in concrete. Destined for the court testimony and the pages of her future book. Any response would be a step down a path I couldn't backpedal from without raising suspicion.

"It's like there are two sides of him. He's a good man—a great husband, most of the time. I could tell you . . ." I looked up to the ceiling, blinking rapidly as if to keep from crying. "I could tell you so many stories, so many moments where he did something that just touched my heart."

"Can you give me an example?" she asked. This woman had way too much patience. If it had been me, I would have brushed right over the *my husband is wonderful* dribble and cut right to the chase—his other side. Instead, she was all big ears and captive eyes, waiting for me to come up with an example.

That was no problem. I had dozens. "Well, when we first moved in together, we were in a tiny apartment—this was before I got my trust fund and before he had really started earning any significant income— and we were tight on money."

Really tight on money. When my credit card had maxed out, I had called George, crying, and he had refused to send me anything. Now I realize he was trying to teach me money management, but back then, I had seen it as stubborn cruelty. He had plenty of money; I needed it, so *he* needed to give it to me.

"I got my period, and it was the first time that Grant had seen that . . . experience. I was in so much pain. My cramps were really fierce back then, and I was in bed, sweating and moaning and thrashing . . ." I laughed at the memory. "God, I was such a wimp. Anyway, Grant didn't know what to do. My discomfort was a problem that he didn't have the answer to, and didn't have the data needed to find the answer. He ran out the door and came back twenty minutes later with bags of stuff. I think he bought every single product in the feminine-care aisle. And he did *not* have the money for that. He didn't have any money to spare, but he spent, literally, his few last dollars trying to buy something that would give me some relief." I let out a small laugh. "He's still like that when I get my cycle each month. He brings me things, pampers me. Still worries over me. Honestly, I always pretend that it lasts a day or two longer than it does just so I can soak up that attention."

I glanced at her and flinched at the smile splitting her face in two. Her hands were holding the notepad with a white-knuckled grip. She'd probably never been spoiled by a man. Most women hadn't. Most women took the shit they were given and didn't expect or demand anything more.

"Oh, how sweet," she gushed, and she was right. Grant was very, very sweet. But "sweet" had never gotten anyone's panties wet.

"So anyway . . ." I pulled at the hem of my skirt, making sure it fully covered my knees. "That's the one side of Grant."

She waited, her pen still stubbornly tucked into the ring of her notebook. I didn't know how she expected to remember all this. I glanced around, looking for cameras. "Are you recording this?"

"Oh, no. I don't record any sessions. I find my patients are more comfortable if they don't feel like they're being spied on."

"So you don't have any cameras in here at all?" I pressed.

"Not a one." She gave a merry shrug, as if that were something to be proud of. It was idiotic, that's what it was. She should have one for security's sake, if nothing else. Especially with these rows of notebooks just sitting out, full of people's secrets. "Should we continue?"

I pushed my opinions to the side. So what if she had lax security protocols? I wanted everyone to know what I talked about in these sessions. Not right now, but later . . . The notes from this session would be gold to the public. Gold that could be exploited in a number of ways.

I glanced at my watch, fiddling with the silver band and adjusting it on my wrist. "Well, the other side of Grant isn't as . . . sweet." I grimaced. "You have to understand that he's an extremely focused individual. When he zeroes in on something, he can obsess over it. And there are certain things, especially from his past, that he does that with. Lately, he's begun to do it with Sophie."

"Wait—" She held up her hand in the same way a crossing guard would. "What's an example of something in the past that he obsessed over?"

This example, I had at the ready. While it wasn't the best, it—if ever shared with police—could lead them down a treasure trove of rabbit holes and Easter eggs on Grant. "Well, there was a man I used to work with. He did maintenance on one of our complexes." I smoothed the line of my skirt down again, watching out of the corner of my eye to see if the shrink picked up on the nervous tic.

She didn't. I continued on.

"Grant and I were at dinner, and we ran into him. Just briefly. We passed on the sidewalk, and I introduced the two of them; then we went home. I didn't think anything else about it."

The psychiatrist was now perched on the edge of her seat. I imagined her falling forward, her large breasts bouncing against the coffee table, her hands not quick enough, her cheekbone smashing into the glass.

"Well, Grant got it in his head that the man was attracted to me. He started to go into my office late at night and review the man's company phone records and cross-check them with mine. He started driving by the man's house each night, to see if he was home. He created false online personas and flirted with him through those, in an attempt to find out if he was single. He posed as bill collectors and called his ex-girlfriends, his relatives, his friends."

I looked out the window of her office, watching as a dark-colored sedan passed on the street outside. "The employee came to me, and I confronted Grant, and it led to one of the worst nights of my life."

"Did Grant get violent with you?"

I shook my head. "That's not what this is about. It's not that Grant has a temper. It's about how he can't stand to not have the solution to a problem. Grant saw a problem: a handsome employee who was attracted to me. He could have just proposed a solution, like firing the man. He didn't. Instead, he created his own solution, and it was a horrible one, for all parties involved."

I waited for her to ask what that solution was, prepped to deliver a big hem-and-haw routine before I told her the story, but instead she took a different, boring path.

"Where is the man now? Are you still in communication with him?"

"No. I don't know what he did after he left the apartment complex. He quit in the midst of all of it. Quit and just left." I shrugged. "Problem solved."

It wasn't a lie, but it wasn't the truth. Frank hadn't quit, but the problem had been solved. More by me but in part by Grant.

I looked at my watch and winced. "I'm sorry. I have to get across town for another appointment." I stood and adjusted the tuck of my turtleneck into my skirt. "Thank you for listening."

She rose and placed her notebook down on the table. I glanced at it; the page was practically empty. So this was what people paid for . . . an hour of someone paying attention to them. What garbage. She hadn't unlocked any of my feelings or fixed any of my problems. She'd just sat there and asked dumb questions.

She extended her hand and I shook it. She had one of those weak half shakes, the kind where our grips didn't fully connect and you felt like she was slipping out. "It was a pleasure to meet you, Perla. Is it all right if I call you Perla?"

"Of course. I'll see you next week, same time?"

"It's a date!" She smiled brightly, like a circus clown.

Out of everything, this part of the plan would be the easiest.

CHAPTER 16

On Sunday, we decided on a family trip to the park for a picnic and bird-watching excursion. We drove north, in the direction of the prison, and I tried not to think about the man who was growing closer and closer with each mile that passed.

I glanced into the back seat, where Sophie was curled up against the leather seat, her journal out and giant blue headphones on. I said her name, testing her ability to hear, and relaxed when she didn't look up.

"She loves that journal," Grant said, following my glance. "Maybe we have a future novelist on our hands."

I scrunched up my nose. "Maybe. She'll have to elevate her interests a bit, first. Right now, I'm not sure anyone wants to read about her obsession with sixth-grade boys and the mall."

He readjusted his grip on the steering wheel, both of his hands in place, body perched forward, his chest almost against the horn. I didn't know how—or why—he always drove like that, but just the sight of it hurt my back.

Putting on his turn signal, he checked his side mirror twice, then eased into the leftmost lane and scoffed. "Oh, come on. I'm sure you weren't into deep theology at her age." He flicked off the blinker. "I mean, you know . . . before."

"Before my father left and I was a ward of the state?" I said tartly. "Yeah, that definitely changed my perspective on things. I was all sunshine and rainbows before that."

He pressed his lips together, and I sighed, irritated at myself for snapping at him. "No, you're right. But I was never into going to the mall." I reached over, pulling his hand off the wheel and threading my fingers through his. "And I always liked the older boys." I wiggled my eyebrows at him. "Like Grant Wultz."

His gaze met mine, and a warmth that only he could deliver hit me. Inside, I was a frigid expanse, but from the very beginning, he had always been able to affect me. Even if it was just a surface thaw, it was there and it was real, and I did love him for it.

Too bad the ability to thaw ice wasn't going to save him. I needed a pawn for my blockbuster crime, and he was the perfect fit.

———

We reached the park and paid the ranger, then parked in the lot next to an ancient RV with a giant satellite dish affixed to its side. Grant took the cooler out of the trunk, his binoculars already hanging around his neck, and I got the bag and blanket. The sky was getting dark, so I added three emergency ponchos, just in case of rain.

We hiked the trail for fifteen minutes before Grant found a spot he was happy with. After spreading out the blanket, I started to unpack the cooler as he paced at the edge of the clearing, his binoculars on his nose, his body straining to every inch of his six-foot frame.

"I don't understand him," Sophie announced from her spot in the middle of the red blanket. "What's so interesting about birds?"

"I have no idea," I said, prying open the plastic lid of the fruit salad. "But it could be worse."

She examined her elbow, then scratched it. "I don't know," she said dubiously. "There are bugs out here. And you have to walk. And it's just so boring, looking for things in the trees."

I had to laugh. "Don't let him hear you say that. He'll be crushed."

"So, what? *Lie* about it?" She smirked, our conversation from the other night still fresh in both our minds.

I gauged her with mock seriousness as I unwrapped the sandwiches. "Oh . . . I'm not sure you have the skills to convincingly pull that off." She glared back at me. "I'm better than you think." I shrugged. "Okay, then, let's see you in action." I checked the time on my vintage men's Rolex watch—a gift from my adoptive father when I had turned eighteen. "See if you can keep up the charade for an hour."

Grant let out a yelp, and we both turned to see him sprinting through the trees, binoculars in hand as he went on the chase of some winged conquest. I gave Sophie a pained look, and she giggled, then quickly wiped the amusement from her face.

"It's not funny, Mom. Do you know how rare the orange-winged flatterbacker is?" She spread her arms in an exaggerated and almost perfect imitation of her father.

"I don't know," I said soberly. "Why don't you tell me?"

She huffed and waved her hand at me dismissively. "Just give me my sandwich. I can't possibly explain it to someone like you, who knows nothing about birds. Me, I find them *fascinating*." She widened her eyes to emphasize the word.

"Not bad," I allowed and passed her a chicken-salad sandwich. "Entertaining but over the top. You'll have to tone it way down for your father."

"I know," she said, settling back down on the blanket and taking a big bite out of the sandwich. "Just watch a master at work. Once I eat, of course."

"Of course," I agreed.

I wasn't daft. I could recognize my own negative influence in her eager desire to lie with permission. Not that it was really lying . . . it was just doing what I liked to do—play a part.

There was nothing wrong with that. It staved off the boredom, and that—at least for someone like me—was good for everyone.

By the time Grant returned, we were both done with the sandwiches. I was lying on my back, growing sleepy. Sophie had her journal out, her pen in motion unless it was time to grab another grape.

"You won't believe what I saw." Grant dropped onto the blanket, breathing hard. "A bald eagle, and I think I see his nest. I climbed up a tree to get a better look, but we might have to get to the next plateau to really be able to tell."

We? I closed my eyes. If he thought I was hiking up to the next ridge to see a stupid bird, he was crazy. I had leg day tomorrow, and I needed to have some muscle endurance left before the deadlifts took them out.

"Really?" Sophie dropped her journal and spun around to face her father. "A bald eagle? Is it still there?"

I unwrapped his sandwich, passing it to him as I watched my daughter warily, wondering if this was part of her act or if she was genuinely excited by the sighting. It was hard to tell, because a bald eagle was fairly cool—way cooler than a split-tag cardinal or a brown spotted dove. And this wasn't the overexaggerated reaction she'd delivered to me just twenty minutes earlier. This was genuine interest.

Or was it?

I didn't like it, I decided as she sat right beside him, peppering him with questions about the bald eagle's lifespan and diet. Her deception was confirmed when she shot me a sly side smile as Grant tilted his head back to down a bottle of water.

Her talent was eerily convincing, the role executed to perfection, and I wondered if it was the only one she was playing in our lives.

———

I knew my husband well enough to know he didn't plan for our bird-watching expedition to journey past the prison, but it still felt almost staged when the big gray building appeared on the horizon. It was stuck on the top of a ridge, like a sentry standing guard, just a dot at first, but then growing bigger and bigger until I thought we were going to drive right up on it. We didn't, of course; the road curved and it moved to Grant's side, and I pursed my lips and let out a long, slow exhale, hoping my husband wouldn't notice how every muscle in my body was tense in expectation.

"What's that?" Sophie called from the back seat. I didn't turn, my gaze stubbornly affixed out my window, looking in the opposite direction of the prison.

I said nothing, expecting Grant to respond, but he didn't and she spoke up again. "Hellloooo?" she sang out. "What's that big gray building?"

Grant tilted his head, looking out the window. "Looks like a prison. See the big circles of wire on top of the fences? That's how you can tell."

"So, like a jail? Full of criminals?"

He reached over and closed his palm over mine. He squeezed, and I pulled my hand away, annoyed by the action.

"Well, yes. It's where people go to serve time for their crimes. They aren't exactly criminals, Sophie. Just people that made mistakes—"

"Yes," I interrupted. "It's full of criminals." I glared at him, fed up with the kid gloves he always insisted on wearing around certain topics.

"I'm never going to go to jail," she announced dryly.

Grant chuckled, returning his hand to the steering wheel. "No, I don't imagine that you would."

No, she would never go to jail. I turned in my seat, tucking one foot underneath myself so I could face Grant. Through his window, I watched the building pass. It was far enough away that the men outside were too small to be distinguishable, but I still tried to look, to see if he might be there. Did he get time outside? Or was he isolated, kept inside?

Grant glanced at me, and our gazes held for a moment, a moment of silent communication. He nodded his head toward the prison. "Have you ever been there?"

The question was so absurd that my jaw dropped. "No," I finally said. "Don't you think you'd know if I went to the prison?" I let out an incredulous huff. "Why, have you?"

It was his turn to give me a look, paired with a long judgmental pause. "No," he said. "But if I ever do, I'll be sure to let you know."

I twisted back in the seat and flipped the AC vents fully open, needing the fresh air on my face. I suddenly felt flushed, like I had been caught in a lie, which was ridiculous. There was no way Grant had any idea what I was up to, and if he did discover that I was researching the Folcrum murders, so what? I had the right to do that. More than enough right.

We drove the rest of the way in silence. Back at the house, I went straight inside, stripped, and stepped into the steam room. Lying back on the teak bench and looking up into the thick air, I thought of those big, tall walls. The sad-looking recreational areas.

The truth was, it wasn't really Grant's business if I'd ever gone to the prison. And maybe one day I *would* go. Maybe one day I would sit down across from one of the most famous killers in the world and introduce myself.

The thought was both horrifying and exhilarating—a moment I wouldn't be able to take back once I did it, which was why I couldn't. Not before Sophie's birthday party.

CHAPTER 17

JOURNAL OF SOPHIE WULTZ

The car ride home was so weird. I think Mom and Dad are fighting. I don't know when it started, but it felt like a coffin when we were driving home.

Speaking of coffins, seeing the prison was cool. I gotta say, it seems like a dumb idea to put all of the dangerous people together, in one place. I mean, it would just take one crazy nut to cause a lot of people to die.

I'll never go there. If I do anything worth being locked up over, I'll make sure I lie my way out of it.

I should probably tear up this entry. If you're reading this, I would confess to any crime I committed. Honesty is always the best policy and the other stuff is all a joke.

CHAPTER 18

PERLA

I wouldn't say that Perla was pretty . . . I guess you could say that she was a handsome woman. Like, not delicate or really very feminine. She was always dressed really conservatively. And her nose had this, like, speed bump in the middle of it.

—*Ann Wiffle, social events director, Brighton Estates*
Country Club

I spent Monday morning calling plastic surgeons, and my stress level grew with each call. I couldn't even get an initial appointment in the next three weeks, and was being quoted surgery dates three to six months past that. I tried sweetness, then aggression, but every one of those bitches on the phone needed a surgical reduction on her ego.

I finally broke down and called Morayi and asked her to lunch. It was risky, going inside our neighborhood's inner circle for help, but I was desperate. I dressed carefully for the event, pairing soft gray cashmere pants with a cream turtleneck and chunky black onyx earrings. I pulled on my highest pair of black slingbacks, aware that I would still fall short next to the ex-model.

I was already seated at the best table in the restaurant when the statuesque African beauty entered. The effect on the room was immediate, a tidal wave of attention that shuddered toward the hostess stand. Morayi stood at the podium, her impossibly long legs accentuated by a short emerald-green silk jumper. Her dark skin glowed, and she exuded confidence as she caught sight of me and waved, then strode forward.

I could spend a million dollars and still never be half as pretty as her. I knew that, yet I still tried to spot her husband's handiwork every time I saw her. I told myself there was no way she was born into such beauty, but maybe she had been. After all, she'd been on billboards and in magazines ever since she was a child.

"Perla." She hugged me and kissed my left cheek, then my right. She smelled like blackberries and vanilla. I forced myself to pull away. "It's been too long! Where have you been?"

The waiter was waiting, Morayi's chair already pulled out, and she dropped into it without looking at him. I tried to remember if anyone had pulled my chair out. I didn't think they had.

"So?" She folded one arm elegantly over the other and leaned forward, raising a brow. "Talk to me—because you were *hot* to get this lunch, P."

I didn't spit it out. I laughed and asked about her kids; then we talked about the newest arrivals to the neighborhood and mused over the sushi selection. It wasn't until we were done with the second course that I brought up her husband.

She tilted her head, showcasing her slender neck, and studied me. "Yeah, I could get you in with Kellan. But what for?"

I gave her a dry look and gestured to my face. "Don't act like this isn't a project that's long overdue."

She lifted one shoulder in a shrug. "What, just some preventative maintenance?"

"I was thinking a nose job and removal of this." I tapped the mole.

She leaned forward, studying me openly. "Turn your head to one side," she instructed. She reached out and gently touched my nose, then

73

sat back. "Your bone structure isn't bad," she commented. "I think a little refinement would make a big difference."

"I'd also like some body work," I admitted. "Just a little bit of lipo in my problem areas."

She shrugged once more. "Sure. Lipo's not really K's thing, but you might as well do it all while you're under." Placing her elbow on the table, she rested her heart-shaped face in one palm. "How does Grant feel about the surgery?"

I bristled at the question. It didn't and shouldn't matter what my husband thought about it. This was my face. My body. I forced a laugh. "He's fine with it. What man wouldn't want a prettier wife?"

She made a noncommittal sound. "Some like a fully natural look. You remember what happened with Lydia Stone."

"Lydia Stone looked like a porn star who'd been stung by a bee," I argued. "I'm surprised she didn't divorce herself when she looked in the mirror." I widened my eyes. "Wait, Kellan wasn't her doctor, was he?"

She snorted. "Please."

"Well, Grant's good with it. He should be, since it's all his idea."

"*His* idea?" Her brows pinched without a single wrinkle breaking the smooth expanse of her forehead. "What do you mean?"

"He suggested it was time for a little improvement. He has a big work event coming up. In fact, that's why I'm under a bit of a time crunch. I need it to be done in the next month, if possible."

She let out a sharp laugh, one loud enough to catch the attention of a passing waiter. "In the next month?" She picked up her wineglass and shot me a look. "Girl, there's getting you on K's schedule and then there's *getting you on K's schedule*, you know what I mean?"

"I know. I'm sorry." I winced. "I wouldn't ask if it wasn't important."

"It's *not* important," she said bluntly. "Kellan's other work is. That's why his schedule for cosmetic procedures is so limited."

Oh yes, we were all aware of Kellan's dedicated efforts to cure the world, one cleft palate at a time. He wouldn't shut up about it. Were their facial deformities really any different from mine?

The waiters appeared, each in a pale-blue linen uniform, and presented the third course. I waited until they left, then picked up my chopsticks. Morayi was busy with hers and seemed to have moved on from the topic, which was unacceptable.

"You always say that you can make anything happen," I reminded her.

"Look, a month?" She shook her head. "Uh-uh. It isn't gonna happen. I could get you in for an initial consultation in the next two or three weeks. And even that's pushing it." She picked up a piece that was covered in pale-brown shavings and popped it into her mouth.

I should have left it alone. Finished up the lunch and accepted the reality. But there was always a way, and this bitch was forgetting that she owed me a favor. I put down my chopsticks and leaned forward, lowering my voice. "M, please don't make me bring up Prince's school."

Her eyes narrowed. "What about it?"

"Remember, three years ago? You wanted Prince to get into the charter program but needed an address in Duarte in order to qualify."

"Oh, that is rich, Perla." She shook her head. "You're talking about the lease you gave us? It was an email. Took you like fifteen minutes."

"It was fraud," I shot back. "I gave you three years of lease records and doctored utility bills to provide to the school, plus had my office prepped and available to verify your occupancy if the school ever called. And look, now Prince is at the top of his class, likely going to . . . where? Juilliard? Assuming he doesn't get kicked out due to ineligibility."

Her perfect jawline clenched. This wasn't a woman I wanted to be enemies with, but this was worth it. I had her. She'd get me the appointment and the precious surgery date. She'd do this for me, and she'd expect me to return the favor one day.

I wouldn't.

CHAPTER 19

JOURNAL OF SOPHIE WULTZ

I have a secret and it's a good one. Jenna told Prista who told Mandolin that my dad's sister was someone famous and that there is a movie about her and everything. I told Mandolin to tell Prista to tell Jenna that I already knew my dad's sister was famous and that she's such a dork.

I don't even think my dad has a sister.

Of course, I'm not going to admit that, especially because Mandolin is finally paying attention to me and her house is the biggest in the neighborhood and she has a pony. Bridget is my best friend now, but I could see Mandolin taking over. Though . . . as rich and cool as Mandolin is, Bridget is way chiller and agrees with everything I say.

It's important that you have friends like that. Mom calls them feeder friends. She says that and I imagine a bunch of those scary fish that all jump together on a person and eat them. Instead, I think of people like Bridget as my cheerleaders. Like a fan club.

I like having fans and I like the idea that Dad's sister—my aunt—is famous. Maybe she'll be my ticket into Hollywood and how I become a star.

Now I just have to find out what she's famous for.

And if she actually exists.

CHAPTER 20

Dr. Kellan Keita stood before me, six foot one inches of pure medical competency. With degrees on his wall from UCLA and Stanford, his talented hands were well known in our circle for seamless and undetectable work. I should have gotten on his books years ago.

I sat on an exam table, in a thin medical smock that opened in the front, exposing my cleavage and belly through a gap down the middle. I had been unsure whether to keep my bra on, the nurse's initial instructions unclear, and had finally removed it. Now, with my nipples pebbling in the cold room, I regretted that decision.

"Your skin has good elasticity," he said, pulling and prodding at my face. He felt along my nose, then used his penlight to look into each nostril. "Inhale," he instructed, and I obeyed.

"The good news is, the size of your nose is very appropriate for your face. We don't need to reduce it; we just need to adjust the shape of it to build up the nasal tip a little."

He moved around to my other side and studied me, then spoke. "We can graft using cartilage from other parts of your nose. Very easy. You'll have puffiness and bruising, but once you heal, no one should realize that you've had work done. They will just recognize that you look great. It will be very subtle but powerful."

"What if I'm under bright lights? Will the scars show?"

"No. You'll have faint scars in the beginning, but they'll fade completely within six months." He clipped his pen to the front pocket of his lab coat.

"Now, you mentioned some upper-body liposuction. Can you remove that for me?" He motioned to the gown, and I took it off, then reluctantly moved the protection of my hair off my neck and over my shoulder.

His gaze immediately found my scar, but he covered it well. "Okay, let's talk through your areas of concern."

I went through an embarrassing tour of the fat pockets that had collected under my chin, encircled my stomach, and sagged over my panty line on my back. All areas that no amount of cardio or weight training had seemed to affect. He recorded them all on his pad of paper, his features quiet and professional, and made no acknowledgment of my bare breasts, which hung between us.

"That's it," I said, once I had mentioned everything.

He took a beat, then tilted his head, meeting my eyes. "Perla, I'd be remiss if I didn't ask you about your scar. Do you mind if I examine it?"

And there it was. I considered rejecting the request, but then nodded. He reached forward and used the pads of his fingers to gently knead across the length of it. The scar was an uneven line, a result of hesitancy during the act. That, paired with the shallowness of the wound, was the only reason I was still here.

"What caused this scar?" he asked mildly.

"I'd rather not talk about it." I pulled away. "It's an old injury."

"The stitch job is . . ." He winced. "It's a bit of a hatchet job. I could open up the wound and clean out the scar tissue. Repair the sutures and make it a lot less noticeable."

I touched my own hand to the spot. "I'd rather not. At least, not right now. Thank you for the offer. I know it's ugly."

He shook his head. "Not ugly. No. Our scars are never ugly. They are proof of what we've been through. Truth be told, they can be the most beautiful parts of us, if we learn to love them."

Oh, I understood that. It was why I didn't want him to touch the scar. It was mine, proof that I could withstand anything and proof that those who love you the most can be the ones who hurt you the most.

"Medically speaking, do you have any issues with shortness of breath?" He was still touching me, his fingers resting gently on my shoulder, and I didn't like it. I didn't like any of this.

"No." It wasn't entirely true, but it didn't matter that I felt like I was breathing through a straw whenever I did physical activity. As I told him before, I didn't want him to fix the scar. After the birthday party, once I'd become famous, I could unveil it. It would be part of my story, a bold mark to make me even more of a conversation piece.

I looked into his eyes. "I need this done this month. Really, as soon as possible."

He sighed. "Yes, my wife has me over a barrel with how urgently you want this done."

Not *want*—*need*. In two months, I'd be famous. I couldn't—*wouldn't*—do that with this ugly nose and shit-colored mole. "Any opening you have, I'll take."

"You can talk to my scheduler when you check out. I've let her know to fit you in." His dark lips were set, his jaw tight, but I didn't care if he was annoyed.

I asked about my recovery time.

"The rhinoplasty is more intensive than the liposuction. Both will be performed in our office, and you'll go home the same day as the procedure. Your face will be puffy and swollen for a few weeks. It'll take six months before you will know exactly how it looks, so don't judge my handiwork too early."

"How long before I'll look normal enough to go out in public?"

"Two or three weeks. You might have black eyes and some bruising. Icing it will help. The liposuction is minor; you'll barely notice any pain from that—though you might want to wait a month or so before you go out in a bathing suit. And of course, the mole . . . it's nothing. You won't even notice it."

I nodded, pleased with the timeline and how it fit. By the time of the party, I'd look normal. A prettier version of my normal. Ready for the spotlight. The interviews. The sympathy. The attention. It would be perfect.

At least, for me. It wasn't such good news for my daughter.

CHAPTER 21

You know, I was there the night that Grant and Perla met. Or *re*-met, I should say. None of us had seen Perla in a decade, and when she showed up, it was like the entire place shut down. She had just changed so much. We'd all heard she had gotten adopted by some rich family up in Burbank, and you could tell. She just, like, reeked of money and confidence. And I had been kind of flirting with Grant—I mean, we all had crushes on him then—but when he went outside to talk to her, I knew he wasn't going to come back. And he didn't. And, like, the next thing I knew, I heard they were getting married.

—Tonya Delron, gas station cashier

Dr. Maddox was late, so I spent the extra minutes lying on her couch and scrolling through *Murder Unplugged*'s forum, trying to find any mention of the email I had sent in. I had been intelligent about it, sending it from an anonymous email account, using a web browser on a burner device connected to a VPN. And apparently, so far, they had ignored it. No response to the email, no mention on their show, and no sharing it on their feed.

I had just gotten into a better position on Dr. Maddox's couch when I heard the office door brush open along the carpet. Turning my head, I watched as the psychiatrist bustled into the room, an overstuffed purse swinging from her shoulder. She had an iced coffee in one hand and shot me an apologetic look as she dumped her purse onto the desk.

"Traffic," she explained. "Sorry about that. Did Laney put you in here?"

I considered lying but didn't. "No. I let myself in. I hope that's okay." I pushed myself up to a seated position.

"Oh, it's fine." She opened one of her drawers and sifted through the contents before pulling out the yellow notebook. "Normally, we ask that clients wait in the waiting room, but it's fine."

I crossed my feet at the ankles and glanced at my watch—a quick dart of a glance, but one she caught.

Taking the soft chair across from the couch, she flipped open the notebook and uncapped her pen. "I'm sure you have places to be, so we can jump right in. How are things going?"

"They're okay." I switched the cross of my leg. "I guess. Same concerns as before."

"And I don't want to invalidate those concerns," she said with that same smile as before, the smile I wanted to smack off her face with a two-by-four. "But we also need to understand what is triggering those concerns and then weigh those in an unbiased way, one not influenced by our own history or emotions towards"—she glanced down at her paper—"Grant."

"Sure, of course." Look at me, easy peasy.

"Last session, we ran out of time before you got a chance to tell me your history with Grant. Let's talk about how you two met. How long ago was that?"

"Ages ago. I was only twenty-one."

"How nice." She wrote that down. "Were you in college?"

"Yes. I met Grant when I had gone home for an anniversary event of sorts. Grant and I had mutual friends, and we ran into each other there . . ."

"Hey." He found me under the tree in the church's backyard. He had a cup in hand and held it out. "Want a drink? I got two."

I glanced at the red plastic cup briefly, then shook my head. "No, I'm good." I held up the joint I had pinned between two fingers. "Don't tell the others."

He glanced over his shoulder at the church. "Wow. Bold. Aren't you afraid you're going to catch on fire?"

"If only I could be so lucky," I said dryly and held it out toward him. "Want a hit?"

He paused, but only for a moment. He placed the drinks on the ground and stepped closer, his dress shoes crunching on dead leaves. When he carefully took the thin joint from me, our fingers brushed, and a shiver of pleasure ran through me. He brought it to his lips and closed his eyes as he took a deep hit. Holding it in, he passed it back to me, then slowly blew a stream of smoke from his lips. "I'm Grant Wultz. Lucy's brother."

He pointed at his chest as if I didn't know who he was, but I had worshipped Grant Wultz for as long as I could remember. I hadn't been back here since my dad was taken away, hadn't seen Grant in a decade, but he had only grown more handsome since then. Gone was the thin teenage boy with dots of acne and a smattering of facial hair. He was a man now, one with a deep voice and muscular shoulders and biceps underneath his pale-blue button-up shirt.

"I'm Perla." I leaned against the tree and took my own quick hit. "Perla Thomas. That's what I go by now. I was—"

"Adopted," he finished. "I know. I heard. My parents told me." His eyes were trained on my face, as if he didn't notice the low-cut top or tight jeans. I'd worn both for him, on the chance that he would be here—and now he was.

I looked away, aware of how important it was for me to play the right role. "You still live in Summerland?"

"Fuck no." He laughed. "I moved to San Diego. Well, I went to Caltech, then moved to San Diego."

"Caltech? For what?"

"Corporate law."

"Really? You're a lawyer?"

He tucked his hands into his pockets and gave me a sheepish look. "No. I just thought that sounded cool. I was trying to impress you. I'm a data scientist."

I brought the joint to my lips and met his eyes. "I always thought you were cool, Grant Wultz. No impressing needed."

He grinned and the expression was slightly lopsided in the most adorable way. "Yeah?"

"Yeah. Especially in your football uniform." I returned his grin. "You still got that in a box somewhere?"

He winced. "No. Can't say I do."

"Tough break." I stubbed out the joint on the bark of the tree. "I'm going to get out of here."

"Oh. Sure. Yeah. I'm sure everyone wants to talk to you."

I rolled my eyes. "Yeah. Everyone loves the freak show."

"You're not a freak show." His gaze was back, diving into mine, and I wanted to curl up in it and never leave.

"Okay." I shrugged. "Well, good to see you." I reached down and grabbed my purse off the ground. "Stay cool, Grant. See you in ten years. Maybe you can dig up the uniform by then."

I was halfway up the hill toward the parking lot when he caught up to me, his fingers curling around my arm and tugging me to a stop. "Hey, Perla . . ."

I stopped, and this was it—the moment when he would either make my dreams come true or crush them into pieces.

"Take me with you."

I raised an eyebrow. "Where do you want to go?"

"With you?" He gave me a smile that managed to be both shy and cocky all at once. "Anywhere."

"I took him to my hotel room, where we fucked to a news report that was doing a recap on the Folcrum Party." I laced my fingers together and tucked them in between my knees. "That should probably have been my first clue that something was off. When he didn't turn off the TV."

"I'm sorry, the news was doing a recap on what?"

I lifted my gaze to her face, which was blank. This woman couldn't possibly be that out of touch. "The Folcrum Party."

"I'm not familiar with that term. What is that?" Her pen was perched on the page as if she planned to write down whatever I was about to say.

Part of me was relieved that she was so uninformed of depravity. The other was alarmed that the crime had fallen so far off the public radar. Then again, this was a clear sign that if I didn't step in, Leewood would rot in prison forever, forgotten.

"It was a crime that happened . . ." I looked to the side, trying to place the date, as if I didn't know it. "I don't know when, exactly. Maybe twenty years ago."

"Why do you think Grant should have turned off the broadcast?"

"It was, um . . ." I shifted uncomfortably in my seat. "Gory."

"In what way?" She leaned forward. This was why everyone in the nation had obsessed over this crime. When it came to bloodshed, we couldn't help but want to know more.

"It was a birthday party for a preteen. She had two friends there, sleeping over for the party. At some point in the night, her father came in and—" I broke off. "Some of their bodies were stabbed dozens of times. Like human pincushions, I think is what people said."

Her face went white. "Oh my. What a horrible event. They caught the man?"

"A neighbor heard the screams and called the police. They showed up, and the father was still holding one of the girls' bodies—his daughter—in his arms. They arrested him for the murders, but he always said he didn't do it. He claimed someone else had broken in and that he had found the girls already dead."

Her eyes were big, and this was why there had been a half dozen documentaries on the crime. Granted, it was twenty-plus years old, new atrocities replacing the old, which was why we were in a situation like this, where you said the infamous name and got a blank stare in response.

"So he's in jail now—the father?" She wrote something down.

I shrugged. "I guess? I don't know. I haven't kept up with it."

As soon as I said it, I heard the mistake. Once everything came out after Sophie's birthday, if someone reexamined these sessions, it wouldn't make sense for me to not know something about Leewood Folcrum's current standing.

But it was too late. The words were out there, and if I backpedaled now, it would only bring more attention to the matter. At least she hadn't written anything down, probably wouldn't even remember asking me the question.

Just to be safe, I glanced at my watch, then grimaced. "Oh no. I think we're out of time." I pushed to my feet and reached for the handle of my purse.

"No, it's okay. I don't have an appointment after this, if you want to finish out this conversation." She didn't move from her seat.

"I've got to go. Grant doesn't know I'm coming here, so I want to get back before he notices I'm gone. Thanks for the session." I tucked my purse under my arm.

I walked over to the door and glanced back at her. I gave her a short, nervous wave, then ducked out of the office.

It wasn't my best performance ever, but it wasn't half-bad.

CHAPTER 22

Well, let's see. I worked for the Wultzes for three years, because Sophie was nine when I started. Now I work for a family on the other side of the neighborhood. No dead bodies yet—wish me luck! I'm sorry. That was a joke. A horrible one. Can we rewind the tape and erase that I said that?

—*Madeline Franx, housekeeper*

"Mrs. Wultz?" Our maid stood in my office doorway, holding something in her hand.

I pulled open my desk's drawer, scanning the contents until I found the roll of stamps. "Yes?" Peeling a stamp free, I carefully placed it in the upper-right corner of the envelope.

"May I come in?"

I sighed and returned the roll to the drawer. "Yes, Madeline. What is it?"

"I thought you'd want to see this." The older woman stepped forward, her white sneakers silent on the dark-blue Persian rug. Extending her hand, she showed me a stained white cloth.

I moved the envelope to the side and took the cloth. It took me a moment to understand what I was looking at. A pair of panties. Small, Sophie's size. I turned them over, and the question on my lips died.

A bloodstain in the crotch, the mark faded from the wash. I looked up at her. "Where were these?"

"In her hamper. I haven't said anything to her."

"Don't. I'll talk to her." I folded the underwear over on itself, hiding the stain. "Thank you, Madeline."

"I just thought you should know. I mean, she's only eleven but—"

"I got it," I interrupted her. "You can go back to cleaning."

Her face tightened, but she nodded primly and turned to leave, her arms pinned to the sides of her uniform. Grant didn't like the uniform, but he didn't understand what it was like to keep a house—and staff—in line. The uniform was a constant reminder to Madeline of her place in the house, and she needed that reminder. Even with it, she often forgot.

I tucked the underwear in the pocket of my blazer. Here, Madeline had done well. I picked up my pen and wrote the address on the front in neat block writing. Taking my time, I tried not to think about what this development would mean to our family dynamic.

It wasn't good. I closed my eyes, inhaling deeply, and remembered my own first experience. I hadn't had a mother and had gone to my father for help.

Grant didn't need to know about this. For one, I didn't want to see his reaction. For another, I refused to share him, in that way, with her. What I told Dr. Maddox was the truth: Grant was so nurturing and attentive during my cycle. For him to lavish that attention on Sophie . . . screw that. And screw her for trying to take that away from me.

I put the letter in my purse and crossed the hall into Grant's office. It was a room he'd designed, one with a wall of humidors and wine pockets that surrounded the stone fireplace. Between the leather seating, the bearskin rug, and the framed art, it felt distinctively masculine, and was offset by a wall of windows that looked out onto the preserve. I opened one of the french doors and stepped onto the balcony.

From here, I could look left and down to the back lawn, where Sophie had a soccer ball and was lining up to kick it toward Grant.

She was in red shorts and a T-shirt, her skinny arms sticking out of the sleeves. She wasn't wearing a bra yet, her chest too flat—but soon that would change.

Another thing I wasn't ready for and couldn't allow to happen—her bloom into womanhood. She was already starting to flirt, testing out sly secret smiles and crop shirts that showed off her impossibly flat stomach. In comparison, I was falling apart, with a doughy midsection, swells of fat protruding from the upper sides of my hips, and cellulite dotting the fronts and backs of my thighs. Five workouts a week barely kept the decline at bay.

The liposuction would help, but it was only one heat in a losing race, and I refused to watch Sophie grow tall and lean, with perky little teenage breasts and a firm ass you could set a cup on. I was already sick of the teenagers at the club, all shiny hair and glowing skin, turning all the husbands' heads.

Even Grant's. He feigned innocence, but I'd caught the flick of his eyes, the appreciation in his stare, the big smile he flashed, and the ridiculous tips he gave. He always hastened to turn to me, reach for me, kiss me—as if proving to himself and me that he was still loyal, but I knew the desire that was deep in his heart. I stood between him and them, keeping watch on every move.

It wasn't fair to do the same with a woman inside my home. It would be an exhausting competition, day after day, for his attention and affection—one I would lose against the youth and beauty that she would become.

When paired with the overwhelming love Grant already had for her, there was only one way to win.

Remove the opponent from the field.

I fished the underwear out of my pocket and examined it. It was a sign, this happening now. A beacon cutting through the fog, reminding me of the direction to go. No deviation. No wiffle waffle. She might not be a problem now, but I'd fix that with the party.

It would be the all-purpose cleaner in my life. Messy now, clean later.

CHAPTER 23

There are things that you do to preserve your marriage. I learned this early on. I watched my adoptive parents, saw their bond, and took careful notes on how to replicate it. It was interesting, seeing a strong marriage up close. My father's relationships had always been short-lived connections full of arguments and crude jokes, with a backdrop of a blaring television set, a dirty couch, and a coffee table piled with empty beer cans. His relationship with me had been his longest and most meaningful, but not always a healthy one.

When CPS took me away and I ended up with George and Janice, everything was different.

Their home, beautiful and clean, with rooms they never even went into.

Their world, full of money and power and people who were smart and fashionable and didn't reek of alcohol or cars or dirt.

Their marriage, which seemed entirely focused on each other and making that other person happy, yet seemed big enough to welcome me in with open arms and warmth and love.

I tested their bonds, tried to break their seal, and when I was unsuccessful, I switched horses and focused all my energies on learning from it. As they say, if you can't beat them, join them.

I joined them, like a parasite stuck to a host, feeding off it, sucking the goodness out in minute quantities that would never be missed.

I realized then, but especially now, that George and Janice gave me everything. They taught me how to carry myself, how to speak, dress, and spend properly. They put me in the best schools with the best tutors. Every meal was an etiquette class, and weekend parties were a lesson on social networking and manipulation.

Not that George and Janice were manipulative—at least, they weren't intentionally so. But I was a tiny fly buzzing through those parties, one that listened to and watched everything. I heard the whispers and the side conversations, saw the hidden kisses and the sneers, the weak moments produced and exploited by alcohol. I saw how much power was created and maintained by my new family's money. And seeing that, tasting that . . . it was like having my first bite of real food.

After that, I could have never gone back.

———

We took the long way home from the restaurant, taking the route that gave us the view of Los Angeles's city lights at night. Rain started to gently pepper the Porsche's windshield, its cadence too soft to be heard over the music, which was set to a Dave Matthews Band playlist. The song on was one I'd heard a dozen times, and I sang along with the words as Grant drummed his fingers on the steering wheel to the beat. Our eyes met in the dark interior, and he smiled at me.

"Song takes me back," he said, turning on the wipers.

"Me too. God, that storm." I peered through the front windshield, trying to see the sky, but it was too dark out. "Way worse than tonight."

That night, we had driven four hours through a downpour with tickets to a DMB concert, and hadn't even considered changing our plans when they postponed the event by several hours. We had been hyped up on caffeine and lack of sleep, and were absolutely broke.

It hadn't mattered. We had donned ponchos and stood in a field, lighters in hand, swaying with a crowd as Dave sang "Satellite" to thousands of soaked fans as the rain streamed down. During the final chords, Grant had dropped to one knee and proposed with a cherry Ring Pop he had secretly bought at a gas station along the way.

"Satellite" was the wrong song for him to propose to. The following week, I had insisted he research their entire discography and pick the lyrics that best fit his feelings for me. Something other than "Satellite," which is literally just about a big dish in the sky.

He picked "Crush," which was the exact right pick, and when he selected it, I knew I had made the right moves in my seduction and the right decision in marrying him.

"Your seats smelled like mildew for months." He laughed.

I wrinkled my nose at the memory of the ancient Volvo I had been driving at the time. George and Janice had passed down their daily driver to me when I started college, and this trip was just one more instance of abuse that the sedan had endured. When my adoptive parents' estate had finally completed probate, a new car was one of the first purchases I made with my inheritance.

"What are you thinking about?" Grant reached across the gearshift and stole his hand into mine. I threaded my fingers through his and turned his palm over, admiring how well we fit together. We'd always fit well, in part because of our shared history—but also because I had worked my ass off, making sure the tumblers in our lock had lined up perfectly for a successful clench.

"Your proposal. Our marriage. What it takes to be successful."

"A lot of work," Grant pantomimed, in the nasally voice he used whenever he imitated me.

I brought his hand up to my mouth and playfully bit his knuckles, punishing him. "Yes, exactly. I'm so glad you understand." I grinned at him. "But no, I was thinking about George and Janice. What they taught me about love and marriage."

"I wish I'd been able to get to know them more." He squeezed my hand.

A wave of nostalgia welled, and I let the tears come, brushing them away as soon as I was sure he had seen them. "I do too," I said softly. "They were the best."

And that part wasn't a lie. They had been the best.

"What did they teach you about love and marriage?"

He knew the answer to this one, but I was still glad he asked it. We needed continual reminders to keep the ship afloat, and he was as dedicated to putting in the work as I was.

"Well, to always put our marriage first."

"We do that, right?" He stopped at an intersection, and his features were lit red by the light. He was so attractive, especially in moments like this, when concern darkened his features. Concern for us. Sometimes you had to spin the top just to keep it in motion.

"For the most part. You've been working a lot lately."

"That will be over soon. This project is almost finished."

"Try to finish it by Sophie's birthday. I want us to have that week to focus on her." Her last week. I'd make sure it was a good one.

The light changed and he gunned the Porsche 911's engine. The car had been his fortieth-birthday present, a splurge that was well worth it. The 1987 Carrera Cabriolet convertible was his dream car growing up, and he had mentioned it to me once—just once—six years ago, but I hadn't forgotten. I had written it down and then waited, because the present needed to matter, and the wait would only prove my attention and devotion to his needs.

"I hope to have it finished by then," he said carefully. "I can't promise anything, though. You know if I can make it happen, I will."

"I know you will." The comment came out wrong, snide and snippy, and I tried to cover it by kissing the palm of his hand. Of course he would try—for Sophie. He'd try anything for Sophie, more so than he would for me, and that was a festering bedsore in the body of our marriage.

You should love your children. But you're supposed to love each other more.

Another lesson from George and Janice, but one that Grant didn't agree with. He wouldn't say it—he could sense the volcano that would erupt—but I felt his resistance to it.

I also suspected what he dared not say: that maybe George and Janice didn't love me as much as each other because I wasn't their real child.

And perhaps there was a point there, but it didn't matter what the reason was. It didn't defy the logic and proof—you shouldn't love your child more than you loved each other. That equation didn't work. I had never begrudged George and Janice for their stance. I had understood and agreed with it.

"Dinner was good," Grant said, putting both hands on the wheel as he approached the sharp turn by the lake. "What was that thing at the beginning? A rice cake?"

"Yeah, I think that's what they called it. With tuna. Yeah, it was good. *Excellent* choice." I overenunciated the adjective, putting a playful lilt on it. "Want to stop at Cav's for dessert and a drink?"

He shook his head. "No, we should get home to Sophie. It's already late."

I tried to flick the irritation away, but it stuck. "Sophie's in bed."

"I know but I want to look in on her. You know she's always restless with a sitter."

I twisted to face the window, where droplets of water ran like blood down the glass.

"Perla." He reached for me, but I avoided his touch.

"Looking in on her is more important than an extra hour with me? You didn't seem to care about that when you stayed late 'working' at the office the other night." I put the word *working* in air quotes and immediately hated myself for it. This wasn't me. It wasn't us.

"Listen." He reached forward and turned off the radio. "You want to go to Cav's? We can go there."

"Oh great." I rolled my eyes. "Thanks."

He braked and I grabbed the armrest as the car shuddered over to the shoulder and then came to a stop on the side of the road. I looked at him for an explanation. "What's wrong?"

His hand closed on the back of my neck, and he pulled me forward until our lips met. His kiss was soft but dominant, forcing my lips into action, and I yielded, sinking forward and gripping his shirt as the rain rat-a-tatted against the roof, increasing in intensity.

He pulled away and looked into my eyes. "I love you," he said firmly. "Now, stop being difficult, and let me ply my wife with a chocolate torte and expensive wine."

My mouth quirked into a smile. "Fine," I said begrudgingly, as if I weren't getting exactly what I wanted.

I kept him out late intentionally, and after we'd stumbled into the house at 2:00 a.m. and paid the sitter, I kept my hand tight on his, pulling him past our daughter's door and into our bedroom, where I made sure that Sophie was the last thing on his mind.

From: tfk@hotmail.com

To: info@murderunplugged.com

Date: July 1 at 9:12 PM

Subject: don't miss your chance

star light

star bright

the Folcrum party was a pure delight

I wish I may

I will I might

Make another birthday end in fright

CHAPTER 24

TIM

Seven miles outside the town of Carlsboro, in the middle of a heavily wooded four-acre lot, sat Wally Nall's home. The former roofer lived in a small one-story house set a hundred yards off the main road, with peeks of the bright-red metal roof visible from the street. The color tied in well with the metal No Trespassing signs stapled to the pine trees on either side of the driveway.

Dr. Timothy Valden nosed his vehicle past the signage and traveled slowly down the dirt drive. Before he was halfway there, a man stepped out in the middle of the path, a shotgun tucked under one arm. He was short and wiry, with a full head of bright-white hair and a gap between his front teeth that Tim could see from inside the car. He held up his hand in warning, and Tim obediently braked.

He rolled down the driver's-side window. "Mr. Nall?" he called out.

"Yeah, who's asking?" Wally took a few steps to his right, keeping an approach angle on the car.

"My name is Dr. Timothy Valden. I'm a doctoral student who is doing research on Leewood Folcrum." He leaned his head farther out the window, not sure if the man could hear him. "Leewood suggested I speak with you."

Wally took a few steps closer. "You come all the way from Lancaster?"

"I did."

"And you said Leewood sent you?"

"Yes."

He leaned back his head and barked out a shrill laugh. "Bullshit." He made a circular motion with one finger, as if stirring a pot. "Turn that thing around, and don't let my shotgun hit you in the ass on the way out."

Tim didn't reach for the gearshift. "Leewood said you were his best friend."

"Easy to be a best friend to someone who ain't got no friends."

"Also said he had been sleeping with your wife."

The man's finger dropped, and he seemed to consider the statement; then he stepped forward until he was right at the car door, the butt of his gun knocking against the paint as he peered at his visitor. "You're a pretty fucker," he said. "They give out those looks at the colleges?"

"Can't tell you. I brought mine with me."

Wally gripped the sill of the car and bent forward until they were at eye level. He said nothing for a moment, just stared at him with pale-blue eyes. "He didn't fuck my wife."

"Okay." Tim lifted his hands from the steering wheel in surrender. "I was just telling you what Leewood said so you'd know I was legitimate."

"That was a running joke between us because he and Becca could never hold their own with me drinking, so they would pass out in bed together all at the same time. I was right there watching, and *nothing* happened between them." He glared, and at this distance, you could see the pitting of old acne scars on his cheeks. "Hell, that fat cow could barely crawl on top of my scrawny ass, much less a hoss like Lee."

"Understood."

"God rest her soul." He tapped his forehead, then made the sign of the cross on his faded-red T-shirt. Stepping back, he swung his shotgun in the direction of the house and pointed to a spot between an RV and a giant propane tank. "Park there and come on in."

"Thank you. I won't take up too much of your time. I—"

Wally had already turned and was ambling toward the house, gesturing over one shoulder for his visitor to come.

Putting the vehicle in Drive, Tim followed.

———

"So, you said your name was what, now?" The roofer sat on one side of a small round table, a sleeve of saltine crackers ripped open before him. Also on the table was a plastic tub of fish dip, one that gave off a strong scent. Twice, Wally had offered a cracker to his visitor; twice, Tim had refused.

They were in a nook between the kitchen and the living room, and without Tim jumping to conclusions, it was a good bet that the man lived alone. Every surface, save the table they were sitting at, was littered with things. There was a dirty garbage disposal on the kitchen counter, alongside a scattering of tools and screws, a pile of clothes, and two plastic grocery bags of items. Between their feet, a gray cat made figure eights, his soft tail tickling the back of Tim's leg.

"Dr. Timothy Valden. You can call me Tim." An itch formed in the back of his throat, and he tried not to think about the level of cat dander that must be in this place.

"And you're, what, writing a book on Lee?"

"It's a dissertation. Sort of like a report. It's part of my doctoral program."

"Yeah, I know what a dissertation is. But listen"—he stuck a dip-ladened cracker in his mouth and took a moment to chew—"if you're going to write about anyone, it should be me. I did a hell of a lot more interesting stuff than Leewood. Other than that one night—shit. His life was one boring rat race. Work, drink, sleep, repeat."

Yeah, the one word Tim wouldn't use to describe Leewood Folcrum was *boring*. He opened the folder he had brought in and pulled out a thin stack of papers. "You testified in Lee's trial on his behalf."

Wally shrugged. "So?"

"I'm curious why you did that."

"'Why'?" Wally wagged a skinny finger at him. "Look, I knew the man. Okay? Knew him better than any other pig fucker in this county. He wasn't a perfect man—hell, wasn't even close to that—but he wasn't what they said he is."

"Okay, well, that's what I'm trying to understand. Who Lee really is—or was."

"Well, he was an ass. That's the first thing you need to know. And mean as a snake."

"Mean enough to kill three little girls?"

Wally tilted his head, a cruel smile twisting his mouth. "Now, I didn't say that, did I? You're interrupting me, Tim. You here to hear me or hear yourself?"

"I'm sorry. Please, go ahead. But can we start back with when you met Lee? How long ago was that?"

The man leaned back in his seat, his fingers drumming the worn table. His fingers were dirty, dark lines under each nail, his knuckles scarred, the backs of his hands covered in liver spots. Like Lee, he was getting old and living a lifestyle where time hadn't been kind.

"Well, I met Lee when his daughter was a baby, so 'bout a decade before it happened. He was with Jessica, of course. Jessica was his wife. Smoking-hot little number but liked the nose candy. Cocaine, I'm talking about." He met Tim's eyes. "Nowadays, she'd probably be into meth, but back then he was a drunk and she was a cokehead—and then there was that baby, who, let me tell you, spent as much time over here as over there. My wife, God rest her soul, couldn't have kids, so she kinda adopted Jenny as her own. I didn't mind, because whenever I got tired of the kid, we'd just send her back over, and to be honest, I'm not sure if they even noticed where she was."

Nodding, Tim digested the information. "And Leewood was a drunk?"

"Well, as much as any of us are." He rose to his feet, circling the table to open up a large white fridge crammed into one side of the galley kitchen. "Speaking of alcohol, I've got Miller and Busch. What's your poison?"

"I'll take a Miller. Thanks." One beer would be fine. Nothing more, not with the drive ahead of him.

After cracking open two bottles, Wally set one in front of Tim and took his seat. "I guess Lee wasn't really a drunk; I shouldn't have said that. But he'd get sloshy on the weekends and at night. That was also when Jessica— She worked at the Dollar Tree down on Fifth Street. That was when she would get high. Not every night—hell, they couldn't afford that. But pretty often."

"What was Leewood like when he was drinking?" Tim reached for his beer and took a small sip.

"Oh, he was a happy drunk. Real friendly with the ladies. Got a little handsy, but hell . . ." He inhaled, then belched. "Who doesn't?"

Normal, upstanding, moral individuals. That's who didn't. "I guess it would depend on what your definition of 'handsy' is." The cat meowed at Tim's feet and put its paws on his bare calf, kneading the muscle without using its claws. Coughing, he reached for his beer and took another sip, trying to gauge the tightness in his throat. "You mentioned that the daughter was over at your house a lot. What was she like?"

"Smart," Wally said immediately. "You could tell she wasn't like the rest of us. She watched everything, that little girl did. Saw what the drugs was doing to her momma, saw . . ." He grimaced. "She would, like, study you, in a creepy kinda way. Like, whenever you'd look over at her, she was always watching you, or watching something, and taking a mental note of it. My wife hated it. Felt like we were being spied on."

"Did Leewood feel that way too?"

"Nah, I don't think so." Wally scratched underneath one arm, then pulled at the front of his T-shirt to separate it from his sweaty skin. "Leewood and her got real close once Jessica died. Too close, if you ask me."

Tim leaned forward because this . . . this was new information. "What do you mean, 'too close'?"

The man pointed at his beer bottle, which was already almost empty. "You want another beer? I'm gonna get one."

"No, I'm fine, thank you." He watched as Wally crossed the room. "So, what do you mean, 'too close'?"

"I don't know." Wally returned, twisting the cap off with the hem of his shirt. "I don't have any kids, so what do I know? It just felt strange sometimes, seeing the two of them together. It was like they was playing house and she was the wife. Not that he was doing anything—I mean, Leewood wasn't a pervert, that's not what I'm saying. I'm just saying that the girl acted that way. And once the mom died, she was on his case about taking his vitamins and things she wanted him to do around the house . . . Like I said, it was just weird. You had this eight-, nine-, ten-year-old kid, but she acted like she was three times her age."

Yeah, that checked out from everything he knew about Jenny Folcrum. The papers back then had covered the little girl extensively, with teachers all saying she was mature beyond her years and extremely intelligent. She probably had to have been, the lack of parenting requiring her to fend for herself from an early age.

Wally sat back down in his seat and leaned back in the chair, balancing on one leg. "Like one night Lee was over, and we were playing poker. He'd brought Jenny, and she'd wanted to play but Lee told her no, so she was watching something on TV, and whatever it was, it was violent. I walked by to get a beer, and there was some guy getting decapitated on the screen, and I asked her if she wanted to watch something else, like cartoons." He swigged a sip before continuing. "She looked at me like I was the stupidest shit on the planet and said that it was fine and I should get back to the cards because Leewood would need to go home soon, that it was getting late and he had work in the morning."

Wally gave Tim an incredulous look. "Can you believe that? Like he was the kid and she was giving him his bedtime."

Tim rubbed his fingers along his temple, thinking it over. "This is the first I've heard or read about their dynamic. Everyone else has said he was a pretty distant and uninvolved parent, that Jenny sort of fended for herself."

"I'm not sure who was fending for who in that house." Wally shook his head, then paused, listening to something. "Hot damn, I think that fucking peckerbird is back. You hear that shit?"

Tim shook his head. "No."

Wally pressed on the arms of the chair and stood. "Well, I've got one chance to get this fucker before he ruins my olive tree. You need anything else from me?"

"Just one question, then I'll be out of your hair."

Wally tilted back his beer and finished it off, gesturing for Tim to continue.

"Do you think Leewood killed those girls?"

He slammed the empty bottle down on the table, then reached for a shotgun leaning against the wall and shook his head. "Not a chance."

CHAPTER 25

PERLA

I didn't even know about Grant's family. I mean, it's not like we all sit around and talk about each other's siblings. My brother was USC's quarterback in 1987, and no one seems to ever want to talk about that, so why would I ask Perla about Grant's sister? But yeah, someone said something to me yesterday, so I guess now the whole neighborhood knows. I guess I could have figured it out, you know, because of his last name. But there are a lot of people named Wultz. I had a teacher in elementary school with that last name. Miss Wultz. She was a total bitch.

—*Laurelin Hodgkins, entrepreneur*

My watch buzzed and I looked away from Dr. Maddox to glance at the caller ID. *Grant.*

"I'm sorry, my husband is calling me. Let me send him a text."

She didn't respond and I looked up at her. Her lips were pressed together in a flat line of irritation.

"He's with our daughter," I said tightly. "Something might be wrong."

"Oh sure." She waved off the response, but the annoyance was telegraphed by the rigid set of her frame and the cluster of lines on either side of her mouth.

I tapped back a response. Can't answer. At the doctor's for my annual exam. All okay?

I placed it on my knees, on the platform created by my soft pencil skirt. "Okay. What were we talking about?"

"Your husband. You were telling me about when you got pregnant."

"Oh. We don't need to talk about that. I just thought it was important to mention that Grant never wanted to have a child. Sophie was an accident, one he wasn't pleased about."

"Getting pregnant can be very disruptive to someone's life, and to a relationship," she said gently, as if I were tender on the subject.

I wasn't. The real truth of the matter was that Grant had been positively giddy over the news of my pregnancy.

I had anticipated his elation, which was why I didn't tell him I was pregnant. I had planned to terminate the pregnancy as soon as I could get the paperwork handled and the appointment made. Then Christmas Eve came. The Christmas Eve that changed everything . . .

I stood on the cabin's front porch and watched as the snow came down. The moon was full, and the fresh layer of snow glowed, an undisturbed white carpet that stretched between the pine trees.

Our car was parked to the side, the windows already iced over even though we'd only been in the house for a few hours. I wrapped my arms tightly over my torso and considered going back inside and finding the gloves and scarf I had packed.

"Wow." Grant joined me on the porch, closing the cabin door tightly behind him and locking the knob. "It's freezing out here. You sure you want to go into town?"

"Yes." I rubbed my hands together. "Better now than in the morning. What if we get snowed in?"

He turned away from the door and wrapped his arms around me, hugging me to his chest as he briskly ran his hands over my arms, warming me up. He kissed the top of my head. "Okay, let's go before the store closes. You okay to run through the snow?"

I looked down at my new boots, my jeans tucked into their fur interiors, laced tight. "I'm good."

"Because I can carry you," he offered.

"No, let's go." I took his hand, accepting his help down the stairs, then gingerly stepped onto the snow, where I promptly sank knee-deep in the snow. Cursing, I turned to him for help.

He was grinning as he traversed the stepping stones, stopping beside me and lifting me, fireman-style, over his shoulder. My stomach cramped from the position, and I thought, for the briefest of moments, about the three-month-old fetus inside me.

Just ten more days, then I would have my appointment and it would be gone. No harm done. No one the wiser. Especially not my husband, who was opening my passenger door and carefully depositing me into the front seat. He paused before me, his mouth inches from mine, a goofy smile on his face, and when I moved forward, our lips touching, his nose was cold.

We were almost at the grocery store, rounding the final curve, when the minivan ahead of us slowed, its taillights glaring red. Grant immediately braked, but our sedan went into a skid. I grabbed the door handle and inhaled, holding my breath as we careened forward. Grant yanked the wheel but nothing happened, the woods rushing up on us in a second.

I woke up in the hospital, Grant beside me, his face gray with concern but his eyes shining bright with excitement. I was strapped to the bed, a neck brace keeping my spine in line, but my eyes moved, catching everything.

Grant's hand protectively on my stomach.

The doctor's mouth moving, his gritty voice sharing the age of the fetus. Undamaged by the crash. A miracle.

They told me the news and took my tears as ones of joy. Grant covered my face with kisses and told me how much he loved me. How happy he was. What great parents we would be.

I had almost died, and yet he couldn't stop celebrating an embryo he hadn't even known about twelve hours earlier.

They kept me in the hospital for two months while my body healed and the baby grew fatter in my belly. Eating my nutrients. Fueling my husband's joy.

It was horrible, a prison sentence I couldn't avoid and didn't deserve. An invasion in the relationship and plans I had worked so hard for.

". . . new relationships and that dynamic," Dr. Maddox continued, and I nodded as if I were listening.

Grant texted back. Everything's fine. Just call me when you're free.

"Now, how did Grant adjust once your daughter was born?" Dr. Maddox had chosen paisley capri pants and a gray jacket. The ensemble didn't match. I tried not to obsess over it.

"He learned to deal with it." Another slight rewrite of the truth. Grant's joy quadrupled the moment the screaming, red-faced infant came out.

The pants had lilac accents, and this was why I only wore neutrals. Janice had taught me that. Wear expensive, quality staples. If you must add color, do it with accessories. Take my outfit today. Gray pencil skirt. White turtleneck. Red coral necklace. Black purse. Black pumps.

Classic.

Conservative.

Quality.

"'Deal with *it*'?" She tilted her head. "You're referring to Sophie? Sophie is the 'it'?"

A mistake. I cleared my throat. "Not Sophie. I was referring to the act of parenting. It was hard for him at first, but he got better—or rather, hid his distaste better. I'm not sure that he's ever been happy being a father."

No, not happy. Boisterously ecstatic. Annoyingly exuberant. When the nurse deposited Sophie's screaming body into his arms, his entire face changed into a combination of fear and love I had never seen before.

I saw then the power Sophie had over him. Naively, I thought I would be able to use that power as a tool of manipulation. I didn't realize that power was going to grow up and have its own ideas, its own desires, its own evil motivations.

CHAPTER 26

LEEWOOD FOLCRUM

Inmate 82145

On December 6, I was the first one at the scene. We got a
9-1-1 call from a neighbor who had heard girls screaming
in the Folcrum trailer, which was in the Daisy Acres trailer
park. I'd actually been to that specific trailer before, when
Leewood's wife died. We knocked on the door, but no one
answered, so we started looking in the windows. I looked
in one, which turned out to be Jenny Folcrum's bedroom,
and I could see the dead girls and Leewood. He was sitting
in the doorway and holding Jenny in his arms, and he was
crying. That's something I don't hear people talking about,
but he was actually bawling. Bawling and saying that he
was sorry. He said that over and over again, and then he
clammed up and wouldn't say anything to anybody.

—*Luke Plakenhorn, Los Angeles County Sheriff's*
Department

"This motherfucker is more regular than a high school girl's period." I peered in the window of the visitor room and waited for Redd to unlock the door.

"Next time, ask him to bring a few extra sandwiches. You're eating better in there than we are." Redd knelt on one knee, his movements slow as he worked the key into the lock. I glanced over at Johnson, who leaned against the wall and watched, one hand resting on his protective vest.

Both men were hefty—two hundred pounds, at least. If I tried to run, I wouldn't get far. The doors on either side of this hallway were locked, cameras recording the space, and between the two of them, I'd be flat on my back within sixty seconds, even if I did manage to land a swing during the process.

It wasn't worth the swing, and I wouldn't cause trouble for either of these two. We had bad COs and okay ones, and they fell on the better end of that spectrum. They didn't fuck with me and I didn't fuck with them, and that's how everything stayed smooth.

"This guy some sort of reporter?" Redd twisted the key, and the tumblers loudly clanked open.

"A researcher. Once I'm gone, you all can read about me in an academic journal somewhere." I smiled down at him. "Well, not you, Redd. But someone who can read. Maybe Johnson has a friend who knows a friend who can sound out the big words."

Both men chuckled as Redd hefted upright, his breath wheezing.

"You good?" I asked.

"Shut the fuck up. You ready to go in?"

"Ready."

He shuffled me back a few steps and nodded to Johnson, who swung open the door. On the other side of the glass, Tim Valden rose to his feet as if I were a king, making my entrance.

"I went and talked to Wally."

Today, he'd brought Chick-fil-A. I'd never had Chick-fil-A. If it was in business when I was out, it hadn't been in our town, and the idea of a fast-food restaurant based around chicken wasn't something that appealed to me.

That opinion changed the moment I bit into a fried-chicken sandwich worthy of a county fair gold medal. I set the sandwich down on its wrapper at the mention of Wally Nall. Bet he'd ended up losing all his hair.

"He bald yet?" I asked.

"Uh, no." Tim linked his fingers together in front of him, his elbows sticking out from his body like two chicken wings. "Has a full head of white hair."

"Damn." I shook my head and picked the sandwich back up. "What'd old Wally say?"

"Some interesting things."

"Yeah? Like what?" There was also a pile of waffle fries, and I eyed them as I took another bite.

"He talked about your wife, Jessica."

"Yeah, he didn't really like Jessica." I wiped at my mouth with one of the brown napkins. "He call her a cokehead?"

"He said she did drugs and that you drank a lot."

"Real insider information you got there, Timmy," I said sarcastically. "Your book's going to be a bestseller."

He smiled, but the gesture was starting to run thin on the edges. "I'm not writing a book, Leewood. You know that. Everything you tell me, it's only going to be read by the doctoral-review team and myself."

I didn't really care if he shouted our conversations from the rooftop. I shrugged. "Yep. We partied. Call DFS."

"And he said that you and Jenny were close."

"What father-daughter ain't?" I sat back in my chair and wiped off my hands.

"Is that what you and Jenny had? A typical father-daughter relationship? Because I got to tell you . . . most fathers don't take a knife to their daughter."

Anger swelled, but I learned years ago to contain that shit. It didn't even make it up my chest. "I'm innocent—or didn't you discover that in your research? Someone came into the house and did all that. It wasn't me."

"Right. Even though your fingerprints were on the knife—"

"I'm sure yours are on the knives in your kitchen."

"And you were sitting there, covered in blood, holding Jenny's body when the cops arrived."

I sighed. "Find your child bleeding to death and tell me you won't hold her in your arms."

"You didn't find them, Lee. The police dug into this. Your defense team exhausted this. They looked for evidence of an intruder. None was found. No outside DNA or prints. No one came in, killed those little girls, then left. Didn't happen."

He thought he knew so much. I shook my head. "Don't know why you're here if you already know everything."

"I'm here to understand why."

"Why the girls died?"

"Yes."

"People kill people all the time. This isn't a new thing, Timmy. Go bother one of the other three hundred convicted killers in this building."

"People kill people all the time . . . due to motive." He spread his hands. "What was the motive?"

"I didn't have one."

"Exactly. So why do it?"

I leaned forward and leveled him with a look. "Why are you here?"

He blew out an irritated breath. "To understand your motivations."

"To understand my motivations for killing those girls?"

"Yes."

"Then you're wasting your time, because I didn't kill them." I glared at him, not knowing why I was even talking to the guy. Why did I care whether he believed me? Why didn't I just tell him what he wanted to hear, then go back to my cell?

Because then he'd leave.

I started to stand, then sat back down. "Look, I can't explain something that didn't happen."

He groaned. "Listen, Leewood. I'm sure there's some part of you that wants to tell your side of the story. The real story, not this bullshit that you've claimed for the last twenty years. In fact . . ." He made a big show of closing his notebook and reaching forward, turning off the recorder. "What if I make a deal with you? I won't publish anything. Won't include you in my research. I won't breathe a word of anything you tell me, not until after you're dead and in the ground."

"No," I said flatly. "Doesn't work for me."

"So, there *is* something for you to confess."

"I didn't say that, but yes, there's shit about this situation that you wouldn't understand."

"I know that you're dying."

I frowned and took a beat, processing the information. "Where did you hear that?"

"It doesn't matter, and I didn't need to hear it from anyone. You've looked like hell, and getting worse each time I've come. How long have they given you? Months? Weeks?"

I folded the wrapper around the final bite of the chicken sandwich and pushed it away.

"Look, my dad passed from cancer. He thought he had two months left, then didn't wake up the next morning. Whatever you have, life is delicate. You don't know when it will end. Do you really want to take this to the grave? Once you die . . . that's it. No one will have closure. No one will ever know the truth."

He thought that was a bad thing, but there was a reason I was keeping my mouth shut. The threat of death wasn't going to change that. If anything, it meant I was almost to the finish line.

"I'm sorry." I stood. "Like I said, I can't tell you about something that didn't happen."

He stared at me, incredulous, as if I should be champing at the bit to confess everything. But his "offer" was a worthless one. I was in jail. It wasn't like confessing to the crime would change that. Confessing the truth, though . . . that would.

CHAPTER 27

PERLA

"You don't ever talk about your father." Grant's voice came out of the dark, breaking the quiet hush of the room. I opened my eyes, and the shapes of the room came into focus. The blur of the overhead fan. The wall sconces. The rectangle divisions of the trayed ceiling.

I considered pretending to be asleep. It had been a few minutes since we had said our good nights. It was feasible, and I closed my eyes, warming to the idea.

"Perla." Grant reached over and patted the top of the covers. "Perla, wake up."

Dammit.

"Yes . . . ?" I said, letting the irritation soak the word.

"You don't ever talk about your father."

"Who, George?"

"No." He rolled onto his side, facing me. "Your real father."

"He wasn't a father to me," I said quickly. "You know that. He was barely there."

"I don't really know that. I mean, you have never talked about him. Not in the fourteen years we've been together."

I let out a strangled laugh. "Do you blame me? I have therapists for that. Forgive me if it's not something I want to talk about outside of that."

"But I think it would be—"

I reached out and grabbed his arm, squeezing it hard. "Careful, Grant. I won't go down that rabbit hole just to satisfy your morbid curiosity. I had a complicated relationship with my dad, and then it was over. Just leave it at that."

He didn't like that. I could feel the stiff hang of disapproval in the silence, but I didn't care. There were certain things I would share with him. That portion of my life . . . it was nothing he ever needed to know.

"Oh, princess. My beautiful, beautiful princess."

I pinched my eyes shut against the memory, locking it back down. When I reopened my eyes, the emotion was gone. "You don't ever talk about your sister. Want to dive into that, Grant? All the happy memories? What about the other ones? What about the last time you saw her?"

"Don't do that," he said, his voice strained. "Why would you say that?"

"There's a reason we don't talk about certain things." I rolled away from him and tucked the pillow tighter underneath my head. "We should keep it that way."

CHAPTER 28

"Do you think I'll ever get a sister?"

I turned away from the stove and looked at Sophie, who was perched on one of the high stools at the island. She had her journal out and was doodling in the margins, her pencil in motion, her attention down on the page.

"Why are you asking?" I glanced back at the stove, checking to see if the water was boiling. It was, so I turned down the burner and replaced the lid.

"I was just curious. I mean, you don't have any brothers or sisters."

"That's right." *Thank God.* I would not have reacted well if George and Janice had had a kid already in the house when I arrived. Competition was something I didn't do well with, especially when it threatened the relationships with the people I loved.

"And what about Daddy? Does he have any?"

Her pencil was moving, her eyes on the page, but there was something unnatural about her hyperfocus. This wasn't a casual conversation. My daughter was trying to figure something out.

"You know he doesn't."

She lifted her gaze and put down the pencil. Turning her head, she met my eyes. "Someone told me that he has a famous sister."

A famous sister. It shouldn't have irritated me, but it did. Lucy Wultz wasn't famous. Her name had been a *Jeopardy!* answer once, and none of the contestants had known who she was. I was probably the only home viewer who had blurted out the answer without hesitation.

"Your father doesn't like to talk about his sister." I stepped away from the stove and took the stool next to her, giving her my full attention.

"Did they have a fight?" This, she understood. Her friend group was rife with drama, all over the stupidest things.

"No, they didn't have a fight. But thinking about her makes him sad." I smoothed down the left side of her hair, putting it into place.

"Is she an actress?" Sophie bounced a little in her seat at the idea.

"What?" I laughed. "No, she isn't an actress. Why would you ask that?"

"Every famous person I know of is an actor or actress."

So much for the fortune we were spending on private school. "People are famous for a lot of things. But I hate to inform you that she isn't famous. Not really." *Not at all.*

Her face fell. "Oh. That's a bummer."

"Sorry for disappointing you." I rose from the stool at the sound of the pot lid, which was beginning to rattle from the steam. "Can you get me a block of pepper jack cheese and the grater?"

"Sure."

I was adding handfuls of pasta to the pot when she joined me at the counter, the grater and cheese in hand.

"Do you think I could meet her?"

I kept my eye on the pot, flinching when a hot droplet of water splashed on my arm. "I'm not sure, sweetie. Let's talk to Daddy about it after your birthday, okay?"

"Okay." She drummed her fingers on the top of the grater. "Do you need any more help? I want to call Mand before dinner."

"No, you can go on. But, Sophie . . . ?"

She pivoted back to face me, her journal in hand.

"Don't talk to your friends about your father's sister, okay? I don't want rumors flying around."

She shrugged. "'Kay."

'Kay. That's what this generation had been reduced to. Single-syllable, if not single-letter, responses. I didn't bother correcting her. I waved her off and watched as she swooped through the arched opening and bounded up the stairs.

CHAPTER 29

Finally, *Murder Unplugged* was covering the emails. They had dedicated an entire episode to the two they had received so far, and the comment section was getting flooded with opinions. Gabrielle thought it was something they should ignore, but Rachel was already "coordinating with law enforcement" to get to the bottom of it. I listened to their discussions with a smile, amused at how far off they were. This episode was already blowing up and feeding traffic to their full breakdown of the Folcrum Party.

My cell rang when I was driving down the 210, heading into Daisy-Villa. The call was from a Los Angeles area code, and I pressed the button on my steering wheel to answer it.

"Hello?"

"May I speak to Mrs. Wultz, please?"

"Speaking."

"This is Tina Anthow, the director of Tom Pullic Academy. I'm calling about Sophie's upcoming registration. We met at the orientation."

Ugh. A horrible decision by Grant, one that we both agreed was a mistake. The two-week-long private soccer camp would run into Sophie's fall schedule, and the instruction was extremely expensive . . . more than we could justify for an instructor who was good but not great. I'd looked into the contract, but their noncancellation policy was ironclad, and they already had our 50 percent deposit in hand.

The silence had stretched too long, and the woman spoke again. "Mrs. Wultz? Are you there?"

I could hang up, but that wouldn't make this problem go away. An idea emerged, and I jumped on it before it disappeared. "I'm sorry," I whispered, my voice cracking. "Sophie died last weekend. I thought—I thought my assistant would have called you by now."

The woman gasped. "What? Oh my gosh. I—I'm so, so sorry to hear that."

"It was a car accident. On the way back from soccer practice, actually. I—" I inhaled loudly. "I'm sorry. I can't. I can't speak about it without crying. Is there a way to cancel the camp?"

"Oh, of course. I'll handle that right away. Let me get an exception and refund your deposit. Again, Mrs. Wultz, I'm so sorry. Is there anywhere we can send flowers?"

"No, but thank you. Please just handle the cancellation and remove her record from your system. We're trying to stop any future mailings or calls . . . it's just too painful."

The woman tripped over herself apologizing, then finally hung up. Pleased, I lifted my Starbucks cup out of the cup holder and took a sip, enjoying the hot hazelnut blend and savoring the reaction I had just gotten.

It was a small taste of what was to come, an amuse-bouche of the upcoming meal. Once the party had occurred, the floodgates would open and I would be swarmed with condolences and pity. They'd probably name a park after Sophie. I imagined myself at the dedication, a black veil on, voice shaking. I would need to give a speech, thanking everyone and sharing a fond memory.

I would bask in it. Enjoy every moment—all with an anguished look of sorrow on my face. I'd already started practicing my demeanor, the lines of my televised interviews, the quotes I would give—ones that would go viral.

I smiled at the thought.

CHAPTER 30

Grant's reaction to me getting Sophie out of soccer camp was overblown, to say the least. I thought he would be happy about it, but he stared at me as if I had devil horns growing out of my head.

"What?" I dropped the set of dumbbells on the mat and moved over to the squat rack, ducking to position myself under the bar. I was in the basement gym with a 50 Cent song playing over the speakers, my workout halfway through.

"I swear to God, you better be joking with me right now." Grant was dressed in his work attire, his stiff short-sleeve button-up still tucked neatly into his powder-blue slacks, his security lanyard hanging around his neck.

"You act like we didn't discuss the cancellation policy and the fact that Sophie doesn't need this camp. It was bullshit, and it's still, what, a month out? They can fill her spot." I spoke with effort, huffing out the words as I completed the deep squats in quick succession and with perfect form.

"So you told them Sophie *died*? What the fuck's wrong with you?"

I finished the set, counting silently in my mind until I hit fifteen, then reracked the bar and ducked underneath it, coming face-to-face with him. "Nothing is *wrong* with me," I said evenly. "Don't make this about me. There was a problem, and I solved it. I don't understand why you care. They aren't going to find out the truth. They're in Minnesota, for God's sake."

"It's not about them finding out the truth, it's about . . . I don't know, karma! There's shit that you just don't do, Perla, and this tops the list." He raised his voice to make sure I could clearly hear him over the music.

God, he was such a wimp. I rolled my eyes and picked up the remote, turning the volume of the song down. "Karma? So when you tell the office that you're late because you got stuck in 'traffic'—you're saying that the next day, you're going to run into traffic as a result? That's bullshit, and you of all people, with your love of statistical probabilities, know it." I reached up on my toes, grabbing the upper bar, and began a series of pull-ups, my knees raising, biceps working.

"You're going to call them and tell them the truth. We'll pay the remaining balance and accept the loss. That's what is going to happen here."

I went to ten, then dropped back to my feet and shook out my arms. "Yeah, I'm not going to do that, Grant. There's no scenario where I'm going to call them back and tell them I lied. They're going to think I'm crazy."

"Yeah," he said through gritted teeth, "because it is *crazy* to say that to someone. And if it's hard for you to fix that mistake, it should tell you something about the gravity of it."

I sat back down in front of the dumbbells and prepared for my extensions. "I'm not doing it," I said flatly. "I solved the problem. Just leave it alone."

I didn't look at him in the mirror. I focused on making sure that my triceps were fully engaged, the weight movements slow and precise.

A new song came on, this one by Eminem. I heard the gym door scrape across the rubber mats, and when I looked up at the end of the set, he was gone.

It didn't matter if he was mad. He would get over this, as he did with everything. There were perks that came with having the "rough childhood" I'd had, and one of them was my husband's acceptance of certain behaviors and decisions. It was like a lifetime *Get out of jail free* card, one that would double in value after Sophie's party.

I reached over and turned up the volume on the song.

CHAPTER 31

Grant was with me on the Christmas committee for the neighborhood. Each year, we decorated the front gates and organized a toy drive for needy kids. Grant was always pretty quiet but the sort of guy who would jump in and help, no matter what. We try to get everything on each needy family's list, but sometimes we're short, you know? Last year, Grant went out himself and bought everything that was missing and anonymously donated it. I know right now a lot of crazy things are being said, but he was a good guy. A really good guy.

—*Russell Stern, financial adviser*

With five weeks before Sophie's birthday, I needed to expand the cluster-fuckery of the event. Grant was a great fall guy for the original Folcrum killer to set up, but I needed to provide a motive if I wanted the police to seriously consider him for the crime. A motive, and another potential villain or accomplice. Someone the police could examine before they settled in on or eliminated Grant.

After careful consideration, I decided a nanny would work. A nanny with an obsession for my lifestyle—one who would kill to get it for herself. She would have to be slightly unbalanced in order to be believable. A few worrisome traits that would increase in intensity leading up to the crime.

She would need to be perfectly flawed, and perfection didn't exist, so I set out to build her, starting with an ad placed in the country club bulletin, the *Pasadena Gazette*, and on three online job sites.

> WANTED: A Nanny for a Brighton Estates family. Pay is excellent, references not required.

If that didn't bring the crazies out of the woodwork, what would?

I'd never wanted a nanny before. It was a ridiculous idea, pawning your child off on someone else, especially when being a mother was so easy.

Maybe not in the beginning. In the beginning, there had been the diapers and the crying and the latching on to my teat, sucking the life out of me as I vacantly stared out an upper-story window and considered throwing the infant down onto the pavement. The beginning was horrible, especially with a child whom my husband wouldn't stop raving about.

I'd only kept her back then because of the way Grant looked at me every time he saw her in my arms. It was so drenched in love, that look. So wistful. So powerful. It was like I was the goose and I was holding the golden egg in my arms, and I would have been stupid to drop it, stupid to get rid of the one thing that, at the time, was holding our marriage together.

By the time we moved into Brighton Estates, Sophie was four, and while every woman in my new circle complained about the chore of parenting, I still couldn't see the issue. If you raised your child right, then they minded. They took care of themselves. I knew that better than anyone. Sometimes less parenting was better than overparenting.

Sophie amazed them. The four-year-old who ate Italian roulade and cauliflower steaks without hesitation, a napkin tucked under her chin, her tiny hands using her adult-size knife and fork with awkward but precise dexterity. They gushed when she used her manners; giggled when she asked if she could be excused from the table; and all but fell over in their chairs when she scraped her dish into the trash, then pulled her stool over to the sink and washed her plate before loading it into the dishwasher.

It wasn't rocket science. She did it because she had been taught to do it. Because it was expected of her. When I had only had a father, one who worked long hours at a hard job, I was the one who had cooked. Who had cleaned. Who had made sure that his clothes were washed and my own lunch was packed. I signed permission slips and took money from his wallet when I needed it, and each of those small things fortified the woman I eventually became.

Thanks to me, Sophie was independent, intelligent, and aware. She knew she had certain responsibilities, and she knew what the consequences of not doing those responsibilities were.

Granted, those consequences were weak and mild. Earlier on, I had thought they needed to be harsh and scary, but it's pathetic how little influence and threat it took to manage a child.

Maybe that wasn't a surprise. If anyone knew the power of an adult's dominance over a child, it was me.

"Well, I think it's a good thing you're finally getting a nanny." Tracy Maldivik set her spoon down and put her skinny elbows on the table, linking her fingers together and looking over them at me. "The fall festival is coming up. Now you can finally chair the committee."

"Oh no." I stirred my tea with my straw. "Joey does a great job as chair. I'm happy to help, but I'm too busy to chair, even with this help."

"Joey had cupcakes at the raffle table," Suzanne said flatly. *"Cupcakes."*

I nodded somberly. It was true—the cupcakes had been an idiotic choice, especially the ones he chose, which were clearly from the grocery store bakery when Beth's Cakes was just fifteen minutes up the road and created couture-worthy bites. Not that cupcakes should have even been in the conversation, much less lined up before the raffle displays like we were an afternoon bake sale at the public library.

"You know who would be a *great* nanny?" Chun chimed in, pausing right before she took a bite of her blueberry-salmon salad. "Estelle, Yolanda's girl. She retired, but if it's just Sophie, I know she'd take the job. She didn't want to deal with Yolanda's girls, but Sophie?"

All the women at the table murmured in agreement. "Estelle's good," Tracy said.

I knew Estelle. Estelle was a battle-ax ex-librarian with an impeccable reputation. Likelihood of killing three preteen girls? Zilch. I made a face. "I was actually hoping for someone younger. Someone who could be more of a friend to Sophie."

"Oh, you don't want a young nanny." Chun leaned forward, and everyone followed suit, curious as to what she was about to say. "You know Stephanie's girl? Definitely sleeping with her husband." She glanced at me. "I mean, not that Grant would ever cheat on you—"

"No, never," Suzanne murmured, and I wondered if Stephanie's girl was up for grabs.

"—but you have to be careful about these things. The younger girls, they just don't respect a household—a family dynamic—in the same way."

"The older, the better," Tracy said. "I like a wrinkly hag, myself."

I laughed. "I'm not choosing a nanny based on whether or not I think she'll want to sleep with my husband. Like you all said, Grant would never." I pierced a cube of melon with my fork and then a folded strip of prosciutto.

Looks darted between them, ones I pretended not to see.

"It's not him that we worry about," Chun tried again. "It's just that . . . Look, we've all had nannies. We all have nannies now. And the young ones . . . they just lead to a disaster, every time."

Exactly what I was hoping for. I hid my smile by popping a big purple grape into my mouth. I shrugged and took my time to chew it.

CHAPTER 32

This event was too important for me to flub. This wouldn't be like before. This scene would be examined with a fine-toothed comb. Every detail had to be perfect, which was why the framework needed to start now.

Cue my surgery, which would require recovery time.

Cue a new addition to my home, in the form of a nanny.

Cue her spending long hours around my husband and child.

Each one was a domino, and I needed to have a dozen in place before the birthday party.

A few hours after the birthday cake was cut, I'd tip over the first one and watch them all fall around her.

The nanny wouldn't understand her role in it, not right away. It would take her days, weeks, maybe even months, before she really understood what had happened. By then, the noose would be tied, she'd be in jail, and I would have my new life.

My first instinct in a nanny had been for flash—something that would cause the media to foam at the mouth. A local beauty queen or an Instagram star. A "perfect, rich teen" . . . the sort of girl Sophie would have turned into five or six years from now.

In my first interview, with Kayla Dearden, I saw the error in that mentality. The guy at the table beside us wouldn't stop staring at her. In addition to being annoying, it also brought to light a problem: Kayla was both beautiful and interesting. The media would focus all their attention on her and I would be forgotten, a second-class citizen, an *Oh, by the way* feature.

Screw that. I needed to be the main event. The star. If they ever put us side by side, I needed to be the more interesting choice in every category.

I told Kayla I would call her if she was selected, then tossed her résumé into the stack with the other rejects.

My fourth interview looked to be a lot more promising. Paige Smith had sounded meek on the phone, and she'd informed me that she was one of the waitresses from the club. I liked that connection, and was curious if she was one of the regular staff who waited on Grant and me.

Paige was ten minutes early to the interview. She took the seat across from me in a white button-up shirt and cheap black dress pants. She wore dingy tennis shoes that were double-knotted and had a single gold ring on her index finger. Cheap, fake diamond studs in her ears. Clean but thin brown hair in a low bun that was losing pieces every time she moved her head.

She looked exactly like what I once was. Slightly white trash and neglected. Looking for a way out.

On one side, that was perfect. She'd have no resources to defend herself. If the rewards were flashy and in easy grasp, she'd make mistakes and overlook red flags.

On the other side, if she was like my early self . . . There was something very dangerous about a woman with nothing to lose. I would need to watch her carefully and make sure our similarities were only in circumstance and not also in cunning.

"You're in school?" I asked, scanning her résumé.

"Yeah, I take classes at the community college."

"What are you studying?" I placed her résumé to the side and picked up my glass of ice water. I had selected the Stag House as the location for the interviews. A neutral location was best, and I wanted to see how the applicants handled themselves in the upper-class restaurant.

Kayla had been right at home, tossing her purse onto one of the free chairs at our table and flagging down the waiter to demand a sparkling water with a slice of lime.

In contrast, Paige had her bag tucked between her knees as if someone might steal it. She'd nervously reviewed the menu before ordering a side salad and a cup of soup—the cheapest items, but they would still total almost forty dollars before the tip. I smiled to myself, warming to the brunette. This could work. I'd have to give her some confidence, get her out of her shell a little, but there were a lot of ways to do that.

I thought of my first month with Janice and George—the day that Janice took me to her salon. It had been all modern surfaces and gold accents, and I'd been given a robe, then seated in a chair before a mirror as two people swarmed around me, peering, touching, fingering the ends of my hair, and speaking as if I weren't there.

"A bob, definitely."

"Look at her bone structure. We can work with this; we just need to get rid of the mess."

"Poor thing. You can just see the pain in her eyes."

Chris, the stylist, had tapped my jaw. "Chin up."

I had glared at him in response. He had paused, then glanced over at his assistant with a loud laugh. "Look at her, Bea. I do believe we have a lion under this mane." He ran his thin fingers through my hair, pulling it off my face. "It's Perla, is that right?"

Perla. Back then, I wasn't used to the name. It sounded strange, like a brand of tampon. Still, it was one that Janice had picked, and I was frantic to make her happy, no matter what.

I nodded and Chris had leaned forward, his cheek next to mine, both of us facing the mirror. "Are you ready to remake yourself, Perla? Are you ready to become a different person?"

I met his eyes in the mirror, and it was like signing a contract with him. I gave him my looks and trusted him to make me beautiful—or at least someone who was unrecognizable from the girl I had been.

And he did that.

He had done that for me, and I could do something similar for Paige, though her story wouldn't end up like mine.

Mine would have a happy ending. Hers would end in tragedy. Jail. A life sentence, maybe several.

"History," she said. "Well, initially."

"I'm sorry?" I stopped, my glass halfway to my mouth.

"You asked what I was studying." Her napkin was still before her, folded in an arched fan on top of her salad plate, and I couldn't concentrate on anything she was saying while it was there.

"As soon as you sit, you should place your napkin in your lap." I nodded toward it, and she flushed, then quickly grabbed it and placed it on her lap. "It's not a big deal," I said kindly. "I didn't know, either, when I was your age."

"I should have known," she said bluntly. "I mean, it's like the first rule of fine dining. I just didn't think. I'm nervous. Sorry. I shouldn't have said that. I just really want this job."

I smiled, and this one was more genuine, because I would be able to cancel the other interviews. I didn't need to hear anything more from her.

Paige was perfect.

CHAPTER 33

LEEWOOD FOLCRUM

Inmate 82145

Leewood,

My daughter caught a butterfly the other day. She brought it to me, cupped in her hands, then cried when she realized that she'd accidentally broken off one of its wings.

What was your daughter like, Lee? Were you close to her? Did you love her? Can a man like you love? If so, what does that look like? Does it look like a knife cutting open her skin? Does it look like a dead stare? Does it sound like a beg, a plea, a scream of pain?

I don't know how a man like you ever got married, but I understand why your wife numbed herself with drugs. At least her death protected her from finding out that the man she loved was a monster.

I've looked at photos of the two of you, and I do believe that she loved you. There are some photos that make me think that you might have loved her too. I've enclosed one here, not that you deserve it. I hate to even extend this kindness to you, but I hope that it reminds you of the innocence of love and I hope you repay this favor with one of your own and tell me what happened that night. Tell me why. Then I'll stop bugging you. Or I'll keep writing you. Whatever you want, Leewood. Just tell me before you die. Please, I'm begging you.

I took the photo out of the envelope and looked at it. It was one of me and Jessica, in the parking lot of the plant where I used to work. I was in my electrician coveralls, standing by the back bumper of the red Chevy I drove back then. She was holding a foil-wrapped casserole and wearing a big smile. I turned the print over and wondered where my pen pal had gotten it. It looked like something he had just printed off a computer, so maybe this was floating around the internet.

God, I remembered those casseroles. My favorite was her broccoli-cheese-rice one. She'd bring them to me on the nights I worked late, and I'd share them with the other guys on shift. She was a good cook. A good woman.

I rose and walked over to the sink, carefully wedging the photo into the framed edge that surrounded the mirror. I had a few other photos there—one of Jenny's old school photos and a couple from my other pen pals. It didn't seem right to have Jessica's photo next to some half-naked whore, so I removed the more risqué ones and dropped them into the trash can beside the sink.

I caught my reflection in the small square mirror. It had been a while since I had taken a look at myself. In a place like this, looks don't get you anything except the sort of attention you don't want.

Now I took my time and examined my reflection. My beard was full and wild. Normally, I'd visit the barber and have it all buzzed off when it got to this point, but it wasn't bothering me, so I'd leave it. I couldn't imagine dying with bare cheeks like a young tart. I winced at the realization that I would never again see a girl's bare legs. Touch her cheek. Feel her tremble.

That, out of all of it, was the worst thing about dying. The realization that the final pleasures you experienced in life were done without the proper appreciation.

I might have been dying, but I didn't look that bad. The beard hid the weight loss in my cheeks. I was pale, sure. A little weak around the eyes. But did I look like a walking corpse?

I didn't think so. Which meant Tim Valden hadn't just "figured out" I was dying. Someone had told him, and it damn sure wasn't me. He didn't look or seem like a man with connections inside this joint, but then again, you never knew what you were dealing with when you had a smart adversary—and he was smart. I could tell that. Not just book smart . . . he also had a bit of calculation going on in that head. A wolf can recognize a fellow wolf, and while Tim might never be on trial for murder, I was beginning to suspect his visits to me weren't altogether professional in nature.

Just tell me before you die. Please, I'm begging you. The words of my pen pal—the blonde's brother—chimed in my head, reminding me that there were a few other people whom I had shared my diagnosis with. Him. A few of my female fans. Almost all the fellow lifers knew. It wasn't exactly a secret within these walls, which meant that maybe it had gotten through them. Maybe it was all over the internet. Maybe everyone knew and Tim Valden wasn't special.

I rubbed my fingers across the prickly hairs of my mustache and then bared my teeth, checking them in the mirror.

Something felt off about Tim Valden, and I didn't like it. Not one bit.

CHAPTER 34

PERLA

I heard they sent an ambulance to the Wultzes' house after the 9-1-1 call. We were in bed; I mean, gosh, it was like three in the morning, but I woke up when I heard the sirens. I remember going to the window and looking out and seeing the red and white lights reflecting against the trees as the ambulance passed our house. Of course, it wasn't needed. By the time they got there, it was too late.

—*Nikkila Matthews, homemaker*

On the back deck, just beside the pool, we sat under the stars. It was a full moon but cloudy, with a snap in the air. I had opened a 2016 bottle of Masseto merlot and brought Grant a cigar, then curled up in a big afghan in one of the rocker lounges that surrounded the firepit. He had turned the flames to low, and I scrolled through the playlists on my phone and selected one of his favorites. "Ole Man Trouble" by Otis Redding began playing through the hidden speakers, the soulful tune floating on the evening breeze. It, along with the crackle of the fire, instantly turned the dial down on my stress.

I rested my head back on the chair's cushion and closed my eyes, humming along with the song. After that was a Sam Cooke tune, and I kicked off my slippers and rested my feet up on the pit's wide rim, twitching my toes to the beat. Grant smiled and took a deep draw on his cigar as he watched me.

I waited until Grant had finished three glasses of wine before I brought up my surgery. I tried to downplay it, but he was a detail lover, and I sighed after his fourth question. "I don't have all of the details, Grant. The details don't matter. It's a nose job. It's with Kellan's office. It's all above board. You know how I am with things like this. It will be safe."

"Okay, but you mentioned a recovery period." He stretched to one side and dug into his pocket, withdrawing his slim silver phone.

"I'll need to take it easy for a little bit. There will be a week or so where I'll need to stay at home, take some pain meds."

He fiddled with the touch screen and moved his chair closer so I could see his calendar. "What day is the procedure?"

"It's in three weeks. On a Wednesday."

"The eighth? Or the fifteenth?"

"I'll have to look." I placed my hand on his forearm and squeezed the muscle, his hair soft and golden from the sun. "It's okay. I'll arrange transportation to and from the surgery, and I'm bringing in extra help to take care of Sophie while I recuperate."

He lifted his gaze from the phone, and I steeled myself for an argument. We had never before discussed a nanny, but it was understood that he carried the same opinions I did regarding pawning our child off on a stranger.

"What do you mean, 'extra help'?" His thick brows pinched together, creating a sea of deep wrinkles and stress lines across his forehead.

"There's a waitress at the country club who's going to help with getting Soph to and from school, with her homework, that sort of thing." I cupped my wineglass with both hands and brought it up to my lips.

"But you hate the idea of nannies."

I made a face. "That's not true. I've—*we've*—raised her to be independent. I don't let people coddle her, and I don't believe in tossing her off to a stranger instead of doing our duties as parents."

Grant chuckled. "Please, tell us how you really feel."

I smiled. It was possible my voice had risen an octave in that last sentence. "Okay," I conceded. "I'll get off my high horse. But I'll be fully involved and supervising. I just want to make sure, if there's an accident or if anything happens while I'm impaired from pain or medicine, that there's a capable and responsible adult here at home while you're at work."

There. He couldn't possibly say anything about that.

He looked out toward the darkness of the backyard and slowly swirled his glass, considering it. "Okay," he relented. "You know best with Sophie. You always do. If you think someone is needed while you're healing, then someone is needed. Do you like the girl?"

I nodded. "I do. You will too."

And he *would* like her. I'd bend over backward to make sure that happened.

And she'd love him, at least on paper. On paper, she'd love him so much that it would drive her to kill.

Sweet, quiet, shy Paige. A girl who would enter a world of wealth and power and fall for the king of the castle—a man she would see as a path to the life she wanted, a life that could be hers, if not for his wife and child. A life she would kill to have.

It could play. I could make it play.

I leaned forward and held out my wineglass toward Grant. "Cheers to a beautiful life."

"I'll drink to that." He clinked his glass to mine, and we both sipped in silence.

And that moment . . . under the stars, a cool hush to the night, his eyes warm from the wine, his leg against mine, a promise of more in the air . . . It felt pregnant with perfection in the way that only something with an expiration date can.

Our expiration was looming, and I was both giddy and nostalgic for it.

CHAPTER 35

"Are you excited for your birthday party?" I pushed the grocery cart, keeping pace with Sophie's slow strides. She was in a purple Lululemon leggings-and-tank-top set that would have made me look like a grape.

"I am, but I don't understand why I can only invite two people." She scanned a display of cake toppings. "Do you *know* how many friends I have? It isn't fair."

"It's your dad's decision." I stopped at the section of spices and searched the labels, trying to find cumin. "Respect it."

"But if I just talked to him, I could explain." She hung on the side of the cart, her earlobes sparkling with the small diamond studs Grant had given her for Christmas.

"Don't talk to him about it," I said sharply. "He told you once, and you already pushed it then."

"But—"

"Sophie." I turned to face her and bent so that we were at eye level. Grabbing her shoulders, I squeezed tightly, making sure I had her full attention. "Look at me. Do not talk to your father about it again, do you understand me? I will plan a pool party for all of your friends the following weekend, okay? It will be a secret, something we don't need to tell Daddy until after your birthday, okay?"

She winced, squirming underneath my hard grip. "You're hurting my arms."

I studied her insolent face and had a brief moment when I realized how much I would miss her. No one would ever be able to say that I wouldn't mourn my child, miss her giggle, the way she slipped her hand so confidently into mine. I enjoyed those moments.

It was sad that this had to happen. Sad—that was the emotion I should assign to it. Emotions like sadness were harder for me. They were like communion wafers—void of taste. Envy, greed, passion—those I felt vividly. Those I savored. They were explosions of flavor, a spicy conch salad of emotion.

I loved conch salad.

And I would love this. Maybe not the initial bite but certainly the lingering taste.

"Mom?" She wiggled, trying to pull away from me.

"I need you to promise me," I said firmly, keeping her in place. "Don't bother your father about it."

"Okay, okay." Her body sagged in defeat. "Fine."

I stood and turned back to the rows of spices, my mind ticking through everything that still needed to be put into place before the party.

There was a lot, but that was okay. The planning was part of the fun.

CHAPTER 36

LEEWOOD FOLCRUM

Mr. Folcrum,

You know, you're a hero to some of us. There's three of us that go to a cabin each winter and spend a weekend together, sharing our stories. Each of us does one event during the year, and that reunion is where we share our stories.

I haven't picked the source of my event yet, but I have to say, you're my biggest inspiration. The drama of the setting in yours . . . it had bite, man. Theatrical effect, if that makes sense. I mean, it's been twenty years and people are still talking about it. You're being listed next to Lizzie Borden and the Black Dahlia, dude. If that's not iconic, what is?

I don't plan to be iconic. The problem with iconic is that it typically involves getting caught, and I got to tell you—I don't think I'd do well in prison. That is one of the things I don't understand about you, man. Why didn't you just get out of there? Why wait, when you had to know that they were coming?

United in solidarity,
Your friend

Redd was off, which meant I was delivered to the interview room by the thin guy with the lisp, whose name I'd never remember if it wasn't printed on the front of his uniform. I glanced at his name tag as we got on the elevator. PERDUE.

"How's it going?" I asked.

"Shut the fuck up, Folcrum." He stared dead ahead, his right cheek bulging with a wad of gum. "I'll be so glad when you're dead."

The doors opened and I stepped out, lifting my chin at a passing prisoner who I sometimes played dominoes with.

We journeyed the rest of the way in silence. It was probably this prick who'd told Valden about my cancer. "You know who's in visitation?" I asked as we entered the left wing.

"What the fuck I look like, your social coordinator?" He stopped at the door and glanced up at the camera, waiting for the buzz. It sounded, and he pushed the door open.

Yeah, definitely a possibility.

As we passed the visitation room, I glanced in the window. Tim Valden sat at a table, his knees pinned together, his back straight, a paper bag and drink in front of him.

"Enjoy that food," Perdue said under his breath as he passed me off to Johnson. "I spit in it."

———

I ate the Big Mac without hesitation, and if Perdue spit in it, I couldn't tell and didn't care. As I chewed, I watched Tim, who seemed on edge.

"What's wrong?" I asked.

"Nothing."

I finished chewing, then swallowed. "I'm good at giving advice. Don't have shit else to do in here."

"Okay. I guess I'm frustrated. I've met with you four times now and don't have anything to show for it, except for a bunch of junk food receipts." He tapped the top of his folder. "You just grunt and argue and talk in circles. Just let me know if I'm wasting my time. I have other inmates I can talk to. You're not the only person in this building who has killed someone."

I shrugged. "Not sure why you picked me to begin with. I haven't talked to anyone in twenty years, and you think I'll start babbling to you?" I wiped at my mouth with the napkin. "Why would I?"

"You'd think a man would want to purge his soul before death." He met my eyes. *I bet the women fall all over this guy. He probably has some hot treat of a girlfriend.* "There's some relief in confession, Leewood."

I chuckled and picked the double-decker sandwich back up. "Really? How do you know?"

"It's been proven in the field of psychology."

I took another big bite, chewed for a spell, then spoke. "I got a confession for you."

He sighed.

"No, no." I held up my hand. "I'm serious. I'm going to tell you something that is true."

"What's that?" His voice was dry, but I could see the interest in his face. He was hooked to whatever I was about to say.

I leaned forward. "I didn't kill those girls."

His mouth flattened and he rolled his eyes. "Okay."

"Listen!" I slammed my palm on the metal table, and the sound reverberated in the small, enclosed room. Tim flinched. The motherfucker was actually listening.

"I. Did. Not. Kill. Those. Girls." I said it slowly and without any ire. "I swear on my daughter and my wife and whatever entity is up there listening. If you came here to understand why a killer kills, I'm not your guy. I don't care what the evidence says and what the jury believed.

Look at me, Tim. Look into my soul." I paused, my eyes boring into his. "I did *not* kill those girls."

There was a moment after that, one where he didn't speak and I didn't breathe and the tie between our eyes was as strong as wire.

And in that moment, even if it only lasted a beat, I think he believed me.

CHAPTER 37

PERLA

When the first email came in from the TFK guy, we pretty much dismissed it. I mean, we get a *lot* of random stuff, and most of it is just attention-seekers, you know? And then the second one came in, and even though it was also bullshit, with two emails, there was enough of something that we could at least build an episode around it. But obviously, it's fake. I mean, come on. Leewood did it. We all know it. But whatever. It stirs up the listeners, which is why we replied to it.

—*Rachel,* Murder Unplugged

In a private training room at the country club's gym, I bent forward, looped my arms around the girth of a tire, and pulled. Stepping backward, I hissed out an exhale as it slid a few feet.

"That's it," Joshua said.

I continued, my legs and shoulders burning from the effort. The tire was a hundred and forty pounds of deadweight. I had to imagine a body would be easier and less cumbersome.

Thankfully, I wouldn't be moving anyone a great distance. I would need to get them from Sophie's bed, down to the floor, then shift and arrange them into place. The girls would be groggy and barely functional, but they wouldn't be deadweight. Not yet.

Plus, Sophie was light. Only eighty-nine pounds, per her last doctor's exam. I would move her last, in case the other two girls took it out of me.

"Almost there . . ." Joshua called out as I staggered the final feet across our makeshift finish line. "Now, drop and give me twenty push-ups. Good ones, Perla. I want your nose tapping the mat with each one."

I dropped into position, spacing my hands apart and lining them up with my shoulders, staying off my knees.

I had increased my sessions with Joshua from twice a week to three, and my home workouts from five days a week to seven. My body was already responding. While I had always been strong and fit, I was going to be in the best shape of my life by Sophie's party, with a new face and slimmer waist to match.

As I performed the push-ups, I thought about my next steps with Paige. Her first day was tomorrow, and it seemed like my job, at least initially, was to woo her into a sense of false security. I needed her to rave about her new job to her friends and be wowed by our lifestyle. Even better if those conversations with friends included a complaint about Sophie.

I finished the set and collapsed onto the mat, thinking up different ways to pit Paige against Sophie.

CHAPTER 38

LEEWOOD FOLCRUM

Inmate 82145

Another week passed, and then, like clockwork, Tim was back. This time, instead of fast food, he had the guards deliver me a soft padded lunchbox with apple slices, two grilled-cheese sandwiches, and a large chocolate chip cookie.

I stared at the food. "This is different."

"It's my lunch. I didn't have time to go anywhere."

I picked up a grilled-cheese sandwich and studied it. "Your mom pack your lunches for you?"

"That's hysterical." He hunched forward and met my eyes through the dusty glass. "Hypothetically speaking, let's say I do believe what you told me last visit—that you didn't do it."

"Hypothetically speaking," I repeated as I unzipped the plastic bag and pulled out the grilled cheese. Grilled-cheese sandwiches had always been my favorite hangover remedy, and I had a sudden and painful memory of my daughter, on her stool by the stove, carefully flipping the bread over in the pan. She'd made the best grilled-cheese sandwiches.

"Wally Nall believes you. You seem to believe yourself. But you got to admit, the circumstances are impossible."

"They seem unlikely," I conceded. "Not impossible." I examined the sandwich, which seemed like a gourmet version of what Jenny used to make.

"So there has to be a piece that is missing. Something that makes the unlikely circumstances more probable."

I shrugged and took a bite. It was good. Crispy but not hard. The cheese was more than I liked, but it was pretty damn good.

"So, what's the missing piece? What are you hiding?" He studied me. "And why?"

"Let's look at this a different way." I spoke through another bite. "You've been meeting with me because you wanted to know the . . . the motivations and justifications? Was that it? Of a killer?"

He gave me a pained look. "What's your point?"

"Well, that's why you *said* you were here. And if you do 'hypothetically speaking' believe me, then you accept that I'm not a killer. So I'm not really of any help in your project." I shrugged, taking another big bite, the sandwich now half-gone. "No reason to talk to me."

"Not being a killer and being innocent are two different things. Are you saying that you're innocent?"

No, I certainly wasn't saying that. I ignored the question. "You're evading the question. I think that you are hiding your own secrets, Tim."

He sighed and shook his head, muttering something I couldn't catch.

"So, why are you *really* here? Why do you need to know the truth so badly?" I tilted my head and peered at him. "Is this just a research project for you? Or do you have a more personal interest in the crime?"

He scoffed, but the gesture felt weak. Wrong. My gut, which rarely steered me wrong, coiled tighter than a cobra.

I'd been blowing smoke, trying to distract him, but it felt like I had hit pay dirt, and that made me very, very nervous.

CHAPTER 39

PERLA

I was so happy when I got that job. I was so broke, and the pay was good—like, ridiculously good. I remember on that first day just thinking that I couldn't do anything to screw it up. Like, whatever they wanted, I would just smile and do it, because I *had* to have that job.

—*Paige Smith, former Wultz nanny*

Paige's first day was a Tuesday, and I watched my daughter closely, curious how she would respond to the new addition in her life.

After a somber handshake and close attention to my introduction, my daughter looked at me. "May I go up to my room now?"

"Yes, of course."

She took off toward the stairs, and I glanced at Paige. "So, that's Sophie. She won't give you any trouble."

"Yeah, she seems really well behaved." The girl stood with her feet spread, her weight on one hip, the stance sloppy. I wondered how much training it had taken for George and Janice to turn me from what I had been into what I was now. I had found them so critical in the beginning, but now I could see how much there had been to fix, and I had to remind myself that I didn't need Paige to be perfect. Her imperfection was what would sell this to the jury. I only needed her to be motivated.

"Let's give you a tour of the house," I said. "I want to make sure that you know where everything is."

———

I invited Paige to join us for dinner. We ate in the smaller of the two formal dining rooms, and I poured her a glass of wine, then hesitated. "I'm sorry, Paige. I don't even know how old you are."

"I'm nineteen." She blushed. "I mean, I do drink, but of course I won't when I'm working."

"Oh, it's fine." Grant gestured for me to give her the glass. "A little won't hurt. And besides, this is too good to go to waste. Knowing my wife, she'll only have a sip."

I shrugged in assent. "More than a glass and I fall asleep." I took my seat and picked up my silverware. Sophie, who had been waiting for the cue, immediately followed suit. Paige was already halfway through her salad and had three bites missing from her fish.

A lull fell, and I waited, certain Grant would fill it. He was a man who hated silence in social situations, not so much for its weight but for what it was—a wasted opportunity in which data collection could have occurred.

"So, Paige . . ." He hunched forward over his plate, a knife in one hand, fork in the other. "Are you from Pasadena originally?"

"No. I'm from Ohio. I came here for school. I'm at the community college but will transfer into the university as soon as I finish my AA."

"What do you plan on studying?"

"Criminology."

I almost choked on my swordfish. "I thought you were a history major." I coughed, trying to clear the thick wedge of food.

"Well, history is the focus of my AA. I'll move into the criminology portion once I'm at the university."

Criminology? This wasn't good. I had selected Paige because I needed a dumb pawn, not someone who might grow suspicious before the big reveal.

Grant was looking at me, his expression guarded, and I wondered what he was thinking. He had his own complicated history with law enforcement, and would certainly approach this from a different direction than I would. I stayed silent, and his gaze flipped back to Paige, who was biting off the end of an asparagus spear, clueless.

"Why criminology?" Grant asked, reaching for his wineglass and finishing off the contents in one deep sip.

"Well, my dad works in corrections," she said, talking with her mouth full.

"Corrections back in Ohio?" I asked.

She shook her head and swallowed. "No, actually close by here. My parents are divorced; my mom's the one who lives in Ohio."

Corrections. Close by here. I straightened my fork beside my plate. "Your father works at a jail?"

"Prison." She leaned back in her seat and patted her stomach. "Oh my God, this is so good. You are such a good cook, Mrs. Wultz."

"Thank you," I said softly. *Prison. Close by here.* Maybe he worked in a women's prison. Maybe. Maybe. Please.

Grant cleared his throat. "That's interesting about your father," he said. "Don't suppose he's at Lancaster?"

"Yeah." She looked up, surprised. "You've heard of it?"

The room closed in on me, and I gripped the edge of the table, willing myself not to faint.

Lancaster. My new nanny's father worked at the prison where Leewood Folcrum was. He probably knew the man. Had talked with him. Maybe they were friends. Maybe they were enemies. Whatever they were, I had invited his daughter into our house. Employed her. Tasked her with taking care of our child and carrying the weight of my future crime. A crime based on and copycatting the Folcrum murders.

It was okay. I pursed my lips and exhaled, then inhaled deeply, filling up my lungs. It was okay. A minor speed bump. Know about something early enough, you can overcome it or twist it to your benefit.

That's what I needed to do. Twist away. And looking at it from that direction, this might even be a good thing. The knot in my chest released, and I took another set of deep breaths.

This could be okay. Maybe even great. After all, here was Paige's connection to the murders—one I didn't even have to fabricate. She already had a documented tie to Folcrum, and maybe even a logical explanation for why she'd hunted down this job to begin with. *Look,* I'd say. *She's clearly obsessed with us, has been from the start.*

Yes, maybe this could work.

Or maybe, quite possibly, I had just royally fucked up.

CHAPTER 40

JOURNAL OF SOPHIE WULTZ

It makes no sense that I have a nanny. Mom always makes fun of the moms that have nannies.

Paige isn't bad. I asked her for a candy bar, and she couldn't find one in the kitchen, but then the next time she came to the house, she had one for me in her bag. So that's cool.

She seems super interested in my parents, but I think everyone is, so that's nothing new. People either love or hate my parents. I can't figure out which side Paige is yet.

I know which side I'm on.

CHAPTER 41

PERLA

I lay back on Dr. Maddox's couch and thought about our recycling bins. Madeline was doing a shitty job with separating the items. Today was trash day, and I hadn't had time to go through the bins and double-check her work, which pretty much guaranteed that there'd be something wrong.

All it took was one wrong item—*one*—and the recycling facility would throw out our neighborhood's entire bin. I refused for my family's contribution to be the one that caused four hundred pounds of recyclable content to go to waste.

"You look worried, Perla." Dr. Maddox took her seat, a cup of tea in hand, and I tried not to fixate on her use of my first name. Maybe it was a good thing, her feeling so familiar with me. Still, weren't we supposed to have some level of professional distance? I was already lying down on her furniture, opening up my heart and head for her examination. Wasn't that enough?

Madeline was supposed to remove the caps on all bottles, and I would have bet anything she didn't comb through the bag to check them. Sometimes Sophie put her water bottles in with the caps on.

"Perla?" Dr. Maddox tapped on my shoulder, and I jerked at the unexpected contact. "Oh dear, I'm sorry. I think I lost you for a minute."

"Yes, I'm sorry. What did you ask me?"

"I said that you looked worried."

So she hadn't even asked me anything. Was I supposed to respond to every comment she had? I bristled, then remembered that looking worried was a good thing, given the purpose of today's session: put Paige on her radar as a potential suspect. "I'm sorry. I'm just thinking about . . . I recently hired a nanny, and I'm wondering if I made a mistake."

"Oh? What kind of a mistake?" Her voice perked up at the idea. If I ever told this woman what was actually going on in my head, she'd probably pass out from excitement.

"I don't know. I have surgery coming up and needed someone to help with Sophie, but now that she's in my house every day, spending time with my daughter and Grant . . ." My voice faltered. "I don't know. It's stupid."

"Stop," she ordered. "Stop that sort of thinking right now. This is your safe space, Perla. The place where you can explore how you feel about things. Your feelings are never stupid. Actually, our feelings can be a very accurate compass to follow. Human intuition is a very powerful thing."

"Well . . ." I waited.

"Go ahead."

"I don't like the way she looks at Grant." I twisted in my position so that I could see her face. "Is that stupid? Tell me I'm being stupid."

"How does she look at Grant?"

I flopped back on the couch. "I don't know. It's probably nothing. She's just too comfortable with him. It makes me uncomfortable. She stands too close to him. Yesterday, I asked her to go get Sophie's bag from upstairs, and she was annoyed at it—I could tell. It was like dealing with Sophie was inconvenient, and that's the whole reason she is here. But Sophie likes her, so maybe I'm just insecure."

"I think you should listen to your gut. I think you're a very intelligent woman. If you are worried, there is probably a valid reason. Has Grant ever given you a reason to distrust him?"

Well, that was a question that would take hours to unpack and was best told with exhibits of police reports and photos.

Yes, Grant had given me reasons to distrust him.

No, that threat was no longer a problem.

Would Paige be one? No, not in the next month or so. If she decided to get naked and ride my husband like a rodeo bronco, more power to her. They'd be the last happy moments in her life.

"No," I finally said. "Not really. I trust him. I just don't trust her."

"Are you able to find someone else to watch Sophie?"

"Not in time. I could deal with it after my surgery. And after Sophie's party."

"That's how far from now?"

"Um . . . a month and a half, give or take." *Forty-two days.*

"A lot can happen in six weeks," she pointed out.

"Yeah." I twisted my head, turning away from her so she wouldn't see the smile that stretched across my face.

A lot could happen in six weeks.

I would make sure that it did.

From: info@murderunplugged.com
To: tfk@hotmail.com

Date: July 7 at 6:02 PM

Subject: re: don't miss your chance

We received both of your emails and find it unlikely that you were involved in the Folcrum Party. Please stop contacting us unless you have proof.

Happy listening,

Rachel and Gabrielle, Murder Unplugged

CHAPTER 42

I never understood what Grant saw in Perla. Before her, he dated the sweetest girl . . . Heather Marigoth. She was a receptionist at a law firm. Actually, she was supposed to come to that event at the church the night that Perla and Grant met. She got horribly sick a week before. Went to the hospital, in fact. They never could figure out what it was, but by the time she got back on her feet, my nephew and Perla were thick as thieves.

—*Gloria Feinbaum, Grant Wultz's aunt*

I watched Paige in the backyard with Sophie. They were over by the back corner. Paige had a blue soccer ball and was tossing it to Sophie, who would hit it with her head.

Such a barbaric and dumb game. I never understood why Sophie wanted to play soccer instead of take ballet. From the start, Grant had encouraged it, and I honestly thought it was so he could yell in some stands instead of sit in an air-conditioned auditorium and watch a bunch of girls pirouetting to classic music.

The games weren't bad; except that half of the girls didn't understand or care, so you had a bunch of yawning preteens who were complaining as much as they were playing.

Sophie wasn't one of them. If she was going to do the stupid sport, she was going to excel at it, which was why I'd hired private coaches early on. She was the best player on her team, which made attending the games enjoyable, at least for me. Grant seemed happy to just sit in the sunshine and clap. Once, he told a girl on the *other* team that they had done a good job. He had absolutely no concept of competitive edge.

I tripped that same girl when she was walking to her bus. I waited, made sure no one was watching, then stuck out my foot while shoving her forward.

Now Paige sprinted forward and dived for the ball, ending up face-first in the dirt. Sophie jogged over to help her up, and even from here, I could see that both of them were smiling.

A wave of annoyance rolled through me. Sophie shouldn't trust strangers so easily. Was I this easily replaced? Sophie had all but tossed her journal to the side when Paige had suggested they go outside and play.

I reached into my pocket, withdrawing the small smartphone I'd purchased in one of the thrift stands at the farmers' market. Its service was disconnected, but its Wi-Fi worked, connecting to the virtual private network that shielded our location and IP address from any future law enforcement inquiries, should they occur. Clicking on the web browser, I navigated to the email login page and entered the details.

ONE NEW EMAIL.

Surprised, I clicked on the message from *Murder Unplugged*. It was short and nasty, and I read through it a few times before logging out and closing the browser window. I shut down the device and slid it into my pocket.

They had already covered the emails on their podcast, so I could stop while I was ahead . . . Though a single episode . . . one that hadn't yet gained traction with any major media outlets . . . Was it really enough? On the episode, Rachel had said they were speaking with law enforcement, but this response didn't seem to lean that way. Instead, they seemed to be dismissing it, and calling me a liar. *We find it unlikely . . .* They wanted proof? Fine. I'd give them proof. I just had to figure out what.

The front door slammed shut, and I tilted my head, listening as Grant's familiar stride sounded down the main hall. "I'm in here," I called out.

The faint scent of his cologne preceded him, and I closed my eyes and inhaled it, appreciating the masculine scent. His hands settled at my waist, and he brushed his lips along the back of my neck, nuzzling the skin before kissing it and pulling away. "What are you looking at?" He joined me at the window, then spotted Sophie for himself. "Oh, that's good. Look at them."

I glanced over at him, not thrilled about the warmth in his voice. "Yes, Paige seems to be very athletic."

He nodded. "Good. Maybe a nanny won't be the worst thing in the world."

I folded my arms across my chest. "I told you." My words came out lightly, and he wrapped his arm around my side and rested his chin on my head.

"It's odd that her dad works at Lancaster," he said.

I stayed in place, resisting the urge to face him. This topic was a land mine, one I would need to tread past carefully. "Yeah, I thought that was strange. I mean, not *strange* but . . . well. You know. Small world."

"Probably just a coincidence."

I coughed out a laugh. "Of course it is. The alternative is—what? That she hunted down this job because of her dad? Because of *him*?"

I turned to look at him, hoping he would warm to the idea as his own.

"Yeah," he said thoughtfully, and it was enough to let me know that the seed had been planted. "Good point." He chuckled, shaking his head. "Yeah. Just a coincidence."

I held his gaze, searching those dark-brown pupils. He wasn't entirely convinced, but he wasn't suspicious either. That was fine. I didn't need him to be suspicious right now. Right now, I needed him to be clueless, and Grant was good at that.

I turned back to the window and pointed. "Oh my God, I think that's one of those tangerine birds."

He stiffened. "A tanager? Where?" He looked, then dashed over to the desk, where he pulled a pair of binoculars from the drawer.

And just like that, the land mine was cleared.

CHAPTER 43

I stretched out on my side of the hot tub, spreading my toes under the water and watching the distorted movement of my feet. Beside me, Grant clipped a cigar and tossed the end toward the bushes that lined the pool area. I watched where it landed. I wouldn't be able to sleep tonight until I fished it out of the azaleas and threw it in the trash.

He placed the cutter on the side and picked up the lighter, running the flame carefully over the end. Sophie shrieked as she ran along the side of the pool, Jordan just behind her. Our daughter dived into the deep end, and her friend kept going, up the stone steps and out of sight as she climbed onto the top of the grotto.

"They're going to sleep well tonight," Grant remarked.

"They should already be in bed." I reached for my glass of wine, which I'd set on the hot tub's ledge. "I told Jordan's mom I wouldn't let them stay up too late."

"Oh, let them have fun." He twisted to the right, finding our daughter in the lit turquoise pool, her red suit shimmering under the water like a pool of blood. "Where is she?"

"Top of the grotto. She's probably coming down the slide."

As if on cue, Jordan's dark form traveled down the curve, her arms crossed over her chest, hand clamped over her nose. Sophie splashed toward her as she hit the water.

Grant's eyes met mine, and I knew what he was going to say.

"Don't," I warned, and took a big sip of the wine.

"She's one of Sophie's best friends," he began.

"I don't care," I said. "Two friends is enough. She's not planning an orgy."

"Sophie doesn't understand why she can't invite her." He hung his arms on either side of the tub's edge, the pose accentuating his shoulders and chest muscles. "Neither do I. It's her birthday. The house is certainly big enough. Let her invite a hundred kids if she wants to."

"Sophie doesn't need to understand. She's eleven. And you aren't the one doing all of the work, Grant. I am. I don't put my foot down on many things. This is one."

He let out an incredulous laugh. "You don't put your foot down on many things? Oh, that's funny."

I smiled despite myself and hid the gesture behind a sip of wine. I put the glass down and swam over to him, then grabbed his shoulders, straddling him in the water. He immediately reacted, pulling me to him with one hand while he held the cigar out of harm's way with the other. I gave him that look—the one he could never say no to—and he sighed, and I knew right then that I had won.

"Ewww, Mom!" Sophie stood beside us on the pavers, dripping wet, her blonde hair plastered to her head. "You guys are so gross!"

Grant detached from me, pushing me away, and if I could have drowned my daughter right then, I would have.

CHAPTER 44

LEEWOOD FOLCRUM

Inmate 82145

With the Folcrum Party, you had twelve stab wounds in Lucy and eight in Kitty. Plus, of course, Jenny Folcrum's slit throat. But there was a lot of psychological speculation over that difference between the victims. Lucy and Kitty were—and I testified to this opinion—much more aggressive, almost angry, which would fit what we knew about Leewood Folcrum, especially if the young girls had spurned his advances. In contrast, Jenny Folcrum's wound was designed for one reason—to kill her as quickly and painlessly as possible. Maybe he did her first so she wouldn't interfere with his attack on the other girls, or maybe he did her last. We never got that information out of him or out of the crime scene evidence.

—*Dr. Aubrey Jones, expert witness (psychiatrist)*

"I have a theory I'd like to run by you." Tim seemed relaxed today, in a T-shirt and khakis. He had on hiking boots, and a backpack instead of his briefcase. I noticed the change but kept my mouth shut.

"What's that?" I unwrapped the first of four tacos, excited at the prospect of spicy ground beef, cheese, and a crunchy shell.

"Do you think people are capable of change?"

I lifted my shoulder in a shrug. "Depends. What kind of change?"

"Well, mental state. For example, do you think you were always the type of person that could kill someone?"

"I think anyone could kill someone if they're put in the right situation," I responded. "Maybe not physically—maybe some spaghetti strap doesn't got the strength to get it done, but I think everyone's got that point where, if they was pushed to it, they'd take a life."

"I don't know . . ." he said, and it clicked what else was different about him. He was wearing glasses, these round-frame ones that the nerds wore. "I think it takes a certain element . . . a piece that not everyone is born with."

"Inner grit?"

"No, that isn't it." He looked annoyed.

"I'm telling you, the average person, assuming they aren't some sniffling weakling, will kill if they are put in the right situation."

"Says the man who's spent the last twenty years in prison. You've been surrounded by animals too long. You've forgotten what normal people are like. The majority of people are good."

"You can be good and still kill someone, Tim."

His mouth flattened into a thin line. "We'll have to agree to disagree on that point."

"So, you wouldn't kill someone?"

"If you killed someone that I loved, and I had the opportunity . . . I could see *wanting* to kill you."

I smirked, amused at where this chat was going. So far this was much better than our typical visits, where he hit me with the same old questions, like he didn't understand I wasn't going to answer them.

A. R. Torre

"But I wouldn't go through with it," Tim continued. "Wanting someone to die and killing them are two different things. We can't help our emotions, but we can control our actions."

"Must be nice to know everything about everybody." I bent back in the chair, reaching my arms out in an attempt to stretch my chest. It was tight, like someone was sitting on top of it, and I coughed to try to clear my lungs.

"So, to return to my earlier focus . . . I was asking about whether you think that people change. Take yourself, for example."

"Yeah?" I dropped my arms, interested in where this was going.

"If we look at a week before the party, we had one version of Leewood Folcrum." He pulled a photo from his folder and held it up against the glass.

Curious, I leaned forward and looked at it. It was a photo of me, my weight against the railing at Pop's BBQ. Jenny was standing beside me, her skinny legs on display in short shorts. She was leaning against me, her head resting on my shoulder. It had been taken at a classic car showcase. Neither of us looked at the camera, but I was smiling at something she had said.

"Where'd you get this photo?" I wanted to reach for it, but the glass was in the way. Annoyance spread through me. Suddenly, there wasn't anything in the world I wanted more than that picture.

"It's a crop of a photo someone took of one of the cars. You were in the background. That's why the quality on it is so bad."

I remembered that day. It had been hot, with a shitty showing of cars but one sweet '39 Ford De Luxe.

"Almost everyone says that you were a good guy. Good father. Reliable employee. Hard worker. Someone who would give you the shirt off his back."

"Guess I had them all fooled," I said tartly, my eyes still on the picture. On her smile.

"Two weeks later . . ." He pulled out my mug shot and held it up beside the other.

Like night and day. Before and after. I stared at my mug shot and remembered how pissed I had been when the photo was taken. It was right after the intake. Right after I'd realized the hell that was about to be my home.

"So, what happened to change you from this to this?" He tapped the glass above the two. "Or . . ." He paused. "Was this first guy always a monster, and on December 6, your Mr. Perfect Father mask just slipped down for a moment?"

I lifted my gaze from the photos, not sure I had heard him correctly. "What?"

"It's a theory I have. That people don't change; sometimes their mask slips off and you see the real person they are." He tapped on the mug shot. "The monster behind the mask."

Sometimes it's not the people that change. It's the mask that falls off.

"This is your personal theory?" I asked.

He shrugged. "Not exactly. It's something they say about narcissists. It can also be applied to violent individuals."

Sometimes it's not the people that change. It's the mask that falls off.

"So it's a common idea? I mean, that's something a lot of people say?" My chest was growing tight, and I coughed again, then hit the center of my chest with my fist.

He looked at me as if I were crazy. "What's something that people say?"

"The thing about the mask falling off," I said impatiently.

"It's not something that normally gets brought up in dinner conversations." He grinned and I didn't return the gesture. Instead, my mind was flipping through where I had heard that line before.

A letter. Had to be from a letter. Not a book I read, not a conversation, not from him in the past. I remembered it because it had stuck in my craw for the next week or two.

Coincidence? Probably not.

"You haven't answered the question." He put down the photos and sat back in his chair. "Were you always this 'monster'?" He put the word in air quotes, but we both knew he meant it. Despite whatever form of friendship we had between us. Maybe he didn't see it as friendship. Shit, I wasn't sure I did either. But for someone used to no one, he had become a someone to me in the last three months.

Maybe a someone who was hiding something.

Sometimes it's not the people that change. It's the mask that falls off.

Maybe he had his own mask on. Maybe that line . . . this conversation . . . it was a slip of it.

He was staring at me, brows raised, and I struggled to return to the discussion before he started to wonder what I was thinking on. "I've always been a monster," I said. "You see a good father . . ." I nodded toward the picture of me and Jenny. "I wasn't one."

"So you—"

I didn't let him finish. Standing, I caught Redd's eye and lifted my chin, beckoning him. "I got to go. Bathroom's calling."

Tim didn't move, his eyes narrowing. Maybe I should have played this off better, but I needed to get to my room and figure out where I'd read that line before.

Redd came in and I looked at Tim. "That picture of Jenny and me. Put it through the slot?"

"You want it?" He picked it up slowly. This asshole was lucky the glass was between us.

"Yeah." I gestured to the thin slot in the glass, the one just wide enough for legal documents and papers to pass through.

He waited for a second, like he was considering it, then leaned forward and inserted it through the opening.

I didn't say *thanks*. I grabbed it and then showed Redd the photo and my shackles, letting him check both.

On the other side of the glass, Tim stood and silently got his backpack and headed for the door. "See you next week?" I called out.

He stopped, his hand on the door handle. "Probably."

I didn't like that response. I watched the door shut behind him and had the feeling that I had fucked up somewhere in this relationship.

—

Sometimes it's not the people who change. It's the mask that falls off.

I repeated the line as I hurried along the wide hall, past the commissary and the library, to my block and then to my cell. Entering the narrow space, I retrieved my files of letters and carefully combed through the stacks.

For my regulars, I kept them grouped by sender, and I thumbed through the women until I got to the men. It was likely the brother, Mr. Anonymous. I pulled out his stack and started there, kneeling on the hard concrete floor and spreading out the pages.

The collection was thick, over fifty or sixty pages, and I forced myself to be careful not to rip anything.

How long ago had I heard that? At least a year, maybe a few.

I'd worn a mask for decades. One that only a couple of people had ever seen behind. Hell, I had adopted a new one once I got here, for survival more than anything.

> *I don't understand how a man like you can look at himself in the mirror.*

I flipped to the next letter, scanned it quickly, then the next. A dozen more letters passed.

> *She was the only pure thing in my life. What did she do to deserve this? How did you justify this in your mind?*

Maybe it wasn't from him. Maybe it had been from—my finger stopped mid-scroll on a paragraph of handwritten text.

> *I've been reading about narcissistic behavior and the differences between a narcissist and a sociopath. Both work very diligently to appear normal but hide their true*

nature behind a mask—their public persona. When they act outside of that public persona . . . say, killing a group of innocent children . . . it's not a psychological break, it's just an interruption of the play-acting . . . i.e., their mask slipping off. To say that another way . . .

Sometimes it's not the people who change. It's the mask that falls off.

That is so disturbing to me . . . the idea that the people in my life could be like you, and just . . .

I stopped, then reread it. Narcissistic behavior . . . That's what Tim had said, right? *It's something they say about narcissists. It can also be applied to violent individuals.*

Maybe it was a coincidence, or maybe this was the scratch that had been digging its way deeper and deeper into my brain with each visit from Dr. Valden.

I pinched my eyes closed, trying to piece together what I had told the pen pal versus what I had told the visitor. I'd always been careful to keep the different pieces of the truth in compartments, but I might have . . . maybe . . . shared too much between the two of them?

I hadn't been the only one with a mask on. The brother had a wife and a kid. Tim had presented himself as single. Who was telling the truth? The brother had been in a long-term relationship . . . surely he hadn't lied in his letters for two decades, but what if he had? What if he wasn't even the brother of one of the girls? What if he had always just used that as a fake connection, a way to catch my attention? It was easier to deceive someone with letters. Plenty of time to line up the lies, think through the wording.

No. It was more likely that Dr. Valden was the one who was lying. Being face-to-face with someone was risky. One off phrase, one slip of the mask, and he would have shown his cards. Like he had tonight.

Maybe it had been an intentional clue. Maybe he'd given me a half dozen, and I'd missed them. *I can confidently say that I know just about everything there is to know about you, Mr. Folcrum.* A big softball right there, and I was too busy jawing through a sandwich to catch it.

I had always believed that my pen pal was the blonde's brother, but maybe he wasn't. Maybe that was a lie. I'd seen the brother in court, glaring at me like he was ready to throw fists. All testosterone and hatred, right there in the front row at the trial, gripping that railing like he'd been ready to come over it at me. It had been easy to believe that he'd start to write me letters, but it wasn't like I had any lack of enemies.

Tim . . . I shook my head, trying to put him and that seventeen-year-old kid next to each other.

Could they be the same person? Maybe. Big difference between an acne-covered, shaggy-headed kid and a clean-cut grown man.

Truth be told, other than the hate in his eyes, the rest of the kid was a bit fuzzy. I'd spent more time searching the audience for *her.*

Searching, and being let down in what I saw.

From: tfk@hotmail.com
To: info@murderunplugged.com

Date: July 10 at 10:19 AM

Subject: proof

There's a detail I haven't seen anyone cover so I'm assuming law enforcement is withholding it intentionally. When I carved up little Kitty Green I cut an S into her stomach.

I won't jump through any more hoops for you. Take me seriously or I'll go to someone else.

CHAPTER 45

PERLA

Paige told me a few weeks into working there that she had
a serious crush on the dad. She said he was like a nerdy
Bradley Cooper. I remember once, he texted her at night
when we were out, and she let out a shriek, she was so
excited.

—*Jeralynn Gutierrez, college student*

It was just a moment. A moment when I came in with the groceries and
Grant was standing in the kitchen, pen in hand, the newspaper on the
counter, open to the daily crossword. Paige was beside him, her finger
pointing to a clue, their heads right beside each other. Innocent, maybe.
I walked in without hesitation and put my bags on the counter, and she
stepped away and he looked up, and then the moment was over.

Even though it ended, it had still happened. And I noted it, added
it to the column of Things Grant Had Done Wrong, and he inched
forward in the race of whom I would set up for the crime. I held that
chip in my hand and loved the feel of power it gave me.

That night, when her car wouldn't start and I gave her a ride home, I planted another seed, this one with Leewood Folcrum's name on it.

———

The Mercedes hummed along the road, hugging the curves, its automatic wipers taking care of the rain that peppered the windshield. Paige pulled a little on her belt and looked out her window. "I'm so sorry about my car. I don't know what it could be."

"Don't worry about it." I flicked my brights at an oncoming car, and he lowered his in response, a streetlight illuminating the car as it swept toward us. An orange Ferrari. Paige craned her neck, watching as it passed. I bet she'd never been in a Ferrari. Never would.

"Tell me about your mom." I slowed at an intersection, glancing both ways to make sure it was clear. "What's she do?"

"Um, she's in retail?" Her voice rose at the end as if it were a question. "She works at a shoe store in Dayton."

How miserably bleak but also expected. My mother had worked in retail as well. I toyed with what, if anything, to tell her.

"Take a right at the next light. Um, please." She played with the ends of her ponytail, separating the limp strands.

"And you said your father works at the prison. You said it was called Lynncaster?" I pronounced the name wrong and waited to see if she would correct me.

"Yep. He's been there like a decade."

"Is that a men's or women's prison?" I put on my blinker, then took a right turn at the intersection.

"Men's."

A conversationalist, she was not.

I faked a shudder. "I can't imagine being around criminals like that, all day, every day."

She let out a small laugh. "I guess? I don't know. He doesn't really talk about it. I think he just sees them like normal people. Normal people who made some mistakes."

Normal people who just made some mistakes. I'd have to save that and whip it out when it was time for her to be locked away as a murderer. *"I forgive you, Paige . . . you're just a normal person who made some mistakes."*

I hunched forward, peering out through the increasing rain. "So what's the most dangerous criminal he's ever dealt with?"

She looked out her window. "I don't really know." It was so offhand, the way she said it. As if she didn't really know—but the slight pitch in her voice gave her away.

"You should ask your dad. Especially if you're wanting to go into criminology. I bet he could get you in to visit someone big. Ask them some questions, like a mini interview."

"Oh, I don't know." She looked down at her knees, then brushed her bangs away from her face. "This is my road here. Cedar Trail."

I turned down the gravel road, my car bumping over the uneven surface, and wondered how far I should push it. "You're probably right. Sitting down with a killer . . ." I turned where she pointed and then parked in front of a double-wide trailer and a blue Kia Sorento SUV.

"It'd probably be too much for someone like you." I paused, then quickly added, "I just mean, because you're so young and quiet. But if you are wanting to do something in that field . . . I don't know, Paige. It would be a fantastic résumé builder. Trust me on that." I placed my hand on her forearm, underlining the point.

She reached for her bag, then for the car's handle.

"Need help getting your things inside?"

"No, I have it. Thank you." She gave me a nervous smile.

"Tomorrow, I'll have Grant pick you up," I offered. "Then you can drive this car home. Use it for the next few days while we sort out what's wrong with yours." What was wrong with hers was the sugar in the gas tank, a problem I'd created and would blame on Sophie, but only to Paige.

She protested, both about Grant and about the use of the Mercedes, but I didn't let her out of the car until she agreed. She would love the ride and alone time with my husband, and driving the $100,000 Mercedes would give her a glimpse of the life that she didn't have. That, and it would be a highly visible sign to everyone that Paige Smith was aggressively moving into our life.

I'd pay for the repairs to Paige's car and tell her that I'd handle Sophie's discipline myself, that she didn't need to worry about that. Paige would most certainly mention it to someone, and this would be the first of a few manufactured aggressions that Sophie would display—all building on the wall between them that would act as a potential motive for Paige's desire to remove Sophie from the Grant + Paige equation.

Again, I didn't need it to be real. I only needed documented red flags that would raise doubts in a jury's mind. And it would be easier since Sophie wouldn't be around to contradict the history.

I backed slowly out of the spot and pulled a tight U-turn. As I headed out, a smile bloomed on my face.

It was almost too easy.

CHAPTER 46

JOURNAL OF SOPHIE WULTZ

I've decided that I never want to be an adult. They all suck. Even Paige, who I thought was cool, but she's not. Today she asked if I messed with her car. I didn't know what she was talking about, and I told her that, but she didn't believe me. I could tell by the way her face got all hard, and then she said that my mom was taking care of it, whatever that means.

I thought that Mom would talk to me about it, but she didn't.

They're loading her car on a tow truck right now. I don't know why she's glaring at me over it. First of all, I didn't have anything to do with it. Second, she's getting to drive the Mercedes until it's fixed so . . . like, what's the problem?

I asked if we could run some drills in the backyard but she said no, that she needed to deal with car stuff first.

Is she allowed to say no? I mean, aren't we paying her to do stuff with me?

The whole situation is weird, but at least she's not permanent. I told Mom that she was being mean, and Mom told me that she'll fire her after my birthday party, so that's cool.

In the meantime, I'll try my best with her, but . . . whatever. As Mom said to me the other day, our job isn't to be nice to the help.

CHAPTER 47

PERLA

"What are you doing?" I stopped in the doorway to Grant's office and glared at Paige, who stood by the fireplace.

She spun on one foot. At least she was barefoot. Yesterday I'd caught her with her shoes on in the house despite my very clear instructions that everyone remove them prior to entry.

"Oh, I'm sorry, am I not allowed in here?"

"We'd rather you not be. Where's Sophie?"

"Oh, she's taking a shower. I'm just waiting on her to finish, and I was wandering."

Snooping, that's what she was doing. Not that I didn't expect it. I took a deep breath and reminded myself that this was normal, expected. Not a bad thing.

"Is this . . . This is Mr. Wultz?" She pointed to a photo on the mantel, and damn if she hadn't found the only photo in the entire house of Lucy. In the picture, his arm was around her shoulders, hugging her tight to his side, big smiles on both their faces.

"Yes." I moved forward until I was beside her. "That's when he was in high school."

"The girl is really pretty."

"Yes," I agreed carefully.

"Is she related to him?" Her voice rose a little. If Paige Smith had a tell, that was it.

I turned to face her. "Why do I think that you already know who that is?"

She flushed. "I don't," she stammered. "I mean, not really. I didn't see any pictures online, but I know—"

"You know about Grant's family," I said.

"Yes." She looked pained. "I'm sorry. I won't say anything to him about it, I promise."

"When did you find out?"

"Just last night. I was researching some of the prisoners that my dad told me about. One of them—I saw the last name Wultz, and it's so unique. I looked it up and saw Grant's name in one of the obituaries." She wrung her hands. "I'm sorry," she whispered.

"It's okay." I sighed. "It's not exactly a secret. We don't talk about it, but some people in the neighborhood know. I would appreciate it if you don't tell anyone."

"Oh yeah, of course. I mean, I don't know anyone you know anyway. We aren't exactly in the same circles." She let out a nervous giggle.

"Still," I said stiffly. "Your discretion would be appreciated."

"Right. Yeah. I won't tell anyone."

"Does your father know?" I held my breath, afraid of her answer. Surely, if she had told him, he wouldn't share that information. A man who worked with criminals, he would understand the need for privacy, especially in a case like this.

"Uh, yeah." Her face crumpled. "I'm sorry, I told him as soon as I found out."

At least she didn't lie to me. She could have easily done so. The fact that she didn't was another point in her favor. So what if her father knew? I could still pull and control the strings from here.

"I'm sorry," she repeated. This girl really needed to expand her vocabulary.

"Sophie is probably out of the shower." I glanced at my watch. "And I need to change."

"Yeah, of course. Sorry." She turned away from the mantel and walked quickly toward the hall. I waited until she was almost to the door, then called her name. She immediately spun around, her shoulders hunched, steeled for a lashing.

"Don't tell Grant that you know. And please ask your father to keep this confidential. Leewood doesn't know that we live in the area. It's very important that he doesn't find out."

She nodded, but I saw the bit of light that entered her eyes and I didn't like it. "Yes, of course. I'll tell him. My dad, I mean. Not Mr. Wultz. I won't say anything to him."

"Good." I tilted my head toward Sophie's room. "Please close the door behind you."

"Right. Absolutely." She quickly exited, then carefully pulled the tall door closed until it clicked into place.

I waited a moment, making sure she was gone; then I turned back to the mantel and carefully picked up the frame, studying the old photograph.

Lucy had been beautiful. All soft blonde hair and big blue eyes. A laugh like a bell. Skin so pale, it was almost translucent. When they'd found her, her features were unrecognizable from the cuts and the blood. She got it the worst, and the police say that she was alive for most of it, that her screams were probably what the neighbors heard.

I placed the frame back in its place, carefully adjusting it to the exact angle it was before. Grant would notice if it had been moved. He always did.

CHAPTER 48

PERLA

I studied the line of dolls along Sophie's shelf. "You're too old for these."

"I am, but I still like them." She sat cross-legged on the floor of her closet, an American Girl catalog open on her lap, and flipped through the pages. "Look, this one is new this year." She lifted the magazine and turned it toward me.

The featured doll was a pop star with a microphone in one hand, cell phone in the other, wearing a sparkling bikini top and matching hot pants. I'm not sure when American Girl dolls had become so . . . untraditional, but I wasn't crazy about the example they were setting for my daughter.

"I think this is the one I want," she decided, dog-earing the page.

"I just don't know what you're going to do with all of them," I said, counting the line of lifelike dolls on the shelf. Each themed doll stood eighteen inches tall and came with intricate outfits and props. While I had understood Sophie's interest when she was eight, I didn't understand her still wanting one now—or the desire to keep them all.

"They're collector's items, Mom." She flipped the page. "They're going to be worth money."

I grimaced at the thought of dealing with the pile of dolls after she was gone. "Well, I think it was a good idea, moving them into the closet before the party." I glanced back at her bedroom, their prior home—the long shelf above her desk—now empty.

"Yeah, Mand thinks they're babyish." She made a face. "I mean, not that I'm moving them for *her*. It's just to make more room for us to hang out."

Mandolin was right. I looked down at the page she'd flagged in the catalog, annoyed by just the thought of going to the website and placing the order. At this point, we were Berry-level loyalty customers and got a free gift in the mail on her birthday *and* Christmas. Again, mortifying.

"You think there's enough time for this to arrive before my party?" She held up the magazine page and tapped her finger on the doll.

"I'll check. If not, we can just give it to you a few days later." *Never.* "We already have a lot of great gifts, sweetie." Grant had been on a buying spree for her birthday, including a new bike, hiking boots, some perfume she wanted, and two bags full of clothing from the downtown boutique that all the preteens frequented. Everything still needed to be wrapped, and I made a mental note to have Paige do it.

Having a nanny was fantastic. I should have gotten one a decade ago.

I took the magazine from her and studied the page, then nodded, folding it in half and sticking it under my arm. "Bridget and Mandolin confirmed? They're coming?"

"Yep." She moved onto her knees, then stood. "And you said I could have some more friends stay over the next weekend for a sleepover, right?"

"Right." I was loving how easy it was, being able to put off and promise things for a later date that would never happen. *Yes, you can have this ugly doll. Yes, you can invite the entire school over if you want. Yes, we will talk about your father's sister.* Yes, yes, yes—all *after* the party.

"Have you thought about what you want to do the night of the party? Maybe a movie in the theater?"

"Dad said he could set up a screen out by the pool. That would be cool."

I nodded. "Okay, sure. I'll let him handle the tech. Just let me know what you want for dinner."

"What are my options?" She followed me as I walked toward our side of the house. When we'd designed the house, I had specifically created a floor plan that would provide as much space as possible between her bedroom and ours while still keeping us all on the same level. In between hers and ours was the catwalk that journeyed past the vaulted areas of the foyer, library, and living rooms, plus the upstairs laundry, our two offices, and the guest rooms.

I hadn't been thinking of murder when I created the plan, but the configuration meant that even if they screamed the night of the party . . . Grant wouldn't be able to hear it from inside our bedroom. He'd sleep through it all, especially with some pills crushed into his after-dinner drink or inside the vials of his Metamucil.

"Mom?"

"Yes?" Someone had left the light on in Grant's office, and I stopped at the door and reached inside, flicking off the switch.

"What can you make for dinner at the party?"

"Whatever you want."

"Anything?"

"Pretty much." I stopped at the door to our suite and turned to her, waiting.

She bit her lip, thinking. "Pepperoni pizza," she said. "With the stuffed crust. And breadsticks with the alfredo sauce."

I had raised my daughter on the finest food money could buy, and pizza . . . that was the last meal she'd ever have. The same thing, coincidentally, Jenny Folcrum had eaten with her father on a regular basis.

I hadn't had pizza in years, not since I realized how many burpees it took to burn off a single slice.

"Okay." I smiled down at her. "Pizza it is. Now, go find your father and make sure he's aware that he'll need to put a screen up by the pool."

"'Kay." She headed for the stairs, and I waited until she was halfway down them; then I pulled the American Girl catalog out from under my arm and dropped it into the trash.

From: tfk@hotmail.com
To: info@murderunplugged.com

Date: July 15 at 1:22 PM

Subject: 3 little girls

Three little girls

Three little girls

See how they run

See how they run

I slashed the girls on birthday night

Poor Leewood had a terrible fright

I thought it killed my appetite

But now I need another delight

Three little girls

CHAPTER 49

"I just don't know what to do." My words were rushing together, and I forced myself to pause and take a deep breath. I started to brush back my hair, but my hands were trembling, so I fisted them and put them in my lap. Dr. Maddox noticed it all, her gaze twitching from each tell like a pinball in motion, finally landing on my face and sticking.

She had warmed to me in the more recent sessions. Each visit, she sat a little straighter in her chair, her dismissive manner slowly replaced by an eager interest in whatever I had to say. The hook, as my father used to say, was set.

"Okay, just take a deep breath now." She gripped the top of her notepad with both hands as if it were a stroller handle. "Tell me what happened."

"I don't know where to start." I swallowed. "I mean, if you met Grant, you would never think—he is such a gentleman in person. And so handsome. I mean, everyone says how nice he is. Everyone."

"Did something happen?"

I turned my head, looking out the window. It was starting to rain. I had left my umbrella in the car. This cashmere turtleneck would be ruined.

"Perla, pay attention. I want to make sure we have enough time to discuss this before today's session ends."

"Yes, I have to pick up Sophie at two thirty from school," I said faintly and adjusted the band of my watch. "Grant will be furious if I'm late."

She nodded and leaned forward. "Okay, so what is it? You'll feel better once you say it aloud. I promise you will. Then we can examine it together, in a protected space."

I took another deep breath, letting the air fill up my lungs in a deep inhale before releasing it slowly, making sure I had all the pieces of me in place and perfect before I spoke. She was watching every move, and so far, she was following my breadcrumbs perfectly.

Glancing at my watch one more time for good measure, I cleared my throat.

She almost fell forward in anticipation.

Giving her an apologetic look, I wet my lips. "I was in Grant's office, just straightening things up, and I found this file he had. It was filled with photos of dead little girls."

There. Even Barney Fife wouldn't pass that one up.

She frowned. "What do you mean? What kind of photos?"

"Crime scene photos. Close-ups of the blood and their bodies . . ." I inhaled and put one hand on my stomach as if I were going to be physically sick. "Really gory things. They were all from that old crime—you know, the one I mentioned in an earlier session. The one that was on the television the first night when we had sex."

"Oh yes." She nodded. "The Fokeman Gala or something like that."

"The Folcrum Party," I said tightly.

"Okay, but these aren't photos he took. These are police photos?"

I nodded.

"Why would Grant have photos of that?"

"He's become obsessed with the event," I said bluntly. "There was a podcast that recently covered it, and it has just lit this fire in him. I try to talk to him about it, but he gets really scary whenever I do. I can't let him know that I found this folder, he would . . ." I shake my head roughly. "I don't know what he'd do. But twice I've come in and found him watching interviews with the killer. And you know, Sophie is the same age as the victims."

"Do you think Sophie's age has triggered a fatherly concern that something similar might happen to her?"

"No." I shook my head once more. "See, this is why I shouldn't have said anything to you. You're just like everyone else—you see Grant as this perfect father and husband, and I've been trying to tell you . . . this is something else. Something dark and twisted. Something that terrifies me."

She looked bewildered. Maybe I was sharing too much. I should be giving her bite-size amounts, not trying to stuff a porterhouse down her throat.

"I'm sorry, Perla." She reached out and patted my knee. "I'm just trying to understand how all of this connects. You both found out about this event on the night you met, right? Do you think that Grant feels some tie to it because of your initial history with it?"

Oh my word. She was chasing fleas and ignoring the mangy dog. At this rate, it would be next year before she found my next breadcrumb. I let out a huff of irritation, and wondered if telling her about Grant's sister would help or hurt the situation. Probably hurt. She'd dismiss the evidence, find a way to turn it around into being caused by "environments of doubt." That was what she had already done with Paige—pushed my concerns to the side faster than vegetables off her dinner plate.

"No, that's not it." Standing up, I tucked my purse underneath my arm. "Look, I have to go. I'm having surgery next week, so I won't be able to make the Thursday session, but I'll let the receptionist know the dates."

"Surgery?" She stood quickly and almost knocked her iced coffee over. "I hope everything's okay."

"Oh, I'm fine. Just something minor." My swollen face and bruising would give away the nose job, but maybe I could do a few telehealth appointments to cover it up.

"Okay," she said faintly, and I savored the look of worry that crossed her face. Later, she would rehash the conversation and see her failure to acknowledge my fears. She would be concerned that I was upset and that she had damaged our relationship and trust. She would call me and apologize, and I would be gracious but cold, and in the next session, she would play the proper part. I didn't care how it happened, only that it did.

I exited on that note and with that expectation, but I didn't like the taste it left in my mouth.

CHAPTER 50

The problem with that email we got from the TFK guy was, we didn't know if the *S* thing was accurate. It took us calling the police and nagging them until they went into evidence and pulled the autopsy photos. But then they stopped treating us like we were kids and immediately initiated a forensic trace and alert on our email account. After that, we took anything we got from TFK very seriously. And go figure that that was when he shut up. We didn't hear from him for almost a month.

—*Rachel,* Murder Unplugged

I'd planned Sophie's birthday party every year, and each one had seemed bigger and like more of a pain in the ass than the last. Everything nowadays had to be impressive enough for social media, which meant the women in this neighborhood were one-upping each other to a ridiculous degree. I had played along halfheartedly while rolling my eyes and hating every painstaking detail. But this party would be different, with a planning process I was excited to embrace.

My inspiration was simple. The Folcrum Party had started out as most twelve-year-old birthday parties did: a sleepover with cake and ice cream, songs and presents. A limited guest list, with only two attendees. The scant attendance was a detail that had prompted countless internet debates, theories, and opinions. It was widely documented that Jenny Folcrum was an unpopular child. There had been plenty of interviews with her teachers and acquaintances who were frank in the fact that while Jenny was an extremely intelligent child, she was also a loner who could be difficult to befriend.

A loser. That's what Jenny was. Bright and intelligent but also poor and weird. Kitty Green's mother said that Kitty hadn't even wanted to come to the birthday party, that she'd wanted to cancel the morning of, but her mother refused and said it would be rude.

Being rude would have saved Kitty's life. Bet her mother stayed up late at night over that one.

What had added fuel to the internet fire a few weeks after the death was all the preteen girls who had produced invitations to the event. As it turned out, Jenny Folcrum had invited seventeen classmates to the party. Seventeen invites and only two had shown up. Even now, twenty-three years after the snub, I was irate and embarrassed on Jenny's behalf.

Had it not been for the seventeen invitations, the public might not have found the two-person attendance odd. As a grown woman, it was hard for me to generate the names of two people whom I'd be willing to share a hotel room with, much less engage in a sleepover, with all the social gymnastics that involved. But I could also concede that the person I became after George and Janice was different from the girl I was before I joined their life. Difficult to befriend? Yes, that could have accurately described me.

I felt a tenderness for Jenny Folcrum and her sad little life. No mother. No money. No substantial role models other than her father—an alcoholic electrician who would eventually slice her open like a deer.

That wasn't my impression of him; it was the internet's. I understood that Leewood Folcrum was a complex individual who had been put in a unique position and acted without thinking through the consequences.

For example, staying at the scene was idiotic. The thin walls of their trailer had done little to contain the little girls' screams, and the police had arrived before Jenny had finished dying, catching Leewood holding her on his lap, her blood spray all over his shirt and face.

He could have run, but he didn't. He held on to his child, and when the police asked what had happened, he kept his mouth shut. He let them lock him up and then went through months of an investigation and trial . . . all while staying mum, except to say that he was innocent and someone else had broken in and committed the crime.

No one in the history of ever believed his story. At his trial, the jury deliberated for less than an hour before returning the guilty verdict. I'd watched the sentencing video repeatedly, focusing on his face as the judge lectured him on his actions and the impact on the other families.

His face had never changed from its flat canvas. Nothing when the parents started to sob from the front row of the audience. Nothing when the sentence—eight consecutive life sentences, without the possibility of parole—was read.

It was incredibly attractive, his quiet strength. I loved that he wouldn't tell them anything. I loved that he didn't take the stand. He only did one interview—and the rumors were that he had sent the payment for that to Lucy's and Kitty's families.

A noble gesture, though I'm sure they didn't appreciate it. I know how Grant feels about Leewood. His name was tantamount to the devil's in our home, which was one of the reasons I kept my affection and respect for Leewood to myself.

There were certain elements of the Folcrum Party that I wouldn't be able to recreate in Sophie's birthday event. The shitty trailer. The way the floor was soft in some places and the wallpaper bubbled in others. The tiny, cramped bedroom where the girls had been found. Sophie's room would be used for accuracy, but it wouldn't have the same feel. It wouldn't have the same impact.

Poverty produces empathy. There wouldn't be the same emotional tug from the public, seeing our crime scene photos. All of middle

America can relate to a cheap preteen's bedroom. The posters of pop stars on the wall. The overflowing hamper. The worn-out sneakers. The saggy twin bed with a Walmart comforter set.

Sophie's room, with its floor-to-ceiling windows and polished hardwoods, wouldn't play nearly as well. The king-size Sleep Number bed, custom built-in bookshelves with hundreds of hardcover books, and desk. Her kitchenette by the bath, with her own mini fridge, microwave, ice machine, and water-filtration system. The spacious walk-in with countless racks of designer clothes.

But then again, for all those who could connect with an average—or slightly below average—childhood, there was the large swath of America who was fascinated by wealth. They would obsess over the fact that Sophie had an opening in her wall that would suck dirty clothes through it and deliver it to our laundry room. They would catalog the items in her room and their value, and know that her bedroom set cost over $10,000 and the sneakers she was wearing were Golden Goose and that those were real diamond studs in her ears.

This would be the rich-girl version of the Folcrum Party, and I was torn over whether to play up those attributes or mute them. I had to maintain a strong enough tie to the original crime or else it would lose its pizzazz.

I also had to be very careful of the details, with an eye on avoiding implicating myself. If I sent out seventeen invitations or dressed Sophie in a polka-dotted cotton jumper with a red bow in her hair, the suspicion would immediately swing my way. I had to make sure to separate myself enough from the planning to keep my hands clean while also making sure that everything was done perfectly.

I found Paige in the library, lazily flipping through a magazine while Sophie did her homework at the table. I hovered in the doorway and waved, catching the nanny's attention. After gesturing for her to follow me, I walked halfway down the hall and waited for her to catch up.

Her steps were quick, and today she was wearing a long-sleeved Gwen Stefani shirt with jeans and sneakers. She had a green headband holding back her straight, dark hair and wore red glasses. A cute look, though I would have preferred a more professional one. I pushed the thought away before it came out. "Paige, I need your help with something."

"Sure, anything." Her quick response was happy, and I smiled at the eagerness on her face.

"It's Sophie's upcoming twelfth-birthday party. I'd like you to handle the planning of it."

"Oh, cool. I'd love to. Do you have any ideas, or should I just—"

"I have some ideas, but I'd really like this to be your project." A project I would manipulate in every possible way. "Can you come in an hour early tomorrow and we can go over the details?"

"Absolutely." She tilted her head. "Is this a secret, or does Sophie know about it?"

"She knows about it. Grant wants to keep it small—he said just two friends. She's already invited two of the girls in the neighborhood for a sleepover. So it won't be a big affair; I just don't have time to handle the cake, decorations, stuff like that."

She nodded again. "I think . . ." She glanced over her shoulder and toward the library. "I think it's going okay between us. I mean, no more things, like with the car."

The car had ended up being a thousand-dollar repair. We had replaced the fuel filter, all the fuel lines, and then had the tank drained and replaced.

"I told you, you just need to give her some space. And if anything does happen, come to me first. Don't try to deal with Sophie."

"Yeah. Okay."

She looked unsure, and I mentally patted myself on the back for how things were going so far. It was the orchestration of a train wreck— one that, even if derailed, would put the attention of the police everywhere except on me.

CHAPTER 51

LEEWOOD FOLCRUM

Inmate 82145

Hi, my forever,

I can't stop thinking of you, stuck in that place. It seems so cold and horrible from the photos I can find online. I wish I was there to fix you a warm meal and hold you in my arms.

I've been researching the party lately, and I wish you would have just told them what happened. I know you didn't do it, but it seems that the police just didn't have enough to go on to find the real killer. Please think hard about if there's any other details you can remember about the intruder. Even something small. I have connections, Leewood. I could help get you out, and then we could be together.

I believe in your innocence. I love you. You and I, we are connected in ways that others will never understand. You feel it, don't you?

I'm sorry that I haven't written in a while. Things have been very busy here, and I haven't been able to sneak out a letter, but it has nothing to do with how much I think of you and want to see you.

I haven't given up the thought of visiting you. I have so many complicated feelings about seeing you in there—and having you see me. But maybe soon. I really have been thinking about it a lot.

Always yours,

Darcy

PS: Please send me a photo. I'm enclosing a camera and some film. I just want to see what you look like now. All of the video clips online are so old. xoxoxo

The camera was a blue plastic thing, with a thin five-pack of blank photos. I turned them over in my hand, surprised people were still using Polaroids.

"Folcrum." Redd stood in the doorway. "Doc wants to see you."

"On a Sunday?" I stood, my back creaking in protest. I leaned back, trying to pop it, then bent over, reaching for my shoes.

"Don't know what to tell you." He glanced at my desk. "How's the fan mail?"

"Same old shit. Half loonies, half whores."

"No loony whores?"

I smiled as I pulled the back of the sneaker over my heel. "Good point." My chest suddenly seized and I gripped it, inhaling deeply as I tried to get some air in.

"You okay?" Redd stayed outside the cell, but I heard the sound of his radio unclipping.

I held up my hand, stopping any action. "I'm fine," I said tightly, sucking in shallow breaths as I gripped the railing of the bed. My chest finally relaxed, and I lifted my chin, meeting his eyes. "I'm good," I said.

"Maybe it's a good thing, you going to the doc right now." He reattached his radio to his shirt.

"Or maybe the thought of seeing him is what choked me up." On the way to the door, I stopped, taking a moment to cover the next letter in the stack. I didn't expect anyone to step into my cell while I was gone, but you could never be too careful.

CHAPTER 52

JOURNAL OF SOPHIE WULTZ

I searched the internet for "famous Wultz" and "actress Wultz" and didn't find anything that looked right.

Bridget said that she's probably married or has a fake actress name, which makes sense. I think I'm just going to ask Dad, but waiting until after my birthday is just ridiculous. I mean, it's still like a month away.

This summer is agonizingly long. My nanny is a bitch, my mom is even weirder than normal, and getting my period turned out to suck. The only good part about it is that apparently my boobs are going to start growing soon, which is good because everyone is ahead of me. I asked Mom if I could get a training bra, and she looked at me like I'd asked for a machete. I get that I don't really need one, but it's embarrassing when everyone else is wearing one and I'm not. Maybe I'll ask Paige to buy one for me. Even though she turned mean and is stuck up Mom's ass, she still has moments where she seems okay. And she's poor, so she will probably buy me whatever I want if I give her extra to keep.

Yeah, I like that plan. Is that a bribe? Maybe. If so, I like that plan even more. I've never bribed someone before, but it seems wicked cool.

CHAPTER 53

PERLA

I kissed Grant once. I know that you didn't ask that, but I have been thinking about it ever since it all happened. I don't think Perla ever found out. It was at the annual Christmas party at the club. I'd had too much to drink. Jeez, everyone had. Perla was running the toy-donation desk, and I had stepped out to make a call, and he was there, and I slipped on the icy walk and he was helping me up and we just had a moment, you know. Like, just this stupid moment that happened before you know it. But I never dated him or anything. I swear. So if you're looking for, like, a secret mistress—that isn't me, but you should really look at the nanny.

—*Marci Vennigan, salon owner*

In Grant's office, there was a locked file drawer in the far end of his massive credenza. We had never discussed it, but I'd found it when I was snooping through his office. I made the discovery on the day we left for Spain and had to suffer through eight days of vineyards and wine tastings before we finally returned home and I could hunt down the key and unlock it.

The key hadn't been hard to find—a small gold digit on his car-key chain—which cemented my belief that the lock on the cabinet was for Sophie's benefit, not mine.

That day I waited until he left for work and Sophie was at school, then went upstairs and opened the drawer. Inside was a thick stack of neatly labeled folders. I sat on the Persian rug in his office and spread the contents out before me.

Now, with Paige and Sophie at the mall and Grant at the office, I did the same.

The folders were a gold mine of Folcrum data, and I once again wondered how my husband had gotten copies of the original case files. Everything was here, in black-and-white printouts. The crime scene. Lists of evidence. Leewood's fingerprint records. Interview transcripts. Photos of the victims. I stared for a long time at the photo of Jenny Folcrum on a medical stretcher, surrounded by a team of emergency professionals, her neck a bloody, gaping hole. Kitty Green's photos were there, along with Lucy's, and I tapped the photo that showed the jagged *S* cut into her stomach, in homage to the *Murder Unplugged* access it had provided me.

Grant's obsession with the murders wasn't normal or healthy, but then again, neither was mine. I ran my hand reverently over the mug shot photo of Leewood, his handsome face scowling into the camera.

Just one hour away. The familiar surge of fear and desire swelled inside me. As always, I pushed it back down and dropped the photo to the side.

I needed to focus on the crime scene photos, so I studied each one, ignoring the bloody bodies and homing in on the backgrounds, looking for small details I could claim and reuse.

The streamers around the room.

The mini cupcakes with sprinkles, the cheap package open, half of them gone.

The two-liter of off-brand soda.

The white comforter spread on the carpet, acting as a picnic blanket.

There was a lot there that I could use, and the good news was that even the minor things would stand out because they wouldn't fit in our house.

Yes. I inhaled deeply. This could—*would*—work.

I returned my attention to the photos and switched my focus to the bloody carnage, taking mental notes of the stab wounds and body positions.

Could I do it? Would my relationship with Sophie cause any hesitation or issue?

I closed my eyes and thought about my child. Tried to find, in the hollow cavities of my heart, some trepidation or agony around the idea of losing her.

Nothing. It was strange how sensitive I was to triggers like jealousy, betrayal, and competition but so completely void in other areas.

Strange but appreciated. I liked the blank slate that was my heart. I liked everything about myself. This event, it would upgrade my life. Drop some of the bad, bring in some good.

Truth be told, I was excited for it.

CHAPTER 54

LEEWOOD FOLCRUM

INMATE 82145

"Well, Mr. Folcrum, I don't have good news." The doc sat on the metal stool and regarded me. "I'm guessing you have two weeks, maybe three. If you were on the outside, we'd be moving you into hospice right now."

Not a huge surprise, or an unwelcome one.

"I can do my best to make you comfortable, and we can move you into medical if—"

"No." I shook my head. The only worse thing than having your body slowly break down was doing it while handcuffed to a hospital bed.

He nodded. "I figured as much. Come by here twice a day for pain meds. I'll alert the COs and the warden. You're done working, starting immediately."

I wouldn't bitch about that.

"Get your affairs in order, Folcrum. Meet with the chaplain. Any last words or confessions you want to make—now's the time." He held my gaze and I grunted.

"Thanks, Doc." I pushed off the exam table and stood. "Can't say I'm disappointed to get out of this place, even if it is in a body bag."

He opened the door. "I dispense medicine, not advice, but think about the people out there who are looking for closure. Do that for me?"

I met his eyes as I moved past him and through the door. "I got my own closure to find, Doc. But sure, I'll think on it."

———

I thought on it. The doc was right. I had felt guilt over both Kitty's and Lucy's families for decades, so the next morning, with no job to report to, I wrote the brother a letter that was different from any one I had ever sent him.

Part of me—a big part of me—wanted to confront him about visiting, about being Tim, but I didn't. I swallowed all that and focused on what I had done wrong and all the things he hated me for.

> You're desperate to understand why and how that night happened, and I have to say, I don't understand the need to know. There was an outcome: death. Why does the motivation behind the act matter? Why does it matter if it was a mental break or anger or jealousy or perversion or something else? It happened, now we have to deal with the fallout.
>
> I was recently told that I need to provide closure to those that are hurting. You, out of everyone, seem to be hurting the most, so I would like to go ahead and give you that closure. Frame this letter, because it's the only time I'll say this, and it's also the last letter you'll ever receive from me.
>
> You already know that I'm dying. Have been for a while, but the doctors say that the end is close, so if I'm ever going to give you any peace, now is probably the time to do it.

I killed your sister. I did it because I'm a sick fuck who likes to hear little girls scream and I wanted to know what the act felt like. I killed the first girl, and when that was done, I continued on so that there wouldn't be any witnesses.

I'm sorry. I am sincere about that. I'm sorry that that whole night happened and for my part in it. I wish I'd never met your little sister. I wish I'd just killed myself before she was ever born, before any of this could have ever come into play.

But I didn't. And I can't bring your sister back, but know that I have paid the price for her life. I've been locked in this place of hell for two decades. I've thought about the mistakes I've made for every day of that sentence.

Like I said, I can't bring her back. But I am sorry.

I killed her. And for no good reason at all. There isn't anything you could have done to prevent it, no mistakes that you or her parents made, no signs that would have tipped you off that a fucking psychopath lived at my address.

Bad things happen sometimes. Not your fault. She died fast, she didn't suffer, she blacked out from fear and pain just after the first stab occurred. Not to make this all about me, but having your body slowly eaten apart, organ by organ, by cancer . . . it's months of excruciating pain. Nights of trying to sleep, but every part of your body is hurting. Your brain going haywire, obsessing over the pain pills and inventing pain even when there was a moment of reprieve from it.

She had a good, quick death. Way too early, but quick and relatively painless, when compared to others, like mine.

I hope this gives you the closure that you need. Do with this confession whatever you want. By the time this reaches you, I'll probably already be dead.

Leewood

I read the letter over twice, saying the words aloud and testing them on my tongue. It was good. He wouldn't like it, but like the doctor said, it would give him some closure. Who cared if it was all lies? I'd consider it my donation to humanity.

I folded the paper into thirds and slid it into the envelope, then printed his PO box in neat writing on the front. I rose to my feet and headed for the commissary for a stamp.

Tim's next visit would be interesting, assuming he was the pen pal–writing brother. Maybe he wasn't and I had imagined a connection where there wasn't one.

Either way, here was my good deed for the year. Probably my final chance for one in this lifetime.

CHAPTER 55

PERLA

You know, one thing about Perla is that she didn't have any close friends. I mean, she went to lunches with us and would host parties and such, but if you asked who her best friend was? I don't think she had a consistent ongoing friendship with anyone. Which is sad, but I think she liked it like that. She had a wall up around her, and no one had the mental energy to scale that thing.

—*Morayi Keita, retired model*

I had some pep in my step when I walked into Dr. Maddox's office. *Murder Unplugged* had been talking about the Folcrum trial nonstop, and two other podcasts had picked up the scent. I smiled at the psychiatrist, not even bothered by her zebra-striped top and pleated pants.

My mood dissolved with her first statement.

"I was thinking that our sessions might be more productive if Grant was here." Dr. Maddox delivered the opinion with a cheerful beam. "Sometimes it helps to have a dialogue with both parties. It also allows me the chance to see how you two interact with each other." She smiled encouragingly, as if she expected me to just nod like a marionette, pull out my phone, and set up something on Grant's calendar.

"Oh, I don't think so," I said quickly. "I mean, Grant can't know that I've even been coming here. He would be . . ." I inhaled sharply. "He can't know," I said, softer this time. I kept my gaze down. There was no way she was missing this clear sign of spousal trauma.

Couples counseling with Grant was definitely not going to happen. For one, it would destroy the picture I'd so carefully drawn for her. Plus, everyone always loved Grant. I didn't need Dr. Maddox warming to Grant. I needed her to see him as a control freak with dark and adulterous tendencies. One who might seduce a nanny and plot the murder as a way of unburdening himself and honoring the past crime. Whether or not he went to prison didn't matter; I just needed enough doubt cast on him so that I would shine as the pillar of strength and sorrow, one the public would cheer for. One who could divorce her husband without scorn, given all the shadiness he'd been up to.

"Well, okay, now." She switched the cross of her legs. "We don't have to have him here if you aren't ready for that. But you have to realize that everything I hear from you is from your perspective."

"Yes." I didn't know where she was going with this, but I didn't like it.

"And we all have biases on our perspectives. Most of the time we can't even see our own biases. Some of them were built decades ago. Some of them were created more recently, as a result of trauma or circumstance."

My hand instinctively went for my neck, but I caught and disguised the action, pretending to brush something off the breast of my ebony sweater.

I waited for her to continue—I'd been through this song and dance before. She wasn't going to put out a net and have me fall into it. I was the one with the hook here, and I'd put in all the work to make sure it was pierced in her psyche, the line taut.

"Can we talk about your history with men, before Grant?"

I sighed, settling back against the soft leather chair. "There isn't much to tell. I had a few boyfriends but nothing serious. I was a virgin when I met Grant."

She flipped a few pages back. "Oh, that's interesting. So you were . . . let's see . . . twenty-one when you met Grant?"

"Yes."

"Was he your first love?" She peered at me. Today she was wearing black-and-white-plaid eyeglass frames. They looked ridiculous.

Grant wasn't my first love, but I couldn't tell her that. If I said that, she'd want to know the intimate details, and I didn't talk about that love with anyone, especially not her. "Yes." I delivered the lie with a wistful smile.

"And how close were you with your father?"

"Excuse me?" I tried not to recoil, not to show too much, but it felt like her pen was pulling open my stomach and examining the contents.

"When we look at a woman's adult relationships, they can sometimes be influenced by the most powerful male figure in her life, which is typically her father."

"My father died shortly after I met Grant."

"Did you have a good relationship with him?"

I thought of George, and this time, the smile that pulled at my lips was genuine. "Yes. He was wonderful. We were very close." I flicked my gaze back to her, and my anger flared. "No daddy issues, if that's what you're asking about."

Definitely not. I didn't have daddy issues; I had a fucking daddy tsunami that was six layers deep and capable of decimation.

"Would you like some tea?" She placed her notebook on the small gold table beside her and stood. "I'm going to pour myself a cup."

"No." I glanced at my watch, irritated to see that there were still eighteen minutes left in our session. Maybe this would be our last. The point had been to establish a key witness for the defense, and Dr. Maddox was getting a little shaky on that front.

"I'll be right back." She walked toward the office door and I saw she was wearing glittery white Birkenstock sandals, each toe painted a different color. Ridiculous.

I spoke just before she reached it. "Actually . . . I would love a cup of tea. With whatever diet sweetener you have. Preferably Splenda."

She nodded and closed the door behind her, and I immediately stood, taking three short steps over to her chair, resting my weight on the arm of it as I looked at her notepad.

There were only three words on the pad. Three words, neatly written in her clean block writing, with dozens of question marks framing the question.

I stared at the words for a long moment, then returned to my seat, the phrase burning into my mind.

Is she lying?

CHAPTER 56

LEEWOOD FOLCRUM

Inmate 82145

Fun fact: Leewood Folcrum's canteen account had over $74,000 in it. Prisoners can only spend a hundred dollars a week, and he barely did that, so his spending couldn't keep up with the donations that came in. He was real popular with the ladies, and they showed their affection in a few different ways, one of them being money.

—*William Smith, Lancaster Prison corrections officer*

If I was right and Tim was the blonde's brother, it meant that any day, he'd be getting my letter with my faux confession.

Either he hadn't gotten the letter yet or he wasn't the brother, because he was on the other side of the glass, still waxing on with these stupid questions and wanting to know what had really happened.

"Given your condition," Tim said slowly, his pen spinning between his thin fingers, "it just seems that you'd want someone to know. Before you pass and take it with you."

Given your condition . . . Again, if he wasn't my secret pen pal, I still needed to figure out how much he knew about me and how he knew what he knew. As shitty as I looked and felt, it was still a stretch for him to have assumed with such confidence that I was dying.

"Someone to know what?" I spit out. Today was a bad day. My entire body was weak; just moving my hand to my mouth felt like I was dragging shackles. The fries he'd brought were cold, and I was beginning to lose my taste for anything.

"What happened that night. You've got to be itching to tell someone the truth of why you did it."

"Sometimes people just do things, Timmy."

"Only if there's a psychological break. Is that what you had? Did your mind crack open one day, Leewood?"

To that, I kept my mouth shut. This guy was like a boxer. Circling and circling, looking for an opening so he could land a punch. Normally, I'd be getting up and leaving. But frankly, I didn't have the energy to move.

"Leewood?"

I yawned.

"I don't think you had a psychological break. You didn't just snap one day and decide to take out a trio of preteens." He shook his head. If anyone here was losing it, it was him.

"Sounds like you got it all figured out." I picked up the burger with both hands and brought it to my mouth but caught a whiff of the scent and stopped, suddenly turned off by the smell of the chargrilled patty.

"Which means you had a motivation. Hedonistic, financial, jealousy, anger—what was it, Lee? Huh?" He leaned forward, and the glass fogged from the hot blow of his breath.

"I think I know why you did it." He said it with such confidence that I cracked one eye open. He was smiling, but it was a grim smile, like he was pleased and upset all at the same time. It reminded me of the Would You Rather quiz we gave the new inmates. *Would you rather sit on a cake and eat a dick? Or sit on a dick and eat a cake?* It was good 'cause there was cake involved—not that any of us was getting to eat cake anytime soon—but it was also bad because there were dicks involved, and in this place, the chance of getting a dick was uncomfortably high. The question made the newbies hella uncomfortable, as if their answer would decide their fate. Sometimes it did.

That was one thing I'd never sunk to, not even twenty-plus years in. A shrink might say it was because I liked little girls, but the truth was, I lost all sexual inclinations after what happened that night. You hold a little body in your arms, one growing limp and still, and you stop looking at that thing as a sexual object. You pull a knife across virginal skin and have blood spray like a hose across your living room—you start to see that shit when you close your eyes. All you see is blood, and maybe that would be different if they hadn't locked me up in here, but they did, so that's the image I've had stuck in my head when I think about anyone under the age of puberty. Bloody dead girls, one still flopping in my hands like a fish. The way she had stared up at me—her mouth gaping open, hurt filling those eyes—I still saw it when I lay down at night.

"I think you did it because of Jenny," he said hoarsely.

"Whatcha mean, 'because of Jenny'?" I couldn't help it. I was a horse led to water. Damned if I wouldn't drink.

"I think you killed her because you were scared of her."

"I didn't kill her," I said, for the tenth time, as if I had known what would happen.

As if I'd known she would survive.

CHAPTER 57

PERLA

Once Sophie headed to bed, I got her phone out of the lockbox and texted Paige. The text was short and sweet.

> My mom doesn't want you to work tomorrow. Enjoy the day off! ☺

I sent it, then waited to see how Paige would respond. I had spoken to Paige before she left and discussed a long list of items for us to take care of, so this should raise a red flag in her mind.

My cell phone rang, and I placed Sophie's down on the kitchen counter and answered it.

"Hi, Mrs. Wultz. This is Paige."

"Oh, hi, Paige," I said, and walked over to the sink, turning on the water.

"I just got a text from Sophie, but I wanted to make sure . . . She said you don't need me to work tomorrow?"

I paused. "She said what?"

"She just texted me and said that *you* said to tell me I had the day off."

I turned off the water and waited for a beat. "Ummm, no. No. I definitely need you here tomorrow. I'll talk to Sophie. She must be confused."

"Yeah, I thought it was strange. So, uh, I'll see you tomorrow? At eight thirty, right?"

"Yes, exactly. The car is still working well for you?"

"Oh yeah. I told you, mine is fixed, so you don't have to—"

"No, keep driving ours for now. I have surgery this week, so I'll need you more for the next week or so."

"Okay . . . if you're sure."

"I am." I smiled. "Have a good night, Paige. Thanks for calling."

She said her goodbyes, and I hung up, then deleted the text from Sophie's phone. I scrolled through her day's activity, checking her social media accounts, texts, and browser history. It was all clean, and I smiled to myself as I returned her phone to the box and locked it.

It was fun, setting all this up. Too bad it was going to end soon. That ending would be sad, but also the start of a new game, one with higher stakes, more deception, more rewards.

I would win at both.

CHAPTER 58

Grant and I rode in silence to the surgery center. I closed my eyes, willing the Ambien I had taken that morning to hit.

"Kellan's a good doctor," Grant said, his voice tight. "Everything will be fine. He has a good team. A good anesthesiologist."

I looked over, surprised at the tenor of his tone. His fingers were wrapped around the wheel, the tendons in the backs of his hands visible from the strain. "What are you, worried?"

"Of course I am. You're going under. Things happen." He swallowed. "It will be fine," he repeated. "I'm sure it will be."

"If something did happen to me, you'd be okay," I pointed out. "Just add more hours to Madeline and keep Paige on. No biggie."

He glanced at me. "I can't tell if you're joking."

"Well, you would have to get a manager for the complexes," I allowed. "But to be honest, nothing I do with them is that difficult. Anyone with basic organization skills and intelligence could do it."

"I'm not thinking about the apartments," he snapped. "I'm thinking about the emotional impact. The loss of you as a person."

"Oh." That's right. People were supposed to mourn. I needed to add that to my list. "How do you think you would handle it if I died? What do you think your reaction would be?"

"I would be destroyed." He reached over and grabbed my hand. "I know what I was like with Lucy, and it . . . I stopped knowing how to live for a period of time. I was just blinded by hate and rage and the deep, deep sadness. It was like falling down a well of hell, one where no one could reach you, no one could hear you screaming, no one understood. That's what I would go through if you passed. What Sophie would go through."

"Oh." I studied his face and mentally repeated the words, trying to cement them in my mind. They were great. I couldn't use them verbatim—that would raise his suspicions—but what a great visual to think of when I spoke to the media fresh after the event. Maybe I should have a mental episode. Freak out enough to be sedated. That would play well for the cameras and the story. *Like falling into a deep well of hell.*

"I can't believe your focus was on the implementation details of our lives." He squeezed my hand as his attention returned to the road.

"Well, I guess that's because that's what I've been thinking about the last two weeks," I said lightly. "Getting everything handled for this week when I'm out of commission."

"Kellan is a good doctor," he repeated, as if convincing himself of the fact. "You'll do fine."

Impulsively, I undid my seat belt and leaned over, kissing him on the cheek. "I will, don't worry. I'm a hard girl to kill."

I settled back in my seat, glowing from the concern he'd shown. Of course, he'd ruined it with that mention of Lucy. The bitch had been dead more than twenty years, and I was still competing with her, but that was okay. I'd had him in ways she never did. There was no way his love for me wasn't greater. If her death had pushed him down a well, mine would open up a crater.

Maybe Sophie's death will break him. That would be an interesting turn of the coin. I had no interest in nursing him through a mourning period and pulling him out of some well of Sophie-triggered sorrow. That wouldn't sit right with me. I didn't need her to be a martyr in our relationship, and right now, seeing him get this worked up over a simple plastic surgery . . . I could see it happening. Him moping about.

Breaking into tears. Babbling about Sophie to anyone who would listen. Taking my time, my limelight.

Which was why he needed to be clearly identified as the villain. The public could debate over whether he was the original Folcrum killer or just working with him . . . but he needed to have his shiny father-of-the-year crown gone from his head before the press descended and decided whom to shower with love and whom to shit on. I didn't need his grief to be constantly compared to my own. What if mine was found lacking? Wooden?

As he made the turn into the surgery center, any internal debate over his role ceased.

Grant had to take the fall. Otherwise, he'd ruin this for me.

CHAPTER 59

"Good morning, sleepyhead." Grant's voice was muted, like it was buried under piles of blankets.

"Mommmmm," Sophie sang out. "Time to wake up!"

"Give her a minute."

"Can I have some money for the snack machine? They have Starbursts. It's *right* there, in the hall."

"Sweetie, she's about to wake up. Just wait. You can have candy later."

Sophie didn't need candy. I tried to open my eyelids, but they were too heavy. I tried to speak, but my mouth was so dry. I swallowed and licked my lips. "Water," I croaked.

"Honey? Honey, we're right here." There was pressure on my arm; then someone was shaking me. Why in the hell were they shaking me?

I coughed, and then my eyes worked. I squinted, trying to bring things into focus. "Water," I repeated.

"Sophie, go get the nurse and tell her Perla wants some water." He loomed above me and was grinning like an idiot. "Hey, sweetie. Kellan says you did great."

I did great. Like I had done anything more than lie there and drool. I tried to smile, but my entire face hurt. I closed my eyes and let out a sob. Why the fuck did this hurt so bad? It felt like someone had smashed me in the nose with a hammer.

"It hurts so bad," I whispered, and tears leaked out of my eyes as the red-hot pain intensified. "Why does it hurt so bad?" I started to wail as a nurse appeared, a white cone in hand.

"Here you go," she said cheerfully, her hand firm on my back as she pushed me upright and pressed the paper rim to my lips.

I guzzled it. "More."

She lowered me back down. "We'll give you some more in a little bit, but we don't want to upset your stomach. That's enough for now."

That's enough for now. What was I, ten? Rage flooded through me, and I opened my mouth to tell her off, but the action caused another stab of pain, and I cried out, then started to sob.

Grant gripped my arm, rubbing it reassuringly while he babbled on about how strong and amazing I was, that the pain would be over soon and that I looked so beautiful.

He was a good husband, despite all his faults. I turned my head, looking at him through the tears, and felt a wave of affection and remorse. "I'm sorry," I said.

He kissed my forehead as carefully as he could. "You have nothing to be sorry for, my love."

I wanted to laugh at that, but the scrunching of my face triggered another slice of pain.

CHAPTER 60

LEEWOOD FOLCRUM

INMATE 82145

Leewood and I are in love. I've already booked the prison chapel for next spring. That will be the first time we see each other in person, and I'm going to wear an all-beaded dress with this long princess train. All my siblings are coming into Lancaster for the wedding. Well, except for my older brother, who says I'm crazy.

—*Tiffany Rose, veterinarian tech*

I knew Tim had gotten the letter when he showed up on a Saturday. He didn't have any food with him this time, and he was standing on his side of the glass, in a green sweater and corduroy pants. He was half-bent over the table, my letter there, his hands tented on either side of it.

I took my time sitting down. I'd had a week to prepare for this beating, so I was ready for whatever bullshit he had to bring. "Hello, Grant."

It was a shot in the dark. I could have been wrong about which girl he was related to. I could have been wrong about how he'd gotten his hands on the letter at all. Maybe someone had given it to him. Maybe he was best friends with Grant Wultz. Maybe, maybe, maybe. But I felt the odds were big enough that I could take the stab and see if I was right.

He met my gaze squarely, and his jaw clenched for a moment; then he spoke. "So you know who I am."

"I had a pretty good guess. Wasn't sure."

"And this?" He tapped the middle of the page.

"What about it?"

"It's real?"

"Looks real from here."

He exhaled slowly, and it took me a minute, but then I saw the signs. The wobble of his jaw. The quick blink of his eyes. The raw pinch of his mouth.

He was a man on the edge. A man who was a breath away from crying or exploding or both.

I took a mental pause and reminded myself of why I wrote that letter. To give her family closure. To mend some of the pain and suffering that night—and my actions—caused. This was gonna hurt, but it was the right thing to do. "Yes, Grant. It's real."

"So you're admitting it. You did it."

"Yes."

"Why?"

"It's all there in the letter."

He hung his head, staring at the page, his shoulders sagging from the weight. When he lifted his gaze, his distrust was clear. "I don't get it. I've met with you . . . what? Eight, ten times? And then you send this?"

You lead a thirsty horse to water, and the damn thing still doesn't want to drink. This. This was why people just couldn't be happy.

"So you don't believe me," I said. Shit, I couldn't do anything to make this guy happy.

"I don't know what to believe," he said. "But this . . . it feels too pat."

Whatever the fuck that meant. I put my hands on the table and hoisted myself to my feet. "Well, it is what it is, Grant. You think you wasted a bunch of visits, and I feel the same. You could have just told me who you were. It wouldn't have made a difference. Instead, you invent this whole . . ." I gestured up and down, encompassing him. "It was wrong," I said flatly.

And then I left. As Redd locked the door behind me, I glanced back through the window, and he was there, still hunched over the table, and he didn't look at peace.

He looked pissed.

From: tfk@hotmail.com
To: grant@dynamictech.com

Date: July 29, at 7:17 AM

Subject: Call me

Call me. We have less than 3 weeks to go and we have to coordinate on details. Is the nanny in or out?

———

From: grant@dynamictech.com
To: tfk@hotmail.com

Date: July 29, at 7:28 AM

Subject: Re: Call me

I'm working on the nanny. P hasn't caught on to anything. We're good, don't worry. I got this. I'll call you when I get to a good phone. Don't email me here.

CHAPTER 61

PERLA

I sat in Grant's recliner, in the living room, and watched Paige run through French flash cards with Sophie. There were so many possibilities there . . . I just needed to figure out how deep to pull Paige in. I only had two weeks left, and an affair was what I really needed. Some hot and passionate tryst between the two of them. Something that would lend credence and authentic evidence to the emails, which I had sent to and from Grant's phone when he was sleeping.

Paige laughed and I studied her figure as she sat at our table, her legs crossed at the ankle, her breasts pressed against the edge of the table. About the same dimensions as me, though she was certainly more toned in all the places that I was getting saggy. She was plain, that was the issue. Too plain to legitimately catch Grant's eyes, but I could help out her cause a little.

"Paige," I called out, "come upstairs with me for a moment. Sophie, you can take a break."

Sophie let out a whoop of approval and rose. "I'm going to go call Bridget."

"Sure." Gingerly, I lowered the footrest of the recliner and stood, grabbing my cup of ice water from beside the chair.

"You need any help?" Paige asked from her place at the table, where she was stacking the flash cards and wrapping rubber bands around each section.

"No, I've got it. But grab two or three of those shopping bags from the pantry."

"Sure." She trotted down the hall to the pantry as I walked over to the stairs and began to take them up. She caught up to me as I reached the second-floor landing. Falling into step beside me, she didn't ask any questions. That was one thing that was good about Paige. She kept her mouth shut and waited for details. Everyone else seemed obsessed with yanking things out of you before you had a chance to sort them in your own head.

I led her into our bedroom, and if it was her first time in the space, she didn't let on to it. No comment on the eighteen-foot ceilings, the discreetly lit art, the dark-plum walls with paneling details, the fluffy white bed, or the massive stone fireplace. I walked over to one of the sets of double doors that framed the fireplace and opened them, entering my walk-in closet.

"Wow." She halted in the doorway and stared, bug-eyed, at the expanse of shelves and racks. It was a common reaction, and I never knew if it was because it was so meticulously organized or if it was just the sheer amount of clothing, shoes, and bags. "Everything is so . . . gray."

I laughed, then stopped at the pain the reaction caused. Carefully touching the cast on my nose, I nodded. "Yes. Well. Not just grays— neutrals. There are creams also."

She walked slowly down the row of compartments, each organized by garment type. She kept her hands tightly crossed over her stomach, as if she were worried about breaking something. "It's very organized," she said finally.

"Well, Madeline helps me with that. I need to do a bit of weeding out and thought that I could give you some of the clothes, if you'd like them."

She blinked. "Me?"

"I think we're close to the same size." I walked briskly down the left-side aisle. "Now, you're not going to be interested in my suits, but . . ." I stopped beside my shorts and thumbed through the hangers, selecting four that were on the shorter side. They were all white or khaki, and felt like butter. I placed the stack on the marble island that ran down the length of the closet. Returning to the racks, I selected a half dozen blouses, focusing on the only lower-cut ones I had, then grabbed her a cashmere cardigan and sweater, adding them to the pile.

"I can't take these things," Paige said helplessly. She reached out and touched one of the sweaters, which still had tags. Flipping one over, she inhaled at the price. "I—these are too nice."

"You deserve to have some nice things." I walked over to the dresses and combed through the hangers, selecting a black eyelet sundress and a tan sheath dress that would look stunning on her. I had never worn either, preferring items that didn't show my neck. "If there's something you want in life, you need to put yourself in a position to take it, Paige. Remember that. Write it down. It applies to everything. Nice things. Jobs. Opportunities. Relationships." I opened the cabinet that housed my shoe shelves. "What size shoe are you?"

"Nine and a half."

"Damn. Okay. I'll get you some shoes."

"Oh, I have shoes," she said quickly. "Really, it's okay."

I closed the cabinet and turned to face her. "I'm not giving you these clothes because I'm being generous. I'm giving you these clothes because I want you to wear them when you work for me. I want you to look like you belong in this house and with our daughter. I want you to be a good representation of our house, of our family."

She flushed. She would need to lose her meekness if she was ever going to succeed in life. That was one thing I'd never been. At birth, I'd come out swinging. "Okay."

"I want you to try on all of these things and tell me what doesn't fit. I'll get you some shoes this afternoon. Tomorrow, I want you to wear one of these outfits and go to Marci's on Promenade and get a haircut. Do it during your work shift, and I'll handle the bill with Marci. Come here afterward."

"Okay." She nodded, and I could see the excitement in her face, even though she was trying to hide it. She wanted this. She wanted all this, and I was going to give it to her, even if it was just for a few weeks.

"I'll let you know the time of your appointment. You try these things on, and I'll give them a call now." I patted the pile and headed for the door. "I'll be in the bedroom if you need me."

"Okay," she called out after me.

I went to the balcony, opening both sliders and letting the cool California breeze into the room. Sitting on one of the soft outdoor chairs, I placed a call to Marci first, who assured me that they could fit Paige in and gave me a nine-o'clock slot. Then I called my personal shopper at Neiman Marcus and ordered a variety of shoes, size nine and a half, and requested they deliver them this afternoon to the house. I gave my credit card number to both, then dropped my phone in my lap and relaxed against the cushion, satisfied with my work.

Grant loved my style. He said it was one of the things that drew him to me—how I always looked perfectly put together, no matter the occasion. It was an easy task when you had money. Expensive clothes hung well, and my monochromatic-color scheme guaranteed that everything matched. Add in a regimen of hair treatments, facials, Botox, and workouts, and the facade was maintained. It was all easy when you had money and time. I had both, and for a short period, so would Paige.

Would it be enough to catch Grant's attention?

Probably not. But I didn't need their affair to be real. I just needed to plant the idea in a few heads, including hers.

CHAPTER 62

We were all at lunch with Perla one afternoon when she got up from the table and stepped aside to call her husband. She thought she was out of earshot, but we could all hear her fighting with him. It was all about the nanny. I couldn't tell exactly what it was about, but I heard the words "hotel room" and "text messages." We all stopped talking to listen, and it was clear what was up. But honestly, it's her own fault. We warned her about hiring someone young and pretty. I mean, seriously. What was she thinking?

—Chun Andrews, wife

"Paige looks nice, doesn't she?" I passed a bowl of brussels sprouts to Grant, who scooped out a heaping amount and grunted in response. He'd been distracted and moody for the last few days, an evolution I wasn't crazy about.

"Grant." I set down my fork and waited until he looked up from his plate. "Did you notice Paige today?"

He looked around. "No. Is she here?"

I was torn between applauding him for his disinterest in other women and smacking him for the same reason. "Yes, she's upstairs, putting Sophie's uniform in the wash. I sent her to my salon for a makeover and gave her some clothes. You should say something to her, give her a compliment."

He finished chewing, and then spoke. "You mean right now?"

I bit the inside of my cheek so hard that I tasted blood. "No, just the next time you're alone with her. I don't want her to think you're saying it for my benefit."

"Okay." He speared another brussels sprout and chewed noisily.

"She's a beautiful girl," I pointed out. "She just needed a little work, that's all."

"Speaking of beautiful, you know that you didn't need that surgery." He put his fork down and cupped one hand in the other, his elbows on the table. "I loved your nose."

"Well, you'll love this one too," I said tartly. "Once the swelling goes down." It was too early to tell how good my new nose would look, given how puffy I was, but even with my face looking like a marshmallow, I was still prettier than before, and now without that shit stain on my cheek.

"It looks good already," he said. "I just hope you didn't do it for me."

Oh no, Grant. You were the last person I was thinking of when I made that decision. I toyed with the garlic chicken tenderloin on my plate. "No, it's been something I wanted to do for a long time."

"Did Kellan see your . . ." He glanced at Sophie, but she was zoned out, her focus on twirling her angel hair pasta around her fork. He mouthed the word *scar*.

"Yes. He asked about it. I told him I don't like to talk about it and that I didn't want it fixed."

He nodded, and I tried to gauge the look on his face. Grant had never understood my attachment to my scar. Early on, he had suggested I get it fixed. I had staunchly refused, and he hadn't brought it up again.

I knew he hated it. Looking at it reminded him of death and what had happened to his sister. But . . . I think it also reminded him of my mortality. Of the fact that he could have lost me also, and he didn't. I think every time he saw my scar, it endeared him further to me. It was a theory, but another reason why I held such affection for the mark.

Paige appeared in the doorway. "Her uniform is in the wash. Would you like me to wait until it's done, or should I head out?"

"I'll swap the laundry," I said. "You can head on home."

"Okay, thanks." She patted Sophie on the shoulder as she passed. "Bye, Sophie."

"Au revoir," Sophie said without looking up.

"Oh!" I twisted around to see if Paige was still in the kitchen. She was, crouched down and getting her purse out of the cabinet. She was wearing a pair of cream linen pants and the new ballet flats I had bought for her, paired with a simple white silk shirt. She looked good, especially with her new haircut, which was much shorter and wavy. "Paige, I'm blocking you in. Grant, can you move my car?"

"Of course." He leaned forward and rose, holding his tie against his shirt to keep it from falling into the food. Wiping his mouth with a linen napkin, he placed it on the table beside his plate.

I mouthed *Compliment her* to him, and he rolled his eyes but nodded.

I watched as they walked out together, him keeping an appropriate space between them as he held the door and waited for her to pass through. Such a polite man. Such a gentleman. So handsome. All traits I would be competing with once the party occurred.

I turned back to my plate and focused on my chicken breast, sawing back and forth on the delicate meat with the sharp blade.

CHAPTER 63

LEEWOOD FOLCRUM

Inmate 82145

A reporter asked me how come I didn't find it odd that Leewood's visitor was one of his victims' family members, but as a CO, I don't even know those people's names. We pick them up at check-in, walk them to Visitation, and make sure they don't try to cause trouble in the process. And he never caused us trouble. He seemed like a real nice guy.

—*Thomas Redd, Lancaster Prison corrections officer*

I was curled up in my bed like a baby, hugging one of the thin pillows and trying to breathe without coughing, when Redd rapped on my bars. I lifted my head enough to see who it was, then slowly sat up.

"Hey, Folcrum, you got a package. Thought you'd want this one."

I moved to my feet at the sight of the chocolate milkshake in his hand. "Where'd that come from?"

"Your regular. He didn't come in, just dropped this off for you, along with this." He held up an envelope.

"No shit." I took the milkshake from him and sniffed it. "Think it's poisoned?" I coughed into my hand, and a bit of blood came up. I wiped it on my pant leg.

"Hey, your risk. You know the rules." He set the envelope on the table. "Need any more pain meds?"

I waved him off. "Thanks for bringing this in."

"You got it." He met my gaze. "You aren't dying on my shift, are you?"

"Not on this one," I grunted.

"Good, 'cause the paperwork's going to be a bitch." He smiled, then rapped his fingers on the desk and left.

I made it to my seat, where I took a deep pull of the milkshake, which was half-melted but still delicious.

I opened the envelope and pulled out a sheet of paper, with the handwriting I now knew well.

Hi, Leewood,

I'm not sure if I'll come back to speak to you. In case I don't, I wanted to say thank you before you passed. I appreciate your time and what you shared. I am still processing it.

I'm sorry for deceiving you about my true identity. I didn't think you would speak to me or tell me the truth if you knew that I was Lucy's brother.

There is an old Latin saying, "mortui vivos docent," which means "the dead teach the living."

Lucy's death shaped my life in so many terrible ways, but now I can stop searching for answers and learn to live with the knowledge that sometimes things don't happen for a reason and some madness is

unexplainable. I am still learning from my sister, and
I will learn from you for long after you die.
Sincerely,
Grant Wultz

Well, shit. I drummed my fingers on the page and thought of the
one favor I should have asked of him before our relationship—whatever
kind it was—ended. Given the tone of this letter, maybe he would have
granted it.

CHAPTER 64

PERLA

When the police showed up, wanting to get into Grant's email account, I was like whoa, because I mean, come on. The guy is like . . . who's the guy on the show who put his shoes on and opened the door . . . Mr. Rogers? I think that was it. Anyway, he's like a grade-A nerd. Definitely wouldn't have had anything to do with anything like this. But we went and looked at the deleted emails first, and that's where we found the bad ones.

—Douglas Foster, internal IT, Dynamic Tech

"Oh my God, nothing on my phone is working." I groaned and settled back on the couch, then turned my head and looked at Grant. He was at the dining table, his laptop open in front of him, his fingers busy on the keys. "Grant, can you text Paige for me?"

"I don't know her number," he said absentmindedly, his typing continuing at a rapid-fire pace.

"Well, I'll give it to you," I snapped. "Or just toss me your phone and I'll send it."

He closed his hand over the device, then turned to me, gauging the distance, rearing back his arm to throw, then thought better of it. He stood, walked it over, and passed it to me. Leaning forward, he kissed me on the forehead, then studied my nose. "It looks really good. The swelling is down. Do you need a pack of ice?"

"No, that was only for the first couple of days." I carefully touched the area. "You think it looks good?"

He was already heading back to his seat. "It looks great."

I unlocked his phone and scrolled to his contacts, added Paige as "Paige Nanny," and then composed a text.

Hey Paige, this is Grant. Perla said you're going to the store in the morning . . . can you grab some mouthwash while you're there?

Oh, also, please pick up a dozen of the mini cupcakes that are in the deli? I like the vanilla ones with little rainbow sprinkles on the top. If they don't have them at our store, please check one of the others.

I sent the two texts and then waited. It was almost nine, but Paige would certainly be up.

Sure, no problem! ☺

I typed back.

Great, thanks.

You're the best. xoxo

As it delivered, I wondered how she was feeling about the *xoxo*. Flustered? Excited? Creeped out?

Maybe she hadn't even noticed.

But then . . . a heart popped up in the upper right-hand corner of "his" text.

She had "loved" the message.

Definitely not appropriate behavior, and something that would give the technical forensics team something to stew over during their investigation.

I smiled and deleted the final text about the cupcakes and the *xoxo* line so Grant wouldn't see them, then did my customary checks of his call log, emails, and messages before I pushed myself off the couch and returned his phone.

"Oh, I could have gotten that." He peered over his reading glasses at me. "You said your phone isn't working?"

"It's being glitchy. I just did a hard reset to see if that fixes it." I waved my hand in the air, dismissing it. "I'm going to work out, then get in the sauna."

"Okay," he said, the tapping of keys resuming. This was going to be one of those nights when he worked until three or four in the morning.

I'd hide the cupcakes once they arrived. One more item from the original murder, checked off the list and ready for the upcoming event.

CHAPTER 65

While Grant worked a rare Saturday in the office, I took a photo of my future Wultz Party murder victims.

Sophie's two birthday guests posed with her by the soccer goal, their arms around each other, sunny smiles turned to the camera. Mandolin stuck out her tongue for one shot, and the other two giggled, then followed suit. I hid my frown behind the big Nikon camera. Sophie should be the one leading the group. I had never understood why she wasn't more of a social alpha, but maybe that was the issue with a dominant parent. We stifle the child. I read a book on the topic and was uncomfortable with how many parallels there were between me and the stereotypical "dominant parent." For a week, I made a sincere attempt to modify my behavior, but was driven absolutely crazy by the stupid decisions Grant and Sophie made when they were unsupervised and undirected.

I decided that, for the good of the family, some dominant behavior was warranted, and the consequences? Oh well.

I got at least five good shots of the girls and smiled at the knowledge that one of these photos would be iconic. Taken just a week before the murder and an isolated shot of the three of them, happy and healthy, unaware of what was to come.

I would also take photos that night. Not of the crime, of course—the police would do that. But of the party. "Before" photos that would show a stark contrast to the horror of the night.

"That's enough," Mandolin called out, turning away from me. That bitch would get the worst of it. I'd do her last and take my time. I savored the idea of her looking in my face and realizing I was the one who would take her life. Me, the one she so flippantly dismissed and ignored.

"Mrs. Wultz?" Bridget stopped in front of me, her hands clasped at her chest as if she were about to beg for something.

"Yes?" I asked, flipping through the camera photos to double-check that Sophie was in the middle. She was, and I looked back at Bridget.

"My mom wanted to know if you can drop me off at my piano lesson the morning after the party. It's in the neighborhood, on Panlo Street. If not, my nanny can do it."

"Sure." I nodded. "No problem."

"It's at eleven thirty. Do you think we'll be done with everything by then?" She glanced worriedly over her shoulder, making sure the team hadn't reconvened yet. As bossy as Mandolin was, Bridget was anxious. She'd probably stop me midstabbing and ask if the knife had been sterilized.

"Oh yeah. You won't miss anything." I put the camera strap over my shoulder. Today was my first day premiering my new nose for the neighborhood, and I touched it briefly, just to make sure it was intact. No one had noticed it yet, and I didn't know whether to celebrate that fact or be pissed.

"And I have to take my medication one hour before bed," she informed me earnestly. "I'll have a sheet with directions, but it has to be refrigerated, so I wanted to make sure you have enough room in your fridge for it."

"Of course." I gave her a reassuring smile. "I'll make sure you get your medicine." I'd have to check her medication's compatibility with the Ambien I'd be spiking all their milkshakes with. I didn't need Bridget frothing at the mouth and ruining the whole aesthetic of the scene.

I'd already tested the sleeping medication a few times with Sophie. The first time, I'd used a single pill. She'd grown groggy and fallen asleep within fifteen minutes of consuming it, but when I had clapped my hands and said her name loudly, she'd woken up. The second time, I had used two, and she was dead to the world. I'd carried her up the stairs to her room, and she barely responded.

I needed them to be pliable when I went up there. I would pose them into position, then start with the knife. First Sophie, to get her over with. Then the other two. Bridget quickly, then Mandolin.

It wouldn't take long. Ten, fifteen minutes, tops. I had a plastic poncho that I would wear, one with drawstrings that closed it tight around my face, and I had booties that would slip over my shoes. That would keep the blood spray off me. I'd hide the poncho and booties, then crawl back into bed with Grant and go to sleep.

And then, in the morning, the fun of discovery and deception would begin.

CHAPTER 66

LEEWOOD FOLCRUM

Inmate 82145

I don't know what happened in Visitation that day, but both Leewood and his visitor . . . they both came out of those rooms different people than when they walked in.

—*Thomas Redd, Lancaster Prison corrections officer*

I wasn't expecting another visit from Grant, so when it came, I forced my ass to roll over and get to my feet. Who knew why he was here, but I had something I needed from him, so I didn't waste time or breath, given that I was short on both.

"I need you do something for me." I spit the words out before Redd had exited the room and before Grant had a chance to say anything. "It's important."

"What is it?" He looked wary. He was about to look confused, but I didn't have time for any questions. Today was a bad day, and I needed to get back to my bed so I could lie down and try not to die.

"There are certain people I'm not allowed to contact, but I need you to get a message to someone on the outside for me."

He hunched forward, his forearms digging into the table, one hand cupped over the other. "Who?"

"My daughter. She's changed her name—I don't know what it is, and there's a protective order in place, so what I'm asking you for, it's not technically allowed, but . . ." I lifted my shoulders in a shrug. "I don't got much time left."

He slowly sat back, thinking. "You don't know her name?"

"No. She was a minor when her name was changed, so maybe it's hard to find, or maybe it's easy. Maybe she wrote a damn book about what happened." I dragged a hand down the front of my face. "I don't know. But I'd appreciate it if you tried."

"What kind of message do you want me to give her?"

"You'll do it?" It was bullshit, the way my voice cracked on the question, but all I had keeping my blood moving in my veins right now was desperation.

"Depends on the message."

"I'd like her to visit me so I can see her one time before I die. I wanna find out if she has any children. If she had a good life. If she's strung out on drugs or is happy. I want to apologize to her." I sat up straighter. "I have some letters to give her. I wrote her a letter every year on her birthday, for the last twenty-two years. I'll give her those." There was a clog in my throat, and I coughed hard, trying to get it out. "She probably isn't going to want to come, so it's important that you at least give her a specific message." I tapped the glass, looking for his notebook. "It's complicated; you're going to want to write it down."

He hadn't moved, seemed to barely be breathing, and I waited, needing him to look at me, needing him to see how important this was. "Are you listening?"

"I'm listening." He lifted his gaze to me, but I didn't like what I saw there. It was like a snake of confidence was winding through his face, from his eyes to his mouth. He didn't exactly smile, but I knew the look he was wearing. Leverage. This was his leverage, but the truth of that night—it wasn't something I would barter with.

I plowed on. "This last part is important. But you gotta write it down, exactly as I say it."

"I'll remember it." He lifted his chin, telling me to go on.

Maybe he didn't have a pen. From this angle, I couldn't even see if he had his briefcase. Okay, fine. Maybe he'd remember. He had to. "Tell her that if she doesn't contact me or come here, the bunny will start talking about carrots."

The confidence drained from his face. "'The bunny will start talking about carrots'? That's what you want me to say to her?"

I nodded. "Yes. She'll understand what it means. It's important. Say it exactly like that."

He wiped his hand across his face and over his mouth, looking down at the table and thinking. He was trying to decipher the code, but he would never be able to do that. Not without knowing what it meant.

He lifted his head, and his gaze connected with mine. "So you're holding on to a secret of hers? One you're blackmailing her with?"

"I didn't say that." I frowned, not sure how I'd given that away.

"We're talking about Piketo, right? That's the bunny?"

My heart stopped for a moment in my chest, then began to beat faster.

Piketo, right? That's the bunny?

I know more about you than anyone. He'd said that to me the first time we'd met. I'd dismissed it, but now I tried to think back at who I had mentioned that story to, what article, what letter, where, where, where it might have been documented.

"How do you know that story?" I asked, watching as he dropped his head into his hands. There was no more arrogance on his face, no joy at revealing his hand, and that concerned me more than anything because for once in our dynamic, he knew something I didn't, and fuck that flip in power.

"I know that story," he said slowly, "because my wife told it to my daughter when she was six." He took off his glasses and placed them on the table. "A story that she heard from her father."

A story that she heard from her father.

Piketo was a story I'd made up, the name borrowed from a guy I'd once worked with, the tale created with the purpose of making sure my daughter understood the repercussions that could happen if she ever told people about things that were better kept private.

Things like the videos I used to film of her friends at her sleepovers.

Things like the special showers I would give to those friends.

Things like what those friends would tell her and how she needed to handle that.

No-fucking-one knew about Piketo but Jenny and me. For him to have heard it from his wife . . . that only meant one thing, and I shook my head, unwilling to accept that possibility. "No." The word rasped out of me, and I cleared my throat and tried again. "No. Who's your wife?"

He looked at me for a long moment. "You either know or you don't, Lee."

"You're saying that you're married to Jenny?" A cough was coming, and I huffed out a small breath, trying to keep it at bay.

"She doesn't go by that name anymore, but yes. We've been together since she was twenty-one." He didn't sound happy about it. Wasn't lording it over me. He sounded defeated, and hell—any man who married Jenny would be. Together fourteen-some years. Jesus Christ.

"So she sent you here?" I wet my lips. "That's why you're here? She's testing me?"

His eyes narrowed and he shook his head. "No. She doesn't know I'm here. This . . ." He gestured between us. "This was about me trying to find answers. Closure. For Lucy and for myself." He tilted his head. "What would she be testing you on?"

I didn't answer that, because there was suddenly a much bigger issue at play. "Wait, you mentioned a daughter. Jenny's a mother?" It was a thought that might fill some grandparents with glee. I had the exact opposite reaction.

"Yes." His mouth clenched. "And no, you can never meet her. We've always told her that her grandparents are dead. There will never be—"

"I don't care about that," I snapped. I didn't want to meet my granddaughter. That was the last thing I needed to have introduced to my system at this stage, with death so close. "How is Jenny with her?"

He snorted. "That's your question? You want to know your daughter's parenting style? She's not chopping Piketo in bits and leaving him on our daughter's doorstep, if that's your concern."

Nausea boiled at the thought of the bunny's light-brown carcass, one I'd had to dispose of. "She told you about that?" So maybe he knew the woman he had married after all. "Did she say why she did it?"

"Did what?"

"Killed the rabbit."

A moment of uncertainty flitted across his face. "She didn't kill the rabbit. *You* did."

I snorted. "The fuck I did. Who the hell would gut a pet rabbit? I'd trained that thing to come when I called. Jenny killed it. Left it by my work boots like a dog bringing home a prize."

He digested the information, and the fact that he was accepting it was proof that my daughter hadn't been 100 percent successful in hiding her true colors. Finally, he spoke, his words halting, and I wasn't the only one in the room on an emotional roller coaster ride. "Why would she do that?"

"I asked her that, and she smiled. A creepy fucking smile. She said the only way that Piketo was guaranteed not to talk was to kill him." I let out a hard string of coughs. "She was seven when she said that. *Seven*."

Horror rolled over his face, and I understood it but also my part in it. I was probably what made Jenny the way she was. If not my parenting, then my genes. Something somewhere had broken in the chain to cause an innocent little baby to become whatever Jenny Folcrum grew into.

"Is that the secret you're protecting for her?"

I shook my head. "I asked about my granddaughter—" My chest seized at the word. *Granddaughter.* That was something I'd never expected, certainly never expected to discover now, right before I died.

I inhaled deeply, then continued. "—because you have to be careful with Jenny. Very, very careful. She doesn't do well with female competition." I shook my head at the thought. A seven-year-old Jenny had been disturbing. A nine-year-old, scary. A twelve-year-old, deadly.

I had no idea what an adult Jenny would be like. What she was capable of.

"She's our daughter," Grant said tartly. "Not 'competition.'"

"I didn't view her mother as competition," I said carefully. "Then again, I had a unique relationship with Jenny. An inappropriate one, maybe."

He pinched his eyes shut in frustration, then held up his hands. "What are you saying, Leewood? Stop dancing in circles and just tell me. You're saying that she saw her mother—your wife—as competition? She was, what? Nine?"

I had kept my daughter's secrets for over twenty years, and I couldn't spill them now. Not to him. He'd spent the last two months lying to me. Maybe he wasn't her husband. Maybe he was a guy in a bar whom she'd told a story to once. Maybe I was sitting here, vomiting out information to a con man.

"You're telling me that you're Jenny's husband?" I asked, just to make damn sure.

He flinched, then looked at me as if I were crazy. "Yes," he spat out. "We went through this. Remember?"

"Prove it," I said, my chest aching from just the act of breathing.

"What?"

"You've lied to me for what, two months? Why should I believe you now? Are you even a doctoral student?"

I could see the truth on his face. When had I become stupid enough to fall for shit like that?

"My name is Dr. Timothy Valden. I have a card, if you'd like to see it." He half rose, reaching back to his pants pocket. I waved him off, then let my cuffed wrists rest on the table.

I should have taken his card, if he'd even had one. Researched him. Vetted him. Instead, I'd been more concerned with getting a fucking roast-beef sandwich.

"No, I'm not a doctoral student. I'm a scientist."

"And Jenny's husband?" I asked.

"Yes." He smoothed down the front of his shirt. "Scout's honor."

"Prove it," I repeated.

He sighed. "How do you expect me to do that?"

"You're the smart one here. Think of something."

He glanced at the window that separated us from the COs, thinking. "I have photos in my phone."

A photo of her. If it's real . . . I try not to get too excited, but part of me had given up a long time ago at the thought of ever seeing her again. I nodded and tried to keep my features flat.

He fiddled with a thin silver device, swiping and tapping for long enough that I started getting anxious. "Just show me something," I snapped.

"Here." He held the phone up to the glass.

The door to the room opened, and Redd stepped in. "I need to supervise this. No pornographic material, nothing with kids."

"No," Grant protested. "It's just . . . I'm just showing him pictures of my family."

Redd stepped forward and stood behind me, looking over my shoulder. I leaned forward and studied the screen.

It was a photo from a soccer game. There were kids in the background, but this was a close-up of just Grant and a woman, smiling for the camera. Her lips were closed, her face reserved, her eyes intelligent and sharp. I didn't recognize the shape of her face or the dark lines of her eyebrows, the dark-red paint on her lips . . . but those eyes. I would have known those eyes anywhere. Always watching. Always studying. Always demanding.

It was her. I inhaled, then sat back, trying to process what to do with that information.

Nothing. I should do nothing. I should keep my mouth closed, ask him to deliver the message, and continue to keep her secrets. Why should it matter if he was married to her? Why should it matter if he was also Lucy's brother?

He pressed a button on the side of his phone, then returned it to his pocket. "I told you. It's her."

I stared at him, trying to match the idea that this man . . . this dweeb of a man . . . was now the one responsible for my daughter. For protecting her. Loving her. Giving her everything she needed. He was also the father of my grandchild. The one who would carry on the Folcrum bloodline, however fucked up it was.

"I'm heading back out, but I'll be watching," Redd said.

I waited until he had left and the door clicked shut. "Your daughter, how old is she?" I asked.

"Eleven. About to be twelve."

"So she's about to have her twelfth birthday," I said. "That one of the reasons why you're here?"

"No." He shook his head. "But I have put myself in your shoes. More lately than ever. Trying to understand how you could do it. I know . . ." He tapped his chest. "I know how much I love my daughter. How I would do anything to protect her. And I don't know how—"

"We aren't so different," I interrupted him. "You and I. You would do anything to protect your daughter? You love your daughter? So did I. So *do* I." I needed to stop talking. Right now. Before I saw myself in this man, before I tried to get him to understand. It didn't matter if he knew why I'd done what I did.

"Jenny . . ." I sighed and tried to think of something I could say, some sort of warning I could give. "When Jenny killed that bunny, she didn't feel anything about it. When her mother died, when the girls died at that party . . . She's empty inside. Like she missed the step in the process when that thing inside us, the thing that tells us what's right and what's wrong . . . like she didn't get that piece."

"And you did?"

"Yeah," I said. "I did. I never touched my daughter—or let her touch me—in certain ways. But I wasn't like that with all young girls. And I feel bad about those things. Real bad. Believe me or don't. But whatever you think of me, you got to know that the woman you're sleeping with each night, she's worse. She's worse and she's smart. She's *so* fucking smart," I said hoarsely. "So just . . . remember that. And protect that little girl you got. But don't coddle her too much. Don't give her too much attention, at least not around Jenny. That's just my bit of fatherly advice to you." I stood before I said anything else. "Goodbye, Grant."

He didn't move. He didn't stand. He didn't even say anything, not until Redd was walking in and unlocking me from the floor ring. "Was there anything true in the letter, Lee?" he called out.

I watched as Redd undid the clip, freeing my ankles to move. "Yeah," I said. "The last part. The last girl. That one was me."

"You mean Jenny. You're saying that you did kill—or tried to kill—Jenny. You're admitting to it."

"I am." I nodded at him. "Remember what I said. All of it. But don't tell her that I said it. You're the fucking Piketo now."

CHAPTER 67

GRANT

You spend decades thinking something, moving down one path, and then, in a single conversation, everything flips upside down.

Leewood had been fucking with my head, stirring my emotions around in my brain with a giant wooden spoon, but this last visit had upgraded his spoon to a blender.

I knew my wife. I knew she'd had a fucked-up childhood. How she had escaped with any semblance of sanity after a dozen years in a house with a madman . . . It was a question I had asked myself a hundred times, one that had endeared me to her and raised every protective hackle in my body.

The night I reunited with her, at the Folcrum Party anniversary memorial . . . it had been like seeing a ghost. I was frantic to talk to her, spend time with her, cherish the life that was just brimming out of her. Our history immediately drew a cord of connection between us, and damn—she had been beautiful. The pull to her had made me blind to her faults, immune to any frustrations, and I built a pedestal of love and placed her on the center of it. Treated her like I wished someone had been able to treat Lucy. Gave her the love she'd never received but always deserved.

Now I didn't know what to think.

. . . she missed the step in the process when that thing inside us, the thing that tells us what's right and what's wrong . . . like she didn't get that piece.

The statement scared me because it hit home. I believed it because I had seen it. Perla was missing something, and I had always blamed that void on Leewood.

When Jenny killed that bunny, she didn't feel anything about it. When her mother died, when the girls died at that party . . . She's empty inside.

Could it be true? She killed Piketo? I couldn't imagine a seven-year-old Perla killing a cute, fluffy rabbit. Killing and leaving it on her front porch . . . I pinched my eyes shut and tried to remember how she'd told me the story. Had she said that Leewood killed it? Or had I just jumped to that assumption because it was the only thing that made logical sense?

Don't give her too much attention, at least not around Jenny.

You have to be careful with Jenny. Very, very careful. She doesn't do well with female competition.

The warning had been clear in his voice, but he hadn't seen Perla with Sophie. While she had moments of jealousy with Sophie, it wasn't anything to worry about.

When her mother died, when the girls died at that party . . . She's empty inside.

I had never known the order of the girls' deaths. It was one of the details I had obsessed over and desperately wanted to know from Leewood. There hadn't been many signs of a struggle, but the thought of the other girls just sitting there while Leewood moved from one to the other had always seemed strange. Two girls, okay. Maybe one was shell-shocked long enough for him to create a debilitating wound, then move on to the next. But three girls? I had tried to bring it up to Perla once, and she completely shut me out. I'd dropped the topic and felt like shit, but the questions had remained.

I should have chased Leewood's comment deeper. He made it seem like Perla had been conscious when the others died and that she didn't care.

Why even bring that up? Because she hadn't reacted to their deaths? Or had she participated in them?

My mind recoiled at the thought, which felt sacrilegious. She was my wife. The mother of my child. She hadn't been anything but a victim in that horrible crime.

I climbed the steps to the second floor and shut myself in my office. Using the key on my chain, I unlocked the file cabinet drawer where I kept all the Folcrum files. Pulling the drawer all the way out, I reached underneath the bottom of it and untaped the manila folder from its underside.

I uncoiled the wire that kept it shut, then withdrew the stack of letters I'd received from Leewood over the years. I placed them in the center of my desk, then opened my work briefcase and removed the thin folder that held the notes I'd collected during my time as Dr. Tim Valden.

Leewood was right: me adopting a faux persona may have been unnecessary, but I had enjoyed the opportunity to get up close and personal with Leewood under the cover of anonymity. For the first time, I understood why Perla enjoyed pretending to be someone else. It was fun, creating a character. I felt bolder, like I could say anything without fear of consequences, judgment, or repercussions.

But life had all three of those things. I spread out my notes and started a fresh page, where I drew a simple organizational table to record my data.

I would start with the oldest letter and move to the most recent and record anything he'd said or written that provided any sort of clue to the truth. His final confession letter just didn't sit right with me, especially given all his emotions around Perla.

Tell her that if she doesn't contact me or come here, the bunny will start talking about carrots.

He had a secret he was keeping for her, and I was terrified I might know what it was.

CHAPTER 68

PERLA

At first, Paige loved Sophie. She said she was the sweetest girl and so polite. But then it was like Sophie turned on her. One day, she was bringing in the groceries, and Sophie had put tacks all over the floor in the kitchen. And apparently, Perla was super particular about taking off your shoes before you came in the house, so Paige was in socks and stepped right on one and cut her foot really badly. She swept them up and showed them to Perla, and she swore to discipline her, but Sophie never even apologized to Paige. Just acted like she never did it.

—Claire Vasset, friend of Paige Smith

With two days until Sophie's party, I set aside Wednesday afternoon to make her birthday cake. Grant was at work and Paige was getting groceries, so it was a nice moment alone with my daughter.

While I pulled out the ingredients for the cake, Sophie worked on a sketch in her journal. She was still in her dark-purple silk pajamas, her hair in a thick braid that hung over one shoulder. I moved the items to a long stretch of counter and glanced at my reflection in one of the ovens as I passed.

My new nose looked spectacular. I should have had the surgery years ago. I looked five years younger and so much more refined. Tucking a lock of hair behind my ear, I turned my face, admiring my new side profile.

Hidden by my clothes was a girdle-like band around my stomach. It had a foam insert that was supposed to help smooth out my stomach and remove some of the lumps.

That was okay. I needed to look good in clothes, and right now I did. Tomorrow, I had a photographer coming by to take some headshots and candid shots. I had booked it as a session for Sophie, but I would make sure he got several solo shots of me, things the publicist could use.

I should definitely write a book. I could use a ghostwriter since my recent attempts to write a rough draft had all ended with only a few chapters written. Once the photos came in, the first order of business would be to pick one for the back cover. Something atmospheric and powerful.

"Has my doll arrived yet?" Sophie asked, not looking up from her sketch.

"No, not yet. I tracked it, but it looks like it's still a few days away."

"Okay." She bent back over the pad, and I watched her long enough to see what she was drawing. It was a fairy, one with giant wings and a heart-shaped face. Sophie had been on a fairy kick the last few weeks, and her depictions were getting better with each month that passed.

I didn't ask Sophie what kind of cake she wanted. I was making chocolate because it was what I always made and what she always ate. This was a recipe I'd been cooking since I was eight. It was fitting that the exact same recipe used at the first Folcrum Party would be used at the second.

I brought the spoon to my mouth and licked it.

CHAPTER 69

LEEWOOD FOLCRUM

Inmate 82145

He came back the next day, but I told Redd I didn't want to see him.

He came back again.

And again.

I didn't know what to do, and I had too many thoughts in my head to sort them out.

"Folcrum, he's back." Redd stood in my doorway. "What's the verdict? You talking to him or not?"

I was flat on my back in bed, wondering if today was going to be the day I'd die. I'd been wishing for it for the last three days, but apparently no one upstairs was listening to me.

I turned my head until I could see the officer.

"Seems desperate to talk to you," he said. "If you've got anything to say, you might as well do it. I'm not sure you're going to have another chance, because I got to tell you, you're looking like shit lately."

I smiled, then coughed and had to roll onto my side, where I hacked like an old man for a spell. When it finally let up, I stood, then shuffled forward to the head of the cell. "Okay, let's go," I said.

"You sure?" He glanced left and right, down the blocks.

"I'm sure." I stopped at the door and wearily stuffed my feet into my shower slides, too tired to deal with shoes. "Might as well get it over with."

Grant was pacing when I was led in. Stepping up to the glass, he waited until the door clanged behind Redd to speak.

"I just want to make sure I understand everything you told me last time."

I lifted my hands and then dropped them onto the table, defeated. "I really don't want to talk to you about this. Look, my loyalties are with my daughter. No one else."

"Right, I get that, but I also know my wife has a five-inch scar across her neck where you cut her throat."

I met his gaze, daring him to say something else about it.

He raised his palms, as if I was a skittish animal he was approaching, and hell, maybe I was. I was certainly itching to get out of this room. "Look, you probably have some questions for me, right? So you ask some questions, I ask some questions. Win-win." He pulled out his seat and sat down.

"She know that I'm here?" I asked.

"Yes. I mean, she knows you're in this facility. She doesn't know that I'm meeting or have met with you."

"And you live close to here?"

"Little more than an hour away."

I nodded slowly, processing the fact that she was so close yet hadn't come to see me. "She ever talk about me?"

"No. Our daughter thinks you passed away. She doesn't have any idea of what happened."

Not a surprise. I would have kept the details of me from her as well.

"What happened when I was put in jail? What happened to Jenny then?"

"My turn." He leaned forward. "I've gone through every conversation we've had and every letter you've sent me." He moved a stack of pages in front of him and placed his palm on them. "And I believe that—with the exception of the last letter you sent me—you've been honest with me the entire time. Both 'me' as Tim Valden and also 'me' as the man you've corresponded with for the last two decades."

I shouldn't have cared that he believed me, but it still did something inside me. Broke off a little piece of my heart because no one had believed anything I had said, ever since the police had barged in and found her body in my arms.

"I don't believe that you killed my sister." His face tightened, and I could see the toll it took, saying that. "But if you didn't, and there was no evidence of an intruder, and you've never been able to point a finger at the intruder, then it really only leaves one possible killer. My wife." His mouth trembled, and he pinned his lips together, his eyes growing moist as he looked to the side, trying to contain his emotion.

It wasn't easy, but I kept my trap shut and waited for him to get himself under control. He finally did, then continued on. "I do believe that you loved her in some fucked-up way, so that's the only logical explanation of why you tried to kill her. You walked in on her . . . what? What was she doing?"

I shook my head. "You don't want to go down this path. I'm telling you, you don't."

"I do," he rasped. "I need to know."

"She was your sister, man. You've seen the photos of it. You know what happened." I looked down, trying to block the memories before they pushed into my head. "I was too late when I walked in. There wasn't anything I could do. I tried . . . I felt for a pulse. I tried CPR, but they were gone."

She'd pouted the entire time. When I had bent over them, panicking, putting my mouth to theirs, pushing on their chests, shaking them . . . She had glared at me from the other side of the picnic blanket. "God, you ruin everything," she had said. "Just like before."

I had never wanted to believe that she'd had something to do with her mom's death. Even after she had dropped a few odd comments.

Even after I had caught her skipping and humming just hours after Jessica passed. The thought had been too horrible to even consider. But in that statement . . . looking at my daughter, who was drenched in her friends' blood, her face devoid of any emotion other than irritation . . . I knew she was evil.

"I didn't think about it. I couldn't, or else I might not have been able to do it. I just asked her to come and sit on my lap, which she did right away. I turned her away from me, then . . ." I paused. "Then I picked up the knife. The one she had used. I picked it up and I just drew it across. Real quick. Apparently, not deep enough, but I didn't know. I was too busy breaking down to realize that she was still alive."

And then the doors had flown open, and then the police were there, and then she'd been taken away and I never saw her again.

I lifted my gaze to meet his eyes. He looked nauseous, and I didn't think it was over anything I'd done.

"I have to tell the police," he said faintly. "She killed Lucy . . . Kitty . . . what, your wife?"

"I don't know that for sure," I said flatly. "But you're not going to go to the police. Or rather, if you do, they won't believe you. What I've told you . . . think of it as a favor. From one man to another, a warning. I won't tell it to the police, and even if I did, they wouldn't believe me. No one ever believes the man on death row proclaiming his innocence."

He wasn't an idiot. He understood what I was saying, but it took a minute for him to digest the fact that he wouldn't be getting justice for his sister. He fell silent and stared at the table for a long moment, then shook his head. "Fucking hell."

Yeah, *fucking hell* was about right.

CHAPTER 70

JOURNAL OF SOPHIE WULTZ

I found out about my dad's sister. Someone at soccer sent me the link to a podcast interview where they were talking about a really old murder. Turns out, my dad's sister was one of the victims, which is like the most uncool way that someone can be famous.

I'm really bummed, both for my dad and all that—but also because I'd pretty much been certain that she was like actually famous and would take me in and I'd end up being one of those Hollywood nepotism babies who always acted like she wanted to stand on her own but would be grasping at every leg up my last name could possibly get me.

Anyway, I've listened to a few other episodes, and some of them are really interesting. Like, there's this other one where a girl pretends to disappear but is actually hiding in her parents' attic the whole time and watching to see who really cares about her being gone. The two hosts are funny in this kind of macabre way.

Anyway, I guess it's cool that Rachel and Gabrielle—those are the show hosts—know who my aunt is. It's like them knowing who I am, in a way.

So that's cool, even if it sucks that Lucy's dead.

CHAPTER 71

GRANT

I've worked with alcoholic stage moms that were easier to deal with than Perla Wultz. She was so insistent that everything be perfect and that everything was about her. We did a one-hour birthday shoot for Sophie that turned into a four-hour event.

—*Lance Gretchen, photographer*

I sat at our small dining room table, a plate of food in front of me, and tried not to stare at my wife. She sat on the other side of Sophie and cut into a piece of lamb, her expression serene, her face even more beautiful after the surgery on her nose. I used to gaze at her with reverence, but now I studied every movement in horror, wondering how much I actually knew about the woman I had married.

I thought of the annual memorial we did each December, when we drove over to East Los Angeles and brought roses to Lucy's grave. We would each spend a stretch of time alone with Lucy, talking to her and sharing updates on our life and memories with her. At least, that was what I did. Now a new vision of Perla popped to mind—her standing in front of Lucy's grave, her hands tight in the pockets of her cashmere coat, a thick scarf covering her neck scar, speaking to the dead girl she herself had killed.

My wife placed a piece of the fish in her mouth and chewed, her expression content.

I would bet the large diamond on her hand that she hadn't spent any graveside-visitation time apologizing to Lucy. Not Perla, the woman who went on a two-week letter-writing spree to every upper-level employee of the Los Angeles County Post Office until she got Barry Goldstick, our carrier, fired because he'd leaned our packages against the gate instead of ringing the bell, waiting for us to open the gate, and then bringing them down the drive and to the front porch. When Perla succeeded in getting the man fired, she printed out the email from his manager, tracked down his home address, and hand-delivered it to him, a smile on her face.

No, Perla had not been sharing fond memories and updates with Lucy. Most likely, she had been taunting her. Crowing her victory.

I tried to swallow the piece of potato in my mouth but couldn't. My stomach rolled and I half stood, clutching my stomach as nausea swelled.

"What is it?" Perla asked suspiciously.

"My stomach. I need to . . ." I half crawled, half tripped over the chair. "I'll be right back."

I needed to leave her and take Sophie with me. But how? When?

I made it to the small bathroom off the kitchen and shut the door, isolating myself in the space. Placing my palms on the counter, I breathed in deeply, trying to calm the panic ripping through my gut.

Okay, I'd call an attorney tomorrow. Set a meeting, find out my options. Move heaven and earth to do whatever was needed to protect Sophie—protect us both.

My knees felt weak, and I moved over to the toilet, closing the lid and sitting down. It wouldn't be easy. Perla was smart, and as Leewood had pointed out, no one would believe me if I suddenly accused her of a decades-old murder.

But Sophie's birthday was in two days. Maybe after the party, I should just take her and disappear. Let Perla hunt for us while I figured out a course of action.

That plan sounded insane, and as someone who prided himself on organization and foresight . . . the idea of going on the run, incognito, gave me a fresh round of hives.

I stood, my stomach heaving, and flung open the toilet's lid, then bent forward and retched into the bowl.

From: tfk@hotmail.com
To: info@murderunplugged.com

Date: August 16, at 7:17 AM

Subject: it's a good day for murder

look alive, ladies. it's going to be a good day.

CHAPTER 72

PERLA

Day of the party
9:30 a.m.

I moved quickly through the first floor, mentally checking off to-do list items. My stomach was in a knot of excitement and nerves, and the feeling was both familiar and nostalgic. After tonight, I would likely never kill again. This would be so iconic, so sensational, it wouldn't be wise for me to attract any additional attention for a long time. But also, I wouldn't need to. I'd finally have what I wanted from the start—a distraction-free relationship with my father and the recognition and fame I deserved. The glow from this . . . it would follow Perla Wultz forever. Maybe I'd even change my name back to Jenny Folcrum. I'd wait until things started to die down and then do it as a powerful tribute—a phoenix rising from the ashes, wanting to shed her tragic past and reclaim the life she had been forced to surrender.

Yeah, I liked that. That could definitely spin. Tomorrow, or maybe the following day, I would hire a publicist to brainstorm and coordinate these sorts of things with. You had to be smart with your media positioning and opportunities. An expert would know how to best capitalize on that.

I started up the staircase, taking the steps two at a time. I'd given Paige detailed instructions on how to decorate Sophie's door and room, and I checked my watch now, anxious about her progress.

There were boxes of supplies strewn across the second-floor hall. I pressed my tongue against my teeth and carefully stepped around the items. Up ahead, she was standing on a stool and stretching up to tape a banner above the doors. She was barefoot, in conservative gray capris and a white button-up shirt, the sleeves rolled to her elbows. So far, she had affixed the *H* and the *A*. She had already wrapped the doors in birthday-cake wrapping paper and set out two marble plant stands with balloon bouquets on either side of the doors.

"This looks great," I said, meaning every word.

"Thanks," she said brightly, stepping off the stool and looking at her handiwork. "There's going to be a balloon arch also. Balloons are really big right now."

"Yes, I've seen them." I looked around, spotting the balloon pump and boxes of latex. "Guess that's what all this is for."

"Yeah, I found a video that shows how to build one. I haven't done it before, but it seems pretty easy."

I nodded. "Good work."

I peeked into Sophie's room, but it was the same. I gave it a quick once-over, satisfied that the dolls were still in the closet and that Madeline had cleared some of the clutter off her counters and surfaces. There were fresh flowers on each bedside table and in her bathroom.

"You're decorating her room also, right?" I returned to the hall, ducking around Paige's ladder.

"Yep, but not as much. Like you said, streamers and maybe a balloon arch around the balcony doors. I have to see how many I have left."

I nodded. "If you don't finish in time to pick her up from soccer, come find me. I'll go and get her."

"'Kay, but I should be finished no problem," she said, a white balloon in hand.

With the room in progress, I went into our bedroom, closing the door behind me and locking the bolt. I went into the closet and pulled out a big Neiman Marcus shopping bag. It was a high-quality paper bag, big enough to hold all my items.

I set it on the floor in the closet; then I moved to the section that housed my winter suits and blazers. I slid the hangers to the left side and removed the back panel of the closet. There was a hidden cavity there, one of many I had created during the build. And there, for the last few weeks, I'd been accumulating items for tonight.

A white blanket like the one my father had stretched out for us to have a picnic on.

A deck of playing cards and a Ouija board.

A knife from the kitchen, one I'd picked up after Paige had used it to cut up an apple for Sophie. I'd sharpened it, then placed it in a Ziploc bag to keep her fingerprints intact.

A pair of gloves to keep my own prints from contaminating the scene.

The plastic poncho.

I placed everything in the bag, then replaced the cavity door and put the bag behind the suits. Pulling the hangers back into place, I arranged the clothing to make sure it was hidden.

Satisfied, I put on a smile and went downstairs. Less than three hours to go before the girls arrived.

CHAPTER 73

GRANT

The girls drifted on the surface of the pool, each on her own float, their bodies silhouetted by the brilliantly lit water. In front of them, the new version of *Mean Girls* played on the big screen I had stretched across one end of the pool. I'd connected the projector to our exterior surround sound system and couldn't help but flinch when one of the characters' voices would come from the rock speaker behind me.

My fear of Perla was increasing by the hour. I could only stall out here for so long before I would have to go back inside, where she was waiting with a hot drink. *Clingy* was not a word I would have ever used to describe Perla, yet that's suddenly how she was acting. Maybe *suffocating* would be a better adjective.

I was paranoid—I realized that—but I was also suddenly seeing things I'd been oblivious to before. The pause before she smiled, like she was processing what reaction to deliver. The manipulation of the girls, of every single aspect of this party, even the minor details that didn't matter. The way she ordered me to do something and didn't wait to see or hear my reaction or opinion. Like now. I was supposed to be adjusting the sound crackle that occurred when the audio hit a certain frequency. The girls hadn't noticed it and neither had I, but Perla did, and she told me to fix it, so I got up and went outside and spent twenty minutes checking the audio connections and settings, listening to the movie, on alert for this sound that I was beginning to think she'd made up.

I turned toward the house, our home, which suddenly looked ominous—lit up against the dark California sky, almost every room ablaze in light. It was like a dollhouse in its perfection. She'd made it that way, and I always appreciated that about her—how every item had its place and was picked for a specific look and purpose—but now it just seemed psychotic. Like that guy in that Julia Roberts movie . . . *Sleeping with the Enemy*. That's what I'd been doing. Sleeping with. Living with. Loving . . . the person who'd murdered my sister.

I'd told Leewood just a few weeks ago that I didn't have the ability to kill someone. I spoke of the line of morality, how a good person wouldn't cross it and that only someone who was broken in some sense would intentionally take a life.

Maybe I was broken, but I was suddenly looking at the act of murder in a new light. I could suddenly imagine killing this woman . . . this beautiful carcass of a person with a rotten inside. What kind of woman married the brother of the little girl she'd murdered? What kind of woman let her father sit in prison for decades for her crimes? What kind of woman did I marry?

Maybe she's changed.

There it was, that little voice that wouldn't be silenced. The one who thought I wasn't a complete idiot, that I could judge someone with some degree of accuracy, that maybe I—and Sophie—had healed her broken soul. Maybe the woman I loved was not the same person who'd done those horrible things as a child. Maybe that person had died in Leewood's arms, and her life with George and Janice, and then with me . . . it had changed her.

My phone buzzed in my pocket, and I pulled it out and checked the screen. A text from work, the fifth so far this evening. Like the others, I ignored it. Our project deadline, which had occupied the majority of my focus for the last eighteen months, no longer mattered. I wouldn't be returning to the office. I wouldn't log into my email, or check my voicemails, or do anything in the next forty-eight hours that wasn't directly tied to Sophie and getting her and me to safety.

Maybe my wife was healed and maybe she had changed, but we would have to explore that idea somewhere far away from Perla.

Another text lit up my phone, this one from Perla.

Don't worry about it. Just come inside and have a drink and relax.

I looked back at the house, and I could see her through the second-story window, standing there, cup in hand, watching me. And I thought about that morning, when I was getting ready and had snooped through her side of the bathroom, which I'd never done. But in my new life, I was plotting to run away with our daughter and I was terrified of my wife, and so the status quo must change. In one of the drawers of her sink had been her bottle of Ambien, and I'd counted the pills, then cataloged the information along with a few dozen other statistics I was now keeping track of. Anything that could be a weapon or used in conjunction with one. The problem was, the house was huge, and it was her castle, with secrets in places I didn't even know existed.

Twenty-two pills of Ambien.

Eight gallons of bleach.

Two boxes of rat poison.

Twenty-six knives.

Two axes.

One BB gun.

One chain saw.

The list went on, and the problem was, when you started looking at things that could harm someone, everything started to look suspicious. Latex gloves under the sink. Gasoline. Matches. Rope.

Perla waved at me, gesturing for me to come inside, and I stood, then looked at the girls. Sophie had her head resting on the pillow of her float, a wide grin on her face, one of her feet dangling in the water. Mandolin was propped up on her elbows, laughing at something on-screen. Bridget was cross-legged on her float, a bright-red bowl of popcorn in her lap.

Only two friends at Sophie's party. Perla had been insistent on that, and insistent that I lay down the rule as my own. Why? Last year, she'd had more than a dozen. I had accepted it without much argument or thought, just like everything.

A twelve-year-old's birthday party. Three girls, spending the night together.

I didn't like it.

———

Inside, I forced myself to approach Perla and gather her against me for a kiss. She tasted like whipped cream, and I pulled away as soon as it felt long enough.

"Here." She held out the cup, and I knew without looking that it would be an Irish coffee, made just how I liked it.

"Give me just a sec. I need to run upstairs and get one of my heartburn pills."

"Sure." She settled in on one of the couches in front of the windows, tucking her bare foot underneath her as she picked up her own drink. Outside, there was a view of the pool, and from that spot, you could see all three girls and the movie screen.

"I'll be right back. You're watching them?"

She scoffed. "Yes, Grant. I'm watching them."

I didn't even know why I'd asked. I'd probably feel better if she weren't. I took the steps two at a time upstairs and grabbed my antacid medication. On my way out, I stopped, then crossed over to her side of the bathroom and pulled open the lowest drawer, withdrawing her Ambien and twisting open the cap.

I counted it once, then twice, the burn in my chest increasing at the total. Thirteen pills.

This morning: twenty-two pills. Now: thirteen.

I returned the bottle to the drawer, being careful to place it exactly as I had found it, then hurried back downstairs.

Nine missing pills. Where the fuck had nine pills gone to? I thought of the cake and ice cream that the girls had yet to eat, and of the drink that was downstairs, waiting for me.

Maybe she had tucked the pills away for a special occasion. Or maybe she was doing something with them tonight. But what? And why?

The number echoed in my head as I took the spot on the couch next to Perla and allowed her to curl into my body. I sipped the Irish coffee, which tasted off, and as soon as I finished it, I excused myself to the bathroom, where I stuck my finger in the back of my throat and vomited it all up.

Nine missing pills. I sat on the toilet and searched the internet to see how much Ambien it took to kill someone. It was, apparently, the wrong thing to look up, generating a slew of suicide-prevention alerts and websites to click on for help.

I flushed the toilet, aware that I was taking too long. I checked my watch: 9:47 p.m. Nine probably wouldn't kill anyone, just knock us all—or at least one of us—out.

I shouldn't wait until Monday. Tomorrow, as soon as the girls had been returned to their parents, I was taking Sophie and getting the fuck out of here.

CHAPTER 74

PERLA

I stood at my sink and spread an antiaging serum across the planes of my face. Humming softly to myself, I squeezed out a dab of under-eye cream, then patted it under each eye.

On the opposite side of the bathroom, Grant flossed. After dropping the first string of floss into the trash can, he pulled out a second. "You seem happy," he observed.

"Oh, I just love parties." I pulled open the large top drawer and selected my lip moisturizer. I unscrewed the cap and looked in the mirror as I swiped it over both lips.

He put down the floss. "What do you mean?"

It was such an odd question that I turned, meeting his gaze in the mirror. "What do you mean, what do I mean?" I laughed. "It's a party, Grant. Who doesn't like them? Sophie seems to be having a great time."

"Well, maybe I'm sensitive, but we don't have a good track record with birthday parties, especially twelfth ones."

I grimaced, then crossed the wide expanse and wrapped my arms around his torso. Squeezing him, I rested my head against his chest as I inhaled his scent. "Well, this one is our chance at a do-over."

It would be a do-over. An improve-over.

He pushed me away. It was so unlike him that I gawked, shocked at the rejection. "Let's just get through the night. I've got a ton of work I need to get back to." He yawned. "And I'm suddenly exhausted."

I grinned, surprised the Ambien had taken this long to work. Granted, he was a hundred pounds bigger than Sophie, which was why I'd used three pills instead of two.

I followed him into his closet, leaning against the doorframe and watching as he changed out of his work clothes. "You should text Paige and thank her for all of her efforts. She really worked her butt off, getting everything set up."

"Yeah, I'm not going to do that, Perla."

I stared at him, trying to understand where the attitude was coming from after fourteen years of compliancy. "What's wrong with you?"

He unbuttoned his shirt and said nothing, yanking it off his shoulders before dropping it into the hamper and selecting a clean white V-neck from the stack. "I just feel like you never think about it." His words slurred a little, and I tried not to grin. Hopefully, he'd make it to the bed before he fell out.

"Think about what, the birthday party?" I asked.

He shot me an irritated look as he unbuckled his belt and pulled it through the loops. "Yes, Perla. The birthday party."

"I think about it all the time," I said, and it was probably the most truthful statement I'd ever given him.

"Well, you don't act like it."

"What's with you?" I glared at him. "Is it a crime to enjoy our daughter's birthday?"

He sighed, and it was like watching a balloon deflate. "I'm sorry. I'm just stressed out about work."

"Well, don't take it out on me," I warned him sharply. "Come on, let's get you in bed before you fall asleep on your feet." The girls' movie was already over, and they were getting into their pajamas now and crawling into Sophie's giant king-size bed. I'd spiked their ice cream with the pills, so they'd all be asleep within minutes. I'd give everything a few hours, just to be safe, and then the house would be my personal playground. I looked down at my smartwatch, which was set to vibrate, and set the alarm for 1:00 a.m.

Moving to my side of the bed, I crawled under the covers and rolled away from him. "Night."

"Good night." He shuffled into the room, the mattress shifting as he got on his side.

I closed my eyes and, within minutes, fell asleep.

CHAPTER 75

GRANT

I lay in bed next to Perla for hours, my mind whirring through possible scenarios for escape. If she needed to, all our cars likely had the ability to be tracked, except for the vintage Porsche, though she had put one of those Apple AirTags in it somewhere. That was okay—I could probably find and disable that from my phone. And I could turn off my phone's location, which I did every time I went to the prison, so that was already second nature to me. I'd toss Sophie's phone or leave it behind. In fact, I should get rid of mine, too, and just start fresh with new phones.

A light buzzing sounded, and I froze in place as Perla sat up on her side of the bed and stretched, then eased out.

I closed my eyes as she came around the foot of the bed. There were the soft sounds of an approach, and then the blanket shifted and her hair tickled my arm as she leaned over and loudly whispered my name. *"Grant."*

I didn't move, attempting to keep my breathing regular and wondering what she was doing.

"Grant," she said, louder, and then she poked me in the shoulder. Despite every instinct to open my eyes, I didn't.

She left, and I waited until I heard noises in her closet, then peeked. She reappeared in the doorway of the walk-in, dressed in all black, a large shopping bag in hand.

Maybe I didn't have to leave her. Maybe she was leaving me.

I heard the bedroom door open; then she left our suite. I counted to ten before I sat up and reached for my cell. It wasn't on the bedside table, so I groped for the charging cord, then followed it, looking for the phone.

My search came up empty. Perla had taken it. Not good.

I snuck out of bed, then crept to the door and eased it open, looking into the hall.

Perla was coming toward me from the direction of Sophie's room. I jerked backward and was about to hurry back to bed when she turned at the staircase and headed downstairs.

Sticking my head out, I listened to her jog down the stairs. Easing out into the hall, I tried to track her movement on the lower floor. Perla had come from Sophie's direction, and I softly moved forward, wanting to look in on the girls. She had only been down there for a moment. Too quickly for anything to happen, yet I had to know my daughter was okay.

Approaching Sophie's room was like the opening act of a horror movie. The happy streamers and balloons around the double doors, the Happy Birthday sign . . . I halted halfway down the hall and realized the decor was eerily reminiscent of the front door to Jenny Folcrum's house on the night of her party. Similar banner, streamers, and balloons. Of course, Sophie's were elaborate and well done, while Jenny's had been hand-drawn letters on construction paper, affixed to the trailer's walls with Scotch tape. Her balloons had been half-deflated, the single strand of streamers limp and sad by the next morning, when the crime scene investigators photographed the house.

Perla's bag was in the middle of the hall, and I crouched beside it and looked in.

It was a collection from hell, most of the contents present at my sister's crime scene. A Ouija board, cupcakes, cards, and there . . . I saw a long knife blade and backed away from the bag. There was no reason for *any* of this to be here, and my stomach knotted with a nausea-inducing blend of fear and rage.

From downstairs, I heard a noise and froze, listening as the front door swung open. *What the* . . . I quickly walked back to the landing and peered over the railing just in time to see Perla exit through the front door and pull it shut behind her.

CHAPTER 76

PERLA

Everything was going perfectly, and I hummed a little under my breath as I pulled the front door tight and skipped down the front steps. The girls and Grant were zonked out, my props were all un-documentable or linked to Grant or Paige, and now I just needed to set the final wheels into motion. I spun on one heel, looking back toward the dark house, my gaze drifting over the security cameras installed in the eaves—all turned off a few minutes ago with Grant's phone app. A shiver of excitement ran through me at how brilliantly I had orchestrated all this. It was like the final twists and turns of a Rubik's Cube. Click. Click. Click. Everything finally matching up, confirming my superior level of intelligence.

I pulled out Grant's phone as I started down our driveway and made a call to Paige, hanging up as soon as she answered. Then I composed and sent a series of rapid-fire texts.

Everything is going wrong. I need you to come to the house.

Did you get this?

Come A.S.A.P.

The front door may be unlocked, if not, use your code.

Please be quiet and meet me in Sophie's room. Perla is asleep. Hurry.

In ten minutes, I'd send a follow-up text. Something along the lines of . . . Nevermind. I handled it. Go back home, we're in the clear.

I had originally thought that an entry of Paige's gate code close to the time of death would be enough to implicate her, but without knowing where she was or what she was doing tonight, it was too risky. With my luck, she was currently live streaming on social media, with a thousand online idiots able to verify her alibi. So getting her headed this way would help negate or excuse that possibility.

I also sent an email to tfk@hotmail.com. Just one line, but enough to hang my husband.

Everything is in place.

Maybe it was overkill, but maybe it wasn't. I'd never seen someone get off because there was *too* much evidence against them.

CHAPTER 77

GRANT

The minute the front door latched into place behind Perla, I sprinted down the hall and into Sophie's room.

The lights were off, the girls in bed, a night-light bathing the room in a gentle peach glow. I ran to the bed and leaned over to examine the girls, then shook Sophie. She was slow to wake up, unnaturally slow, and I shook her harder. *"Sophie,"* I said loudly. When she finally opened her eyes, they were heavy, her pupils unfocused. *Shit.* Nine Ambien. Four of us.

"Wake up," I said urgently. "There's someone in the house. Someone bad. I need you to help me wake up the girls and get them onto the balcony, then crawl down—the way we did when we practiced the fire drill, remember?"

"What?" she said, pushing herself up, then flopping back down. "Dad, I'm tired."

I shook her harder, so hard that her head snapped back and she winced in pain. *"Sophie, wake up.* This is very, very important. Listen to me carefully." I repeated the instructions, shaking her every time her eyes began to close. "Do you understand?" I asked her.

"Yeah." She yawned. "And then what do we do?"

"Wait for me behind the tree of the tree house. Just lay there on the ground and be quiet. Wait until I come and get you, okay?"

She nodded and yawned again. "Okay. Go on the balcony, crawl down. Lay behind the tree house."

"You need to be very, very quiet when you do it, do you understand? As silent as possible."

"Okay." She leaned over and poked Mandolin in the side. The girl didn't move.

I circled to the other side of the bed and roughly shook Bridget, then Mandolin. "Wake up, girls," I said loudly. "Come on. Now. Get up and hurry."

They both complained, and Bridget rolled onto her stomach and tried to pull the comforter over her head.

"Here, you can each take a pillow. Lay down there and go back to sleep."

I opened the balcony door, frantically gesturing them through, and watched, my heart in my throat, as they trudged to the far end of the balcony. Sophie's room faced the back of the house, but I didn't know what Perla was doing or how quickly she'd be back. As long as Sophie followed my directions, they should be out of sight, but my heartbeat was still running at full sprint through my chest.

Sophie swung her pajama-panted leg over the railing and onto the flat roof. It wasn't ideal, the girls walking along the roof and over to the oak tree, which they would need to climb down to the ground, but it was doable. We had made a game of it when we'd practiced the fire drills, and Sophie had done it in less than a minute.

Our eyes met and she looked more alert. "Be careful," I said quietly.

"I got this, Dad. We're good."

"I love you," I whispered, aware that it might be the last time I had the chance to tell her.

"Love you too." She gestured for me to go, and I hurried back inside. Her bed was glaringly empty, so I snatched at the pillows, stuffing them into body-size shapes under the covers.

Perla would be coming back. Whatever she was doing in the front yard—Disabling the gate? Hiding the keys to our cars?—she would be back, and then . . . what?

I already knew the answer to that. I'd seen the knife in the bag. The props she planned to use. *She hadn't changed.* She had just grown older and smarter.

There was a sound downstairs, and I froze, then carefully sprint-walked to the bedroom door and put my ear to the open crack, listening. The front door clicked shut.

She was back.

It was interesting that my wife, even as she navigated this descent into hell, took the time to remove her shoes. I heard the entry bench creak as she sat down on it. I knew exactly what she was doing. Removing the right, then the left. Pulling the laces tight and tucking them into the shoes before she opened the door to the coat closet and placed them on the appropriate shelf.

That gave me a minute, at most. I moved frantically around the room, making sure that the balcony door was closed, its curtains drawn, the bed realistically full. I considered bolting out of the room, but I needed to see whatever it was that Perla was about to do. My gaze ping-ponged around the room, looking for a hiding spot, and I hurried over to Sophie's closet, where I eased in, pulling the door until it was ajar just a crack.

Placing my eye to the opening, I softened my breathing and waited. My heart felt like it was galloping inside my chest, and I placed my hand on it, willing it to slow down.

The bedroom door eased open, and I watched as my wife stepped into our daughter's bedroom. She nudged the door shut with her heel and was pulling on tight latex gloves as she approached the open area beside the bed. She had the bag, which she set on the floor, then straightened, a clear package in hand. She unfolded it, revealing a clear jumpsuit, and pulled it on over her clothing, then zipped it up, tucking her hair into its cap and tightening the neckline of it. She had booties also, and my concern bloomed as she pulled them over her socks.

It was a kill suit. She looked like the serial killer on one of those shows she loved, and as much as my optimistic mind tried desperately to find some other reason for her to be donning this protective garment, only one made sense. She didn't want blood spatter to get on her, or her DNA to get on one of these beautiful, precious girls.

The next thing out of the bag was a white blanket, which she unfurled like a flag before crouching to let it settle across the open wood floor. The familiar item made me instantly nauseous. I closed my eyes, trying to breathe as quietly as possible while fighting away the crime scene images I always associated with that fabric.

Lucy's hand, outstretched, her palm streaked with blood.

Her hair, matted and mussed, in a red, sticky pool.

Her knees splayed, the soft blue sleep shorts gaping open at the legs, showing a peek of yellow underwear.

Perla straightened out the corners of the blanket, then returned to the shopping bag, where she pulled out a few more items, placing them down on the blanket. I knew what they were, even with the dim light and my limited view. A Ouija board. Cupcakes. Playing cards. She stood, moved the bag to the side, and withdrew the final item, one that flashed in the dim glow of Sophie's night-light. A long and skinny knife.

Oh God. She was going to put the girls on the blanket and then kill them all. Maybe leave our daughter's neck half-intact, just to make the recreation as accurate as possible. But then what? Hope that I woke up from their screams? Rushed in and get caught red-handed, like Leewood?

Unlike Leewood, I wouldn't lie for her. Keep a stoic silence and serve decades behind bars. I would crucify her, but she had to know that—which meant I was probably the final victim of this insane plan.

She crept forward, and if I was going to do anything, I needed to do it now while she was distracted and focused on the bed. Once she realized the girls weren't there, she'd be on the defense and I'd be a sitting duck in a closet, without a way to defend myself.

I opened the door and rushed toward her.

I grabbed her from behind, one arm locked across her chest, the other wrapped in a monkey grip around the wrist of the hand holding the knife. She didn't release it. She bucked back against me, attempting to free herself as she squirmed in my grasp.

"Stop it, Perla." I spoke in her ear, my voice low.

"What are you—" She sagged against me and let out a strangled cry of relief. "Shit, Grant, you scared the shit out of me. What are you doing?"

"I'm stopping you." I squeezed her wrist harder. "Drop the knife, Perla."

"Okay, I will, just let me go. Jesus, is this a sexual thing?" she hissed. "Because it seems a little late in our marriage to play a Dom."

"You can't kill them, Perla. I won't let you do it."

"Kill who? Grant, what are you talking about?" She suddenly raised her foot sharply, and her heel hit the most sensitive part of my nuts. The air in my chest released in a sudden *oomph* of pain, and I staggered back, my grip loosening on her. She spun around and raised the knife, rushing forward, and if I'd ever had any doubt, it vanished in the moment our eyes locked and I saw the dead vacancy there. No emotion about the decision to kill her husband. No torment over the act she had come into this room to commit.

I grabbed her arm, stopping the downward slash of the knife, then twisted the appendage behind her back, yanking it upward. She gasped out a cry of pain. "Okay, okay, please, please, Grant, stop. That hurts."

"You were about to kill our daughter."

"I wasn't," she protested.

I closed my hand over her latex-gloved fist, keeping it pinned to the knife. "Tell me the truth, or I will kill you."

"You won't," she choked out.

"I will, because I know the truth about Lucy."

She went very still at that. There was a full-page confession in that silence.

"My father killed Lucy," she said weakly. "You know that. Why would you—" She let out a sob, but I was done falling for her lies.

"Your father told me what happened."

She didn't ask when or how, and I wondered if she knew about my visits and what they had entailed.

"Why?" I rasped as I wrenched her hand with the knife around and placed the edge of the blade to her throat. There was the scar from when Leewood had cut her, and I wondered if he'd felt the same mix of repulsion and fear when he had been in this same position.

"You can be good and still kill someone, Tim." That's what he had said to me, and I had sneered at the thought. What was it I had said? That wanting someone to die and killing them were two different things? That we couldn't help our emotions, but we could control our actions?

My emotions, right now, were a tsunami, and I didn't have time to sort the good from the bad. Perla had approached our daughter's bed in a kill suit, a knife in hand. Perla had killed my sister.

My hand tightened on hers, but I couldn't bring myself to move.

CHAPTER 78

PERLA

He wasn't going to do it. He wouldn't. When I had stared up into my father's eyes the night of my birthday party, I had seen a strength there. He hadn't wanted to kill me, but he had been man enough to do what he thought needed to be done. And I had seen the love in his eyes when he placed the blade against my throat.

Grant didn't have that specific bone in his body. He had other good traits—ones I had appreciated while we made our life together—but he was not built like me or my father.

Grant put his mouth against my ear. "Did you kill your mother too?"

Kill her? No. She killed herself. She ignored me, wormed herself between me and my father at every opportunity, and spent all our money on drugs. She was high the morning I brought her a cup of coffee. So high that she didn't notice the taste or the powdery flecks I hadn't fully crushed. She was so high, she could barely see that it was me.

I wet my lips. "No," I whispered. "She overdosed. You know that. Grant, you know *me*. Let go of my hand. You're hurting my wrist." If I turned quickly, I could stab him in the stomach or chest. Then kill the girls, then call the cops. Tell them that I'd caught him in the aftermath. He'd attacked me, I'd gotten the knife free and defended myself.

"Tell me why you killed Lucy."

Because he wanted her. Her and Kitty and everyone except for me. He had special time with them, special relationships with them—and I got the leftovers. The dirty laundry, the dinner and dishes, the half hour of television before he fell asleep in the recliner.

My birthday was supposed to be all about me, but when I'd opened my presents, there were two that weren't for me—one for each of *them*. I could tell they were from my dad because he sucked at wrapping and always wrote my name directly on the paper in black Sharpie.

It was my birthday, and he had gotten presents for them.

"Perla." Grant's voice was harder, his grip on me tightening, and he shook me as if it would cause the truth to shake free.

It wouldn't. No one knew what had really happened that night, or what had caused it, or the dozens of little moments that had led up to it.

Long live Piketo.

I tried to pull my hand free, but he fought me, and the blade tip scraped against my neck, a hot rip of pain. I gasped. Maybe I had gone overboard in sharpening it.

"I'm sorry," he said in my ear.

Then he did the one thing I didn't expect.

The one thing I would have bet my life on him not being capable of.

The one thing I did bet my life on, only this time I would lose it.

He pressed my hand hard, pinning the blade so deep against my flesh that it cut into the tendons, popping them like rubber bands. And there was a moment—before the pain hit, before I understood what was happening—when everything stopped.

A moment of clarity. A moment that I wondered if my mother, or Lucy, or Kitty had experienced, a moment of pure pause, where the enormity of the moment hung above me and I had a chance to think.

And I thought about my dad. There were these Oatmeal Creme Pies we used to buy at the gas station down the street from our trailer. And on Friday nights, we would watch a Clint Eastwood movie, and he would drink beer and I would have a sip, and we would each have a creme pie and he would pass me his and let me lick all the icing out of it and give him back the cookie part, and those Friday nights . . . those were the happiest moments of my life. Just me and him and Clint.

Grant yanked my hand to the right, ripping the blade through the thick muscles that protected my carotid artery—and it was different from before. I tried to catalog the distinction, but somehow I was on the blanket, and then I—

CHAPTER 79

GRANT

When she fell to the ground, face forward, the enormity of what I had done hit.

I stood there, my body half-hunched forward, as if I had tried to catch her but hadn't, and attempted to process the drastic step I had just taken.

Her leg twitched and then she was still, a pool of blood beginning to stain the white blanket around her head. Again, like clockwork, the image of Lucy entered my head.

But while I had the familiar ache at the thought of my sister, I didn't feel bad about Perla. For once, just like her, I felt nothing.

I didn't make the mistake Leewood had. A minute after she stopped twitching, I very carefully moved around, making sure not to step in any blood or disturb any item, until I could see her face.

Her head had landed with her face to the left. Her eyes were open and still, her mouth agape. Like a doll. A beautiful dead doll.

That gave me an idea, and I straightened and slowly scanned the room, looking for something. I didn't see what I was looking for.

CHAPTER 80

Under the tree, the girls were curled at right angles to each other, creating a lopsided triangle, each of their faces slack with sleep. I stared down at them, my mind frantic as I tried to piece together what to tell them and what to tell the police. I had her blood on my hands. Figuratively, not literally—not best as I could tell. I had been standing behind her when I yanked the knife, so the blood sprayed outward, and I was very careful where I stepped and what I touched in the room. I had washed my hands and changed my clothes, but it only took one hair, one clothing fiber, and it was over. Just ask Leewood.

The girls were safe, given that Perla was dead, but I couldn't leave them here. I'd need to bring them with me. I crouched down and shook Sophie. She rolled onto her back, looking up at me, then yawned. Precious minutes passed as I got each girl to sit up, their sleepiness fading as they blinked and stretched, then looked around, remembering where they were.

I helped them to their feet, realizing that they were all barefoot save Sophie, who was in a pair of dirty white socks. Shit. I looked down our long driveway. "Okay, let's go."

"I'm tired," Mandolin complained, hugging her pillow to her chest. "Also, I need my phone. This *no phone at night* rule is stupid. My mom said that, by the way. She thinks it's stupid also."

"Yeah, I'm not going to argue with her on that one." I grabbed Sophie's hand. "Okay, we're going to walk to the neighbors' house, but we need to hug the tree line and stay hidden, okay?"

"Walk?" Mandolin looked aghast at the idea. "Like, how far? I'm not wearing any shoes."

"What about Mom?" Sophie looked over her shoulder, toward the house.

"Come on, we can talk as we walk." I pulled on her hand and started off, gesturing for the other two to follow me. Bridget, who hadn't said anything yet, grabbed my other hand, her palm cold and timid. "I have to go to the bathroom," she whispered.

Oh jeez. "Okay, we'll go to the bathroom as soon as we get to the neighbors'. If you have an emergency before then, we can make a pit stop in the woods."

"Ew. Bridget, you are *not* going in the woods," Mandolin stated.

"What about Mom?" Sophie asked, louder.

I shushed her with a warning glance and made a big show of looking around. "Girls, we all need to speak very quietly and move as fast as we can, okay? Sophie, I don't know where your mom is, but right now I just want to get you to safety."

She digested this, and I watched her face as we walked, gauging her response. I don't know that she believed me, but she kept her mouth closed, her features set in determination.

"The ground is hurting my feet," Bridget complained.

"Yeah, I was just about to say that," Mandolin chimed in. "Why aren't we walking on the path?"

A valid question, since I'd just killed the bogeyman, assuming Perla was working alone. Maybe she wasn't. Maybe right at that moment, there was someone else in the house, someone who might run out and follow us. Unlikely, but with what had just happened, everything felt eerie and dangerous. I stared at the ground before me, trying to see any dips or hazards, and attempted to piece together an answer to Mandolin's question. Whatever I told the girls would follow me into the courtroom, if it got to that. "I want to stay out of sight, just in case someone comes by."

"What do you mean, 'in case someone comes by'?" Bridget said, alarmed.

Okay, maybe the wrong thing to say.

"He means a bad guy," Mandolin said importantly. "Right?" She spun around to face me, her expression pointed.

God, this was a stupid idea. So much for the thought that we would be able to traverse in silence and let me sort out my explanation of events on the way. "I don't know who is in the house right now, so I'm just trying to be extra cautious. It's probably nothing, but just to be safe, I'd like to get you all to the Scotts. We're halfway there. There, we can call your parents and the police, and you can use the restroom and get some shoes or socks."

"I thought we didn't like the Scotts," Sophie said.

"Well, your mom doesn't like the Scotts, for a reason that is neither here nor there. They will help us, and that's what we need right now."

"Why doesn't Perla like the Scotts?" Mandolin asked.

"They left their trash cans out on the curb a few times. It wasn't a big deal." I skirted a tree root. The trash cans *shouldn't* have been a big deal, but Perla had made it one. She'd sent a report to the homeowner association, complete with time-stamped photos of their driveway, their cans at awkward angles by their mailbox.

The rule was that cans should be removed from the street by noon on trash-collection day, and each hour that had ticked past that deadline had been like a new thorn in Perla's side.

I was certain they knew that we had been the ones to file a complaint against them. Perla had made several pointed comments to Julie Scott about the cans and had included a flyer with the trash-collection schedule and rules in her Christmas-card mailing to them. I hadn't spoken to Julie or Bill since the debacle, but as I'd told the girls, it didn't matter.

It was too risky to pretend like I didn't know Perla was dead. I needed to tell the police as much of the truth as possible while covering my involvement in the crime.

Okay, so I'd tell the truth. All of it, except for the fact that I had been the one in control of the knife. So I'd tell them a version of the truth. I woke up. I found the bag. I got the girls out of there. And then . . . I frowned. I should have left with them. That's what a normal person would have done. So why didn't I?

The problem was, a normal person probably wouldn't have been alarmed by a shopping bag full of toys. I gritted my teeth, aware of the domino effect of suspicion that might be unearthed by me introducing the Folcrum Party into this equation.

But they would, of course, know of it on their own. If not right away, as soon as they looked into Perla and me.

"How much longer?" Bridget asked, her hand slipping from mine. She covered her mouth with her forearm as she yawned.

"Not far." I moved to Sophie's other side, my stride picking up speed as I approached the small opening set into the bushes on the side of our big vehicle gate.

"Look, the gates are open." Sophie pointed.

I turned and squinted, trying to see where she was pointing. Our vehicle gate was a giant iron fortress–looking set with *W*'s set in the center of each side. I had always thought they were a little gaudy and certainly not worth the ridiculous expense, but Perla had insisted on them. "Are you sure?"

"Yeah, I can see them. Can't you?"

I strained my eyes, but everything was too dark. "No," I admitted. "Mandolin? Bridget? Can you tell if the gates are open?"

"Yeah, they're open," Mandolin said, bored, as if she weren't accomplishing a feat of strength by seeing that far.

"I can't tell," Bridget said, and with her Coke-bottle glasses, I wasn't surprised.

"Okay, come through this gate. We'll leave that one alone." I ushered them through, closing the gate behind them and looking through the darkness, trying to understand why the gate had been open. Was this why Perla had gone out the front door? Probably not. If she had needed to let someone in, she could have just given them a code.

Unless she hadn't wanted a code to be logged by the system. Every time a code was entered, it was stored somewhere. When the police investigated this evening, they would be able to tell who had opened the gate and when. Unless that was why Perla left. Maybe she walked down here and manually opened it.

I thought of my missing phone and the cameras at the gate and on the exterior of our house. She'd probably turned off the cameras. If she hadn't, there'd be footage of whatever she did, as well as footage of the girls' exit across the roof and down the tree.

The footage, or lack of it, was another reason I would need to be very careful with what I told the police and why I should stick to the true timeline as closely as possible.

"The Scotts don't have a gate," Sophie whispered, for Mandolin's and Bridget's information. "And their house is close to the road, so we won't have to walk as far."

"Have you been to their house before?" Bridget asked.

"Just for trick-or-treating."

We were at the cul-de-sac now, and they moved off the grass shoulder and onto the pavement. I was running out of time, and my mind was still piecing together my story for the police.

Sophie was right: the Scotts' house was only a short distance off the curb. They had put their home at the front of the lot and used the rear acreage for their horse barn and paddocks—another checkmark against them, in Perla's book.

Their two-story brick home was dark, save for discreet path lighting and some landscaping uplights. I checked my watch, then remembered I didn't have it on. The girls quieted as we hurried down the driveway and up their front path. They hung back on the steps as I approached the front door and pressed the doorbell.

It illuminated with an electronic chime, and we were most definitely on camera.

I stepped back and waited as the doorbell slowly pulsed blue.

No one answered, and I gave it a minute, then pressed it again.

A scratchy male voice finally spoke through the speaker. "Hello?"

Bill.

"Bill, there's been an emergency. This is Grant Wultz from next door. Can you let us in?"

CHAPTER 81

<1:57 a.m. Call began>

DISPATCH: 9-1-1, police, fire, or medical?

714-555-3612: Police.

DISPATCH: What's your name and address?

714-555-3612: Grant Wultz. I'm at a neighbor's house but need the police to come to 229 Timothy Drive in Brighton Estates.

DISPATCH: What's your emergency?

714-555-3612: My wife just killed herself.

DISPATCH: How did she do that, sir?

714-555-3612: Um, a knife. She cut her throat.

DISPATCH: Do you need an ambulance?

714-555-3612: No.

DISPATCH: Are you certain? Did you check to see if she had a pulse?

714-555-3612: No. I, um . . . no. But I'm pretty sure. Her eyes were open. She looked . . . I-I'm sorry, this is really hard—

DISPATCH: Okay, we're sending officers there now. It looks like this is a gated neighborhood, sir. Is that correct?

714-555-3612: Yes. I can call the guard gate and let them know—

DISPATCH: No, that's fine. We'll coordinate with them. Did you see it happen?

714-555-3612: *inaudible mumbling*

DISPATCH: Sir? Sir? I need you to be here with me.

714-555-3612: I'm sorry, I have to go, my daughter is here.

DISPATCH: Okay, are you going back to your house, sir?

714-555-3612: Yes. I can meet the police there.

DISPATCH: Okay, don't go back inside. The officers are going to meet you in front of the house, do you understand?

714-555-3612: Yes.

DISPATCH: They are about six minutes away. I'm also calling an ambulance just to be safe.

714-555-3612: Okay I'll go over there right now.

<2:01 a.m. Call ended>

CHAPTER 82

I mean, I didn't know what to think when Grant rang our bell in the middle of the night. And let me tell you, when we opened the door, he looked like hell had run him over. Hair sticking every which way, breathing heavy, eyes all wild—and with three girls and no sign of Perla. I told Bill that those officers better look at that crime scene awfully closely. Because I mean, I've seen people in shock before, and I think there was some of that, but there was also something off about the whole thing. When we got those girls inside and gave them something to eat, I kept looking at Grant, and he was just staring off into space. Making up his lies, that's what I think he was doing. The nerds are the ones you got to watch out for. I've always said that.

—*Julie Scott, neighbor*

It was quickly decided that the girls would stay at the Scotts' until the morning. Julie Scott, who was bright-eyed over the drama of the situation, herded them into a guest room, where they all crawled into a king-size bed and promptly fell back asleep.

Bill gave me a ride back to our house. His headlights swept over the white adobe siding, and I realized the sprinklers were on. I reached for my phone to turn them off through the app, but stopped. I swore and Bill looked over.

"What?"

"Nothing. I don't have my phone. It's just—frustrating." Leave it to Perla to take the one thing that would render me useless. Which was probably why she had done it.

I opened the door. "Thanks for the ride. I'll just wait for them out front."

"Oh, I'll wait with you. You never know. They might call back the house and need something. Julie can reach me here." He patted his pocket. *Must be nice to have a communication device just inches away.*

Twin beams of light illuminated the planters to our left, and we both turned to see three black-and-white patrol cars pull through the gates.

"Popular guy," Bill remarked, hunching forward in his seat. "Oh, and there's an ambulance too. Look, I don't want to pry, but you said you thought someone might be in the house. So Perla . . . ?" He raised his brows, waiting for me to fill in the blanks. "I mean . . . is the ambulance for her?"

"I need to talk to the cops." I swung my leg out. "Really appreciate your help, Bill. I'll come by the house and get Sophie as soon as I'm done here."

"Oh yeah, sure. Hey, Grant?" He spoke just before I shut the car door and I paused, my irritation growing.

"Yes?" I asked impatiently.

"If you need an attorney, call Paul Reachen. Real good guy and tough. He lives in the neighborhood, over on Outlook Drive."

I nodded. "Thanks," I said and meant it.

Two more police cars pulled in, which seemed excessive. Then again, it was Brighton Estates. We paid more in property taxes than a hundred houses in the poorer sections of LA combined.

A trim, dark-skinned officer with silver hair and a foreign accent introduced himself as Lieutenant Johnson.

I shook his hand. "Thank you for coming so quickly."

"We were told your wife is inside and you believe her to be deceased, is that correct?"

I gave a tight nod. "Yes, she's in one of the second-floor bedrooms."

"Okay, I'm going to keep you out here while our officers search and secure the home. Is anyone else inside?"

I shook my head. "I don't believe so."

"Any weapons in the house?"

"Um . . ." I tried to think. "There's a BB gun in the garage." *And knives in the kitchen. Big ones, bigger than the one she had.*

"You have any weapons on your person?"

"No." I raised my arms and then lifted my shirt, showing him the waistband of my shorts and my bare stomach.

"Okay. The front door locked, or can they go in through there?"

"I don't know . . . I left around the back. I can give you the code if it's locked."

He turned his head and yelled something, then studied the house. "How do you turn off the sprinklers?"

"Uh—it's an app on my phone, but I can't find it. My phone, I mean."

At the front door, one of the cops tested the front door handle, then pulled it open. Guns drawn and flashlight beams shining, a line of them entered.

The lieutenant's attention returned to me. "Okay. Tell me what happened."

"I woke up and realized my wife wasn't in the bed. Which, um . . ." I inhaled, trying to organize my thoughts in as succinct a manner as possible. "I went to call her, but when I reached for my phone, it wasn't on the charger. I . . ." I paused, frustrated. "This is going to be a long story. Do you want me to just skip to the part where—"

"No." He rested his fingers on his hips, and I tried not to stare into the large camera lens affixed to the center of his uniform.

"Okay, so I went looking for her. And I thought, *Oh, I'll check on the girls*, because my daughter was having a sleepover for her birthday. And outside—"

"Where's your daughter now?"

"My daughter and her friends are at the neighbors' house." I twisted, pointing in the direction of their house. "The, uh, the one who you just got his information."

"Okay, go ahead."

"So, outside my daughter's bedroom was a bag. This big shopping bag. It was odd; it was like, set right in the middle of the hall. And that's something my wife does—she sets things in the middle of a doorway or a hall if she doesn't want to forget something. So I looked in it . . ." I inhaled and felt a string of my composure break.

"It's okay, Mr. Wultz. Take your time."

I took a few deep breaths, then continued. "It was, um, a bunch of items. But all bad things. There was this clear plastic suit and a pair of gloves—and a really sharp knife, one of the ones from the kitchen."

The sprinklers suddenly died, and there was a soft buzz as all the heads lowered into the ground. In another part of the yard, there was the sound of them ticking into action. I glanced at the officer. I had his full attention now.

I continued on. "I got worried about the girls and went in the room, and the girls were there, and they were okay, but I woke them up. It was really hard to wake them up. I think they must have been drugged. Oh . . ." I looked up. "I didn't think about the girls. You'll need to test them. We just put them to bed. I can ask—"

"Just continue on," Johnson interrupted, giving me the gesture to hurry it up.

"Okay, so I woke them up and told them they needed to go out on the balcony and then walk along the roof to the tree and climb down. I wasn't sure what was going on inside the house, but there was too much that was wrong, and I wanted to make sure they were safe until I figured it out."

He held up a finger as a fresh group of officers approached. Turning to address them, he issued a string of orders, then returned his focus to me.

"I told my daughter, Sophie—I told her I'd come out and meet her under the tree house once I figured out what was going on. And once they were off the balcony and headed down, I went looking for Perla." This would be a bit tricky, since I couldn't tell them the truth, that I'd hidden in the closet and waited for Perla, then finished staging the picnic blanket scene after she was dead. I took a deep breath, reminding myself that I had a script in mind, fake tasks at the ready.

"Perla's your wife?"

"Yes."

"Did you find her?"

"Not right away. It's a big house, and I checked the basement and the garage—I wanted to see if her car was there, which it was. I also tried to get into the lockbox to get the phones—we take our daughter's phone away at night, and I thought I could use her phone to call Perla or the police, since mine was missing. But the code didn't work on the box." I spoke confidently, and they never needed to know that my actions had occurred after Perla's death, not before. "Then I heard something upstairs, so I went back up, and that's when I found Perla."

I closed my eyes and took a moment, knowing I had to deliver this part of the story perfectly. "She was . . . I don't know how to describe her. Manic? She had unfolded this white blanket on the floor and was pulling items out of the bag and laying them out on the surface and then . . ." I swallowed. "You'll see it. It's really fucking creepy. And I came in and asked her what she was doing, and she said she was finishing what had been started."

"'Finishing what had been started'?" he repeated.

"Yeah. I told her that the girls were gone, that she couldn't hurt them, and that's when she grabbed the knife." I shook my head and my vision blurred, and the tears were real because this had been a fucked situation from the word *go*. "She said, 'I can still finish the job,' and then she pulled the blade across her neck." I took a deep breath. "I lunged forward, but there was so much blood, it just wouldn't stop. I tried to hold my hand over it, to stop it, but within a minute or so, she was gone."

He nodded as if it all made sense. If it was this easy to commit murder, no wonder Perla had gotten away with it twenty-three years ago. "Okay, so then what happened?"

"Well, I didn't have a phone, so I washed my hands and changed into a clean shirt and pair of shorts. Then I went and got the girls, and we walked to the neighbors, where I called 9-1-1."

"So, you cleaned up after the crime?"

"I mean, I cleaned myself up. I didn't want to scare the girls by coming out all bloody. All of the clothes I was wearing are inside, in the laundry room. It's a bit of a mess. You'll see."

More headlights passed over the house, and he swore, then jerked his head to the nearest uniform. "Thomas, go down to the gate and sit it, make sure no lookie-loos or neighbors come in. You get anyone odd, you radio me."

He pointed at something behind me. "You know that car?"

I turned and held up my hand, shielding my face from the oncoming headlights. When it turned, parking beside a cop car, I could see the older Toyota Camry in the darkness. "Yeah, that's our nanny."

Paige cracked open the door and winced against the glare of the flashlight that one of the officers was playing over her face. "Grant?" she called out.

"Yeah, I'm here." I kept my distance as Lieutenant Johnson approached her, wondering what the hell Paige was doing here at this time of night.

"Miss, can I help you?" Johnson now had his flashlight out, the beam centered on Paige's chest.

"Oh, he told me to come here," she called out.

He? My stomach dropped.

"Who did?"

She looked as confused as I felt and pointed at me. "Grant did."

CHAPTER 83

Everyone's eyes swung over to me. If there was a sign of the disaster ahead, this was it.

"Wait." I started toward her. "You're saying I told you to come here? When?"

Lieutenant Johnson stepped into my line of sight, blocking me from going any farther. "I'm sorry, I have to do my best to keep everything clean until the detectives get here. Miss?" He pointed to the closest officer. "Please go with this gentleman and tell him your story."

He turned to me. "Mr. Wultz, let's get you somewhere you can relax. You mentioned the girls who were sleeping over. I'll need to get all of their names so we can contact their parents."

I glanced over, watching as the officer helped Paige out of her car. She was in leggings and a T-shirt, and our eyes met over the top of the car. She looked scared, and I wanted to reassure her, but I also had no idea what she was about to tell the officers about me.

I followed Johnson up the front path of the house. Someone had flipped on the porch light, and he pointed to the seating area on the right side of the expansive porch. We never sat out here, preferring the back views to the front, and I took a spot on the sectional couch and sank down an unexpected amount.

The other cop was leading Paige around to the back of her car, but they were too far away for me to hear anything. "I didn't tell her to come here," I muttered to Johnson. "I don't ever even talk to her. I've said like, three things to her, ever."

Tell her how nice she looks, Grant.

I need to text Paige. Let me use your phone.

"It'll all get sorted," he said. "Right now we just want to make sure that the scene is contained and we get down the details while they are still fresh in your mind."

I shouldn't be telling him anything more. I'd probably already said too much, given some detail I would be tried and condemned on. "I need to call a lawyer," I said, rubbing my face. "And I need to find my phone, if you could ask the officers to look for it. Maybe it's on her. I didn't think about checking her pockets, if she even had any."

"No problem." He stood between me and the front door, his posture relaxed. "You guys had any problems in your marriage? Any fights? Talk of divorce?"

"No." I shook my head.

"What about in the past?"

"No."

"Any infidelity?"

I thought of Marci Vennigan and that one kiss, the night of the Christmas party. "No."

He nodded. "Okay. Detective Heinwright is on his way. He'll have you run through what happened again; then we'll get you out of here and to your daughter. You mentioned she might have been drugged, so we will need to have her and all of the girls checked." He pulled a notepad out of his front pocket. "Let me go ahead and get their names."

I looked at the house, where flashlights were visible through the windows, dancing over our walls, then back at the car, where Paige was talking animatedly, her hands waving through the air, and wondered what other surprises Perla had in store for me.

CHAPTER 84

Two officers entered the front doors slowly, the strong beams of their flashlights sweeping over the dark interior. At first glance, the house looked perfect. The large expanse was all cream furniture and gold accents, the scent of fresh flowers light in the air.

The officers crept in, their shoes creaking on the polished floors. Sweeping the room, the female uniform pointed to an open marble staircase. "Apparently, the victim is upstairs."

"God, this house is a big bitch," the man said. "This is going to take a while to clear."

"I'll tell J to let in the others."

"This all looks in order; let's go upstairs."

On the second floor, the group stopped at the landing and swept their flashlights to the left and the right, a rusty scent strong in the air.

"Look." She pointed at a bloody heel print and they turned left, following the scent and the print's origin, moving slowly and opening doors as they passed.

An office, all wood paneling and dark colors. Empty.

Another office, this one in delicate blues and creams. Empty.

A bedroom with two queen beds and pale-green floral wallpaper. The beds were made, everything in order.

Another bedroom with a single large bed and a sitting area, everything in place, no personal items in sight.

A laundry room with a long marble counter and two sets of stainless steel machines, everything sparkling and white, save for a small pile of clothes on the floor in front of the washer. Bloody clothes.

"J, we're going to need CSIs up here, ASAP," the male officer said into the radio on his shoulder. "Lots of blood and evidence. Haven't gotten to the vic yet."

Taking care not to disturb the footprints, they came to a stop at the double doors at the end of the hall. The doors were closed, their exterior decorated with limp pink streamers. An arched paper banner was mounted above the doors, each piece of paper a different letter.

H-A-P-P-Y B-I-R-T-H-D-A-Y

One of the doorknobs was smeared with blood, and here, the smell of it was strongest. The duo halted, looking at each other.

"You want to take dibs on going in there first?"

"Yeah, don't mind if I do." He reached forward and turned the unbloodied knob with a gloved hand, then pushed the door open. They both stayed back, guns drawn, and waited as the slow open of the door revealed the scene. He cautiously stepped in. "Well, shit."

Beside the king-size canopy bed, a white cotton blanket was spread over the wood floor, the fabric wrinkled around a woman's prone body, lying face down in a pool of blood. She wore a clear plastic jumpsuit over a black outfit and plastic booties on her feet, which were each stuck in different directions.

Walking carefully around the edge of the display, the male officer played a flashlight over the scene. The beam revealed a bloody knife still in the woman's grip. Her eyes were open and still, her mouth agape.

A second beam joined the first as the female officer crouched beside the man and swung her light from the body to the other faces in the scene.

A blonde girl, sitting upright, her hair perfect, tiny glasses perched on her nose as she held a stack of books against her chest.

Another girl, this one with red hair and freckles, ski goggles on her head, her body encased in a fluffy down ski suit.

The dolls were at perfect forty-five-degree angles to the dead woman, one beside a plastic tin of cupcakes, the other smiling toward the officers, her eyes glassy, head slightly cocked to one side.

"This was called in as a suicide?" the female officer asked, sweeping her flashlight back to the woman's body.

"Yep."

"Detectives are going to have a field day with this one." She stood, then glanced over her shoulder at the others. "Welcome to the party."

CHAPTER 85

GRANT

The next hour passed in a blur. The detective showed up, along with the president of the Brighton Estate's homeowner association and their head of security. I had to go through my story again, then stood by as an officer placed calls to Mandolin's and Bridget's parents, who handled the news in markedly different fashions. Mandolin's parents said their nanny would be over shortly to collect her, while Bridget's mother stated that she needed to call their attorney and that she was going to record the phone call.

I hadn't yet brought up the Folcrum murders and wasn't sure how and when to. I needed to keep my mouth shut, and I needed to call an attorney. The latter was made more difficult by the fact that I still didn't have my phone and was lost without its list of contacts.

The detective arrived, a short man with bright-red hair who introduced himself as Hal Heinwright but said I could call him Hal.

I didn't want to call him Hal. I was going on my third day without more than an hour of sleep, and I was exhausted and neurotic enough that confessing everything was starting to sound like a good idea. I needed to get to Sophie and get us both somewhere quiet and private.

I walked over to Hal, who was resting his forearms on the hood of his unmarked car, a coffee cup between his hands. He straightened at my approach and stopped whatever he was saying to the CSI beside him. "Hi, Grant. What's up?"

"If I could use a phone, I'd like to call an attorney. Just want to make sure I'm not doing anything wrong."

He pursed his lips. "Sure, of course." He unclipped a cell phone from his belt. "Use mine." He unlocked the screen and passed it to me.

Paul Reachen. Bill's recommendation was imprinted in my mind, and I googled his name, pleased to see an emergency contact number on his website. I glanced at the sky, which was just starting to gain light, dawn still at least an hour out, and initiated the call. I didn't have time to wait. I needed someone here, to act as a barrier between me and a confession.

They had already shown me the evidence on Paige's phone. Dozens and dozens of text messages I had never seen and certainly had not created. Nothing horrible, but a lot of back-and-forth communication I'd never been aware of, all with a flirty tone I abhorred.

Most damning, there was a call from my phone to Paige's at 1:14 a.m. She had answered it, but the line had been dead. "I" had immediately followed up the calls with a series of incriminating texts.

Everything is going wrong. I need you to come to the house.

Did you get this?

Come A.S.A.P.

The front door may be unlocked, if not, use your code.

Please be quiet and meet me in Sophie's room. Perla is asleep. Hurry.

My stomach had dropped at the precise *A.S.A.P.*, which was exactly how I always typed it, with spaces and periods in place. Someone—a forensic expert on the stand—would point that out. Use it to prove that I was the one who had sent the communication.

What had Perla planned for when Paige got here? To kill her? Or to frame me and Paige for the crime?

The call to Paul Reachen rang, and whatever part of me had felt guilty retreated a little farther into my chest.

CHAPTER 86

GRANT

I was working the scene with Shirley Priest, and she was the one who noticed that something was strange about the scene. I mean, more strange than just dead bodies and a creepy setup. She picked up on the twelfth-birthday cake, which I guess was identical to the one that was at the Folcrum Party crime scene. And I shrugged it off because lots of twelve-year-olds have chocolate cakes. But she kept finding things that she thought were the same, so we called into the office and had them pull the file, and sure enough, they were like twins of each other. A rich twin and a poor twin, but yeah. Twins in terms of setting, at least. The bodies didn't match up.

—Ethan Way, crime scene technician

It had been hours, and the detectives were still here. Once the house had been cleared and the EMTs had verified Perla was already deceased, a large number of them had left, but the forensic teams were still working, and her body was still inside.

Now the sun was beginning to peek over the tips of the oaks, bathing the house in a warm golden light. The rays shone off the copper porch railings, and I thought of Perla's insistence on the material even though the price had been exorbitant.

We'd have to sell the house. I wasn't sure I could even sleep in it again, not with the awareness of what could have and did happen. I closed my eyes and ticked through where we could go tonight. A hotel seemed cold, but maybe there was a vacation rental somewhere close, somewhere we could stay for a few weeks until we sorted things out.

"Mr. Wultz?" I turned to see Detective Heinwright approaching, his face tight. My chest instantly seized at what it could be.

"Yes?"

"We need to talk to you about your sister and her connection to all of this."

Well, that hadn't taken them long. I rubbed my fingers across my lips, then spoke. "I'd like to wait for my attorney to arrive first. He's on his way."

Detective Heinwright regarded me for a long moment, and it was in that moment when we crossed to opposite sides of the line. He held the stare long enough to make sure I felt it, then nodded. "Yeah, I thought you might say that."

It sounded like a challenge of my innocence, but I didn't refute it.

CHAPTER 87

At the prison, we didn't have any idea what had happened at the Wultz house. I was on my rounds and passed Leewood's cell at 4:42 a.m., and spotted him on the floor of his cell, struggling to breathe. At that time, his skin had turned blue, and he had defecated himself. I immediately called it in, and we moved him into the med bay, who then transferred him to hospice.

—Lawrence Booth, Lancaster Prison corrections officer

The word spread through the neighborhood like a virus, one initiated and fed by Julie Scott, who didn't wait until dawn to start calling her friends. By the time the sun cleared the tree line, there was a crowd of neighbors huddled in our cul-de-sac, their invasion held at bay by a line of officers and sawhorse barricades.

It was the most excitement Brighton Estates had ever seen, and the rumors were swirling, with everything from a heart attack to a sex party gone wrong to a cannibalistic ritual. The preteens were still asleep, their slumber at risk of interruption by Julie Scott, who had opened the door to their room, peered in, then loudly shut it at regular intervals over the last three hours.

Bridget's parents were now in the Scotts' living room, their attorneys on speakerphone, possible legal strategies being discussed and initial filings being prepared. Everyone was a possible defendant, including the Scotts, though they had held off that discussion until the couple had gone outside to mingle with the growing crowd.

Bill was outlining the entire thing in his mind as a novel and envisioning this as the launchpad for his writing career. This had *big book deal* written all over it, especially if he could dress up the facts a little bit. Sophie, for example, should be pregnant, and maybe the nanny and Perla had been engaged in a salacious affair, one that Sophie had discovered. Grant was the guilty party, clearly, and had probably been embezzling funds from his employer while hiding a gambling problem and a growing debt with some unforgiving Italians. It would come out in hardback, and a book tour would be needed, along with a snazzy headshot for the back cover. Maybe he should wear the fedora that he'd bought at that Panama hat store in Key West, a purchase Julie had protested over but would finally see the value of now.

If any neighbors had been unaware of Grant Wultz's tragic family history prior to this morning, they had since been briefed in full, and theories spread among the early-morning dog walkers and lookie-loos. Phones were pulled out and Wikipedia articles read aloud as facts about the Folcrum Party murder were shared and then hypothesized about. It didn't take long for connections to be made between last night's event and Jenny Folcrum's twelfth-birthday party, and the excitement rose to a new fervor.

This was almost better than a cannibal ritual or sex party. A tie to one of the most famous murders in history, happening right here inside their jeweled enclave.

Another hour passed, and the first of the media trucks arrived at the neighborhood's guard gate, where their access was blocked. They parked on the road's shoulder, one stacking beside another, until the entire entrance road was paved in them. Like a sea of locusts, drones popped into the air above the news vans and then buzzed over the gates and toward the Wultz home.

CHAPTER 88

Detective Heinwright stood on the second floor of the Wultz home and tried to understand what was going on.

The coroner's stretcher was in the hall, Perla's body on top of it, her body bag half-unzipped. He stood a few feet from the bag and looked at her face, thinking.

The coroner, a woman with bushy eyebrows and a southern accent he had always found irresistible, came out of the bedroom, a blue-and-white-plaid face mask on. "Good morning," Hazel Grooms said cheerfully.

"Not the best I've had," he said, watching as she zipped up the body bag, then pulled her face mask down to her chin. "What time'd you get the call?"

"Around three thirty. Nature of the beast. People don't like to die during business hours. Especially like this." She patted the bag with something akin to affection.

"What's your gut tell you about the scene?"

Hazel laughed. "Oh, it's a mess of one. I don't envy you your job, that's for damn sure. But in terms of the vic, this one's an exciting one."

"You mean the cut throat?" He shrugged. "Not the first I've seen."

"No, not that." Her blue eyes twinkled. "Put a pair of gloves on; you're going to want to see this."

Intrigued, he reached into the pocket at the top of the gurney and withdrew a set, then pulled them on his wide hands. Nodding at her, he gestured for her to continue.

Unzipping the bag, she parted it so that he could clearly see Perla Wultz's face. The brunette was pretty, but in an unconventional way. Her nose was perfect and straight, her mouth full, skin smooth—but her jawline was a bit too square, her angles a bit too harsh. The image was also marred by the blood, which was all over her lips and chin, the wound of her neck slash gaping open in a way that made her look practically decapitated.

He grimaced, but Hazel's smile grew even wider. She crooked her finger, beckoning him closer. "Feel this." She reached into the open cut and probed the incision. "Here." Grabbing his hand in hers, she pressed it against the inside of the wound.

"I don't know if—" He stopped, understanding what she was trying to show him. "Right here?" he asked, running his fingers back and forth over the thick ridge.

"Yeah. You know what that is?"

"No." He pulled his hand free as soon as she released it, slightly nauseous by the sight, much less the feel of it.

"It's scar tissue. Same angle, same area. Old, old scar tissue, probably from a decade ago, maybe longer."

"Meaning what?" She couldn't be saying that . . . But her brow raised in a knowing way that made him second-guess his doubt.

"Meaning that this isn't the first time she'd had her throat cut." Her mouth curved in a cocky smile. "Seen that before, big boy?"

CHAPTER 89

GRANT

Attorney Paul Reachen was on the property within fifteen minutes of my call. He was in a 49ers jersey and jeans, two coffees in hand, and started lecturing me the minute he got me off to one side. We took a seat on the left side of the front porch, and I sipped the coffee and wondered when, if ever, I would get a chance to sleep.

"Okay, I got too much shit that doesn't make sense, so I'm going to need you to start talking." Detective Heinwright strode up the steps of the porch.

Paul stopped midsentence and turned to glare at him. "We're in the middle of something here, Hal."

"Yeah, and while I respect your process, I got just a few quick questions for Grant, and then I'll be out of your hair. It's up to you if you want him to answer them, but just let me spitball them over before we waste any more time licking our own assholes."

Paul smiled despite himself. "Okay . . ." he said slowly. "Grant, don't answer any question until I approve it, understand?"

I nodded and the effort of just moving my head felt herculean at this point.

"Do you know how Perla's throat got cut? I don't mean tonight—I mean in the past?"

Whatever Paul was expecting Heinwright to ask, that wasn't it. He recoiled, then looked sharply at me. "You don't need to answer that, Grant."

"Yes," I said.

"*Wait,*" Paul commanded. "Hal, let me talk to my client—"

"It's okay." I spoke over him. "Perla's real name is Jenny Folcrum. She had her name changed when she was a teenager, after the—"

"Holy shit," Heinwright swore. "You married Jenny *Folcrum*? You're telling me that you married little Jenny fucking Folcrum? Lucy Wultz's brother? And no one knows about this? This stayed out of the press?"

Paul himself seemed speechless, and they both stared at me as if I had grown a third arm and won the Olympics. It was the first time anyone had reacted to the news—the first time anyone knew the truth other than Perla's adoptive parents and, more recently, Leewood Folcrum. Even my parents hadn't known Perla's true origins, and they would have certainly detested the connection if they had discovered it.

"Yes," I said.

"Holy shit," Heinwright repeated. "This is going to be a media shitstorm."

"I think she—Perla, Jenny—was trying to recreate the murders. I think that's why she freaked out when she got back into the room and discovered they weren't there. And that's what she meant when she said that she was finishing what had been started. That if she couldn't kill them, that she'd at least kill herself and finish what had been . . . left open last time." I grimaced.

"Stop talking, Grant," Paul ordered, though I don't see how it hurt me to tie the strings together, just in case the detective missed them. "Just stop." He turned to Heinwright. "You got what you need, right? I need to get this guy to bed. He's got a funeral to plan and a young girl to break this news to."

"Sure—just one last thing." Heinwright lifted his chin at me, catching my attention.

"Nope," Paul said. "That's it."

"Are you keeping anything from me, Grant? Any other giant tidbits of information that could be holding up our investigation?"

"Don't answer that," Paul said sharply. "Come on, Hal. I'm getting him out of here." He stood between us and waved his arms like he was trying to flag down a plane.

I met Heinwright's eyes but didn't answer the question. I held his gaze for a long moment, then looked away, letting Paul push me off the porch and toward his SUV.

CHAPTER 90

SOPHIE WULTZ

The true-crime community exploded that morning. It went beyond the podcasts and the vloggers and the Reddit threads. We were getting calls from *Good Morning America* and the *New York Times*. Before, we had been pretty much shunned by so-called 'real press'—but since we'd been the contact for the TFK emailer—that stands for 'the Folcrum Killer,' by the way—we were suddenly on everyone's wish list. Gabrielle and I were flying first-class to New York to interview with *The View*, but then her phone rang, and it was little Sophie Wultz. And that, honestly, is what took us to another hemisphere of fame.

—*Rachel,* Murder Unplugged

They'd arrested my dad that morning. Paul said it wouldn't happen, that he'd take care of it, but now he was behind bars and I was at Mandolin's house, and everyone was having whispered conversations they didn't think I could hear about where I'd end up living now that I was basically an orphan.

I was in Mandolin's backyard, kicking a soccer ball against their racquetball-court wall, when Paige showed up. She didn't even go through their house; she slipped around the edge, and I liked that immediately. It was like she knew where I'd be.

Paige didn't say anything at the beginning. She just walked up next to me and put in a cross kick, sending the ball toward the wall. I jogged forward, using the edge of my foot to punt it back, and we worked in silent tandem for several minutes.

She had been under investigation, but unlike my dad, she had been cleared. I tried not to hold it against her but my irritation simmered, and I kicked out harder than necessary.

"Did you pour sugar in my gas tank?"

The question caught me so off guard that I missed the ball altogether. "What?" I turned to her, my chest heaving a little from the exertion.

"Did you pour sugar in my car's gas tank?"

"Why would I do that?" I was so confused, especially because of the way she was staring at me. It wasn't an angry look; it was like I was a puzzle she was trying to solve.

"What about the tacks in the kitchen?"

I swiped some of my hair away from my face. "I have no idea what you're talking about."

She looked toward Mandolin's house, which was like twice the size of ours. If they did adopt me, there'd be plenty of room, but I didn't want to live here. I wanted to be back home with my dad.

"I think your mom was fucking with us."

Despite myself, I grinned at the curse word, which she didn't apologize for or wince at. "That sounds about right. Mom liked to fuck with people." I didn't feel guilty saying it. It was the truth, and I had never minded it, given that her actions typically benefited us.

"The evidence against your dad . . . it's mostly electronic. Text messages . . . emails. That sort of thing. Mostly at night. Just like a few texts I once got from you. Weird texts." She was still staring at me, like I

319

knew something she didn't. I kept my mouth shut, waiting to see where she was going with this.

Then she asked something I really didn't expect, something that made me stand stick straight with interest. "How do you feel about talking to your grandfather?"

CHAPTER 91

LEEWOOD FOLCRUM

INMATE 82145

My daughter doesn't ask for much, so when Paige wanted
to get cleared for her and the Wultz kid to get a visitation
with Leewood, I did it. Yeah, I got some kickback for it,
but you gotta do what you can do for your kids. I haven't
given her shit else in this life.

—*William Smith, Lancaster Prison corrections officer*

The two girls came to my hospital room. I knew something was up
when officers brought handcuffs in and cinched me to the bed. I could
barely roll over to shit, so the security measures were unneeded.

I studied the officer latching the cuffs. "What's up?" I asked.

"Got a visitor. Two. Behave with them, or I'll come back in here
and pull the plug on you myself," he said gruffly, and I didn't bother
telling him I wasn't on life support.

"Cops?" I asked, moving my wrist in a position to give him better
access.

"Nope." He pointed to a camera in the corner of the room. "This isn't your attorney, and you aren't in a visitation room, so be aware that this won't be private. You got ears and eyes on you." He checked the lock, then opened the door, waving someone through. I tried to straighten up in the bed and failed. Looking for the controls, I saw the incline button, but it was just out of reach. Fuck.

Two girls entered, and I'm shit at ages, but the brunette looked to be in college. The blonde was Jenny's age when I last saw her, and my breath caught in my throat when our gazes connected.

Even without the photo Grant had shown me, I would have known. I would have recognized Jenny's child anywhere. She had the same crooked nose. The same sharp, intelligent eyes. The same Cupid's bow–shaped mouth.

"Hey, Lee." She smiled, and my own mouth trembled as a wave of emotion and grief hit me. I tried to respond, but instead started to weep.

———

I told them everything, a final confession of my soul. I didn't care about the cameras and I didn't share that I had told Grant the truth—I just told them what had happened the night of the party and that I hadn't spoken to Jenny since the night I was arrested.

I already knew that Jenny had died—that news had made it to the prison, and I spoke freely about the past, no longer bound to keep her secrets.

I didn't tell them my opinion of what had supposedly happened to Jenny. There was no way my daughter took her own life. I suspected Grant—but to be honest, I didn't give a damn how it had happened. What mattered was that this little girl was okay. Hopefully, history wouldn't repeat itself and put Grant in prison for her crime. If it did, he'd do the time, and without bitching. You did what you had to do to protect your children.

They stayed almost an hour. At the end, the blonde—Sophie—gave me a kiss on the cheek, and I gripped her hand for a long moment, my waterworks springing back to life.

Then they walked out, my vision blurry as I watched them leave, and I realized I didn't even know who the brunette was or why she had tagged along.

CHAPTER 92

GRANT

Our investigation took a bit of a wandering path because so many things just didn't line up. It was like an onion, with more layers and people and different stories the more we peeled things back. We had all this evidence that seemed to point to him plotting to kill the girls . . . but then the girls were safe, and the wife was dead. It was a clusterfuck, pardon my French. We finally got enough to arrest him, but I didn't like it.

—*Detective Hal Heinwright, Pasadena Police Department*

I was in general population for eighteen hours, which was the closest to hell I've ever been. I tried to keep to myself, but I stood out, and that wasn't a good thing. I had a black eye and a swollen jaw, and I was missing a front tooth by the time they moved me into solitary confinement.

At least in prison, I could see and understand the dangers. In my marriage, I had been in a Venus flytrap of hell, stepping in booby traps right and left, completely ignorant to them all.

I wasn't sure I was going to get out of this, and it was terrifying to think of the fact that I was minutes away from being in this same situation, but with three dead victims, including my daughter. In that alternative scenario, Perla would have still been alive and vomiting out all sorts of bullshit to the cops. It would have buried me. I was having a hard enough time keeping my head aboveground with all the existing "evidence" against me.

I'd always known my wife was smart, but I hadn't realized she was evil. My cell phone was recovered from Perla's pocket, along with hers. Mine had a long litany of internet searches for "Folcrum murder," "send untraceable emails," "how to drug someone," and dozens of other incriminating topics. All the searches had been made in the middle of the night, the histories quickly cleared without any time spent in the browser results, and Paul thinks we can prove that the phone events were part of Perla's attempt to set me up, not actual searches on my part.

My phone had also turned off the security cameras, but one of the Scotts' had captured a thin dressed-in-black figure punching in a gate code just before the madness started. That was where Perla had gone. To enter Paige's code in an attempt to place her at the scene. That video is another point in my favor, but I'm not sure it's enough.

The picture the prosecution was painting of me didn't make sense. I'd supposedly been in cahoots with someone who fancied themselves the original Folcrum Party killer—they won't agree that he was involved in the original crime—and me and that killer had teamed up to kill Perla and decorate the crime scene to resemble the Folcrum Party.

It's ridiculous . . . but as a scientist, I could agree that the data points connected.

My "growing relationship" with the nanny. Flirty texts. Requests for her to purchase identical items (like the cupcakes) from the original scene. The frantic texts the night of the crime.

My emails with this TFK guy. There weren't many, but they created another dataset of support.

"My" rule that Sophie could only have two friends at the party. Why had I let her communicate it to Sophie as my directive?

And lastly, my visits to Leewood. I'd screwed myself with those. They had been harmless at the time, but now . . . given this angle the police had adopted . . . they looked like I had been collaborating with him. Plotting, with my visits increasing in frequency until right before the party.

The thing was . . . Perla had expected to kill the three girls, and all her setup of me was designed to point to that goal. It was a small flaw, but it was there and supported my story that she had planned to frame me, gone to kill the girls, discovered they were missing, and killed herself.

At least, to me it supported the story. And it wasn't just that angle of logic that was on my side.

Sophie, Bridget, and Mandolin had blood work and urine tests done, with results that tested positive for Ambien. They all stated that I hadn't given them anything to eat, that everything had been served by Perla.

Even though they'd found texts from my phone instructing Paige to buy a Ouija board, playing cards, and cupcakes, my fingerprints weren't on any of the items.

A psychiatrist had stepped forward, revealing that Perla had visited her thirteen times in the last three months and had been increasingly critical and suggestive of the possibility of me having an affair with the nanny and also an obsession with the Folcrum Party. The doctor's suspicions about Perla's intentions had grown, and she had categorized her as narcissistic and a potential sociopath, though she had not shared either diagnosis with Perla.

And there was the call from the soccer academy, who shared that Perla had told them that Sophie was dead, weeks before the night of her party. It wasn't proof of intent, but it was a strike against her and evidence that my wife was batshit crazy.

My defense wasn't ironclad, but there were enough things that—if this made it to a jury trial—could cast reasonable doubt. No one could prove that I had my hand on Perla's when the knife dragged across her throat. No one could prove that I'd done anything other than witness a horrible event.

The psychiatrist's diagnosis irked me, and it was embarrassing that a stranger had seen the truth in Perla when I hadn't. Granted, Dr. Maddox was professionally trained, but still. I had seen enough evidence of Perla's lack of empathy, cruel behavior, and manipulation that I should have realized the dangers, or at least been more aware than I was. Instead, I let my affection and attachment to Lucy's memory trigger this ideology that, by loving and taking care of Perla, I was, by extension, giving those things to Lucy.

The thought was ridiculous, but one that had fed more than a decade of marriage to a woman who had stabbed my sister over a dozen times and watched her bleed to death.

I didn't regret killing my wife. I regretted not doing it sooner. I regretted that it took the endangerment of my daughter in order for me to take action.

"Wultz." A guard unlocked the cell door and gestured for me. "You have a visitor."

CHAPTER 93

SOPHIE WULTZ

Leewood Folcrum passed two days after the visit of Sophie Wultz and Paige Smith. His personal effects were collected by Wally Nall, except for a package of papers that he left for Sophie Wultz. No funeral was held, and he was cremated and interred in the Lancaster Prison cemetery.

—*Alex Boyton, Lancaster Prison warden*

My mother once told me that a lie only mattered if the side effects did. She was right about that, as she was about most things. After today, people would say horrible things about my mother, but she was right about most things. Like being famous. I once told her that I wanted to be an influencer, and she told me that it was better to be famous for doing something rather than being someone.

After all this, I've become famous. I didn't realize I was until Mandolin and I stepped out of her father's car at the mall and two photographers rushed forward to take my photos and scream a bunch of questions at me. I didn't answer any of them. I looked around for Paige, and she came around the back of the car and screamed at them to get away.

Paige now lives in one of the bedrooms in the Contis' employee house. It's at the back of their property and is where Mandolin's nanny and their housekeeper and chef live. I'm paying for Paige's costs. Dad transferred a bunch of money into my savings account, and the banker came to the house with a bunch of forms and brought me a debit card and a bunch of checks and told me to just use those for anything I need. Mandolin's mom—her name is Gia—told me how much to write it for and showed me how to fill it out to Paige.

Anyway, I digress. That's a new word I learned this week. Gia uses it all the time. Best I can tell, it means that I've gotten off topic. The point of this entry is that right now, I'm famous for being the daughter of Perla and Grant Wultz. No one really knows much about the fact that my mom was trying to kill me (or Mand or Bridget), which is why no one cares about taking their pictures.

I'm famous for who I am, not what I've done. But that will change in two hours. That's when I'm going on television. I told them that I'm going to share the truth about my mother.

And I'll do that. I'll tell the truth in the way that my mother taught me. A way paved in lies.

CHAPTER 94

GRANT

We tried to get a statement from Leewood Folcrum before he passed, but we couldn't get anything from him. We had to go live without a statement from him or Grant Wultz, whose attorney had him on a no-contact gag order. So really, all we—or America, in general—had to go on was what little twelve-year-old Sophie Wultz had to say. And that, of course, was a doozy.

—*Neil McArthur, broadcast journalist*

"I don't understand how this happened. Who set this up?" I spun the small touchpad screen toward me, watching a video of my daughter walking across a stage and taking a seat across from Neil McArthur. The journalist smiled, and I was surprised his teeth weren't fangs. He was going to destroy her. Dig and berate until she was in tears. This was going to be terrible, both for her psyche but also for our case. Sophie didn't realize how much one line, one little bit of information, could sink me. "She's twelve. Doesn't she need parental permission for this?"

Paul Reachen shook his head grimly. "This isn't with the police or the courts. She's speaking publicly. She can do that however she wants. Doesn't matter if it's being recorded. As long as she doesn't defame someone, she's not breaking any laws."

There was someone else with her, a thin young woman with gaunt cheeks. A strip across the bottom of the screen introduced her as Rachel Goodsmith, from a podcast called *Murder Unplugged*.

I rubbed my hand across my face, wincing when I touched the tender ridge of my nose. "Can you try to call her?"

He didn't say anything, and we both knew how futile a phone call would be at this point. We were lucky he'd caught wind of this in time to get to the jail and get me in a private visitation room. That was something I hadn't expected, all those times I met with Leewood. That one day, I would be on the inmate side of the table.

Sophie had moved past the introductions, and they were now showing a photo of her and Perla, one that had just been taken a week or so earlier by the private photographer Perla had hired. We'd never had a professional photo shoot before, and it was just another example of a red flag I had missed. *Stand here, Grant. Smile. Put your arm around me. Dance, monkey. Dance.*

"Tell us about your mother, Sophie," Neil urged.

"A lot has been said about my mom this last week." She fidgeted, her hands rolling over each other in her lap. Nervousness was a look I had never seen on my daughter. Not before a dentist appointment, not before a piano recital or a penalty shot in an important game. I frowned, trying to understand it. "I thought it was important that I tell you about the person I knew."

"Oh, this is not what we need," Paul muttered.

"Just wait," I said, curious about what Sophie was about to say.

My daughter turned to the camera and took a deep breath before she spoke. "My mother was wonderful in a lot of ways. She was a lot of fun. She taught me things constantly. She pushed me to succeed and showed me how to be a strong female and stand my ground and demand the best."

"Yeah, a regular Margaret Thatcher," Paul drawled.

"Do you realize that your father is trying to paint your mother as a murderer? He says that she *killed* her friends when she was your age and had planned to *kill* you and your friends at your party!" Neil hunched forward, and every time he said the word *kill*, his voice rose in skepticism. I wanted to *kill* him.

"My mom did kill her friends." She looked into the camera, and now there was no sign of her nerves. Her face was calm, her eyes steady. "And I have no doubt that she would have killed me, if she'd had the chance."

Whatever Neil had been expecting, this wasn't it. He paused, looked down at his notes, then back at her. "You say that with such authority. Why do you think that?"

"Because it wasn't the first time she tried to hurt me." She pressed her lips together tightly, as if she were close to tears, then inhaled and looked into the camera again. "When I was eight, she tried to drown me in the bathtub. I was clawing at her, screaming under the bubbles, when our housekeeper heard the noise and came in the bathroom. She stopped, and she pulled me out of the water and held me against her chest, and I was screaming and crying, and she told Ana—that was our housekeeper—to go away, to leave us alone, but she whispered in my ear that she would kill me if I didn't stop crying. And when she tucked me in that night, she told me that she'd do it again, would drown me in the pool if I ever told anyone about it. And her eyes . . ." Sophie visibly shivered and she hesitated, then started again. "She would get this look in her eyes sometimes. Like she was dead. Like no matter what you said or did, you couldn't get through to her, you couldn't change her mind. That was the look on her face. Both when she pushed me underwater and when she promised to kill me if I talked."

Paul turned to me. "Did you know about this?"

I shook my head but didn't trust myself to speak. I hadn't known about it because it didn't happen. Not that I would put it past Perla, but it didn't happen. And no one would be able to confirm or disprove it with Ana because she was back in Honduras. I looked into the screen, staring into my daughter's beautiful face, and could swear that the corner of her mouth twitched into the hint of a smile.

Maybe this would do it. I looked from her smile to Paul's face. He was grinning, and I felt my own lips curve in response.

CHAPTER 95

SOPHIE WULTZ

Tech traced the TFK emails best they could. Majority were
sent from an anonymous email and a private VPN server,
but one email—the second to last one that was sent—
wasn't encoded, and we traced it to the Wultz home IP
address. We found it unlikely Grant was sending emails
to himself from two different accounts, so that was just
another big arrow that pointed to Perla's culpability.

—*Detective Hal Heinwright, Pasadena Police Department*

Today they're releasing Dad from jail. Paul got the DA to dismiss the
charges, and while we are probably going to be back in court, thanks
to Bridget's litigious parents, it will be for a civil suit, and nothing that
would put Dad back in jail.

I'm going to live stream his release and add it to the socials I set up
in his name. Turns out, my dad is almost as famous as me. Apparently,
he's hot, according to all the comments and fan clubs that have sprung
up. He's not. He has gray hair already and farts if he eats ice cream.
Also, according to Paul, he's a little beat up, but that's okay. It'll make
for good footage.

I'm certain that as soon as we are away from the cameras and alone, he's going to lecture me on my lies to the cops and Neil McArthur. And yeah, I lied. I had to because Dad needed to get out of jail and I know Mom would have killed us because I was on the balcony the whole time, watching it happen. I saw her walking toward our bed with the knife and I saw my father stop her.

If he starts to get too self-righteous, I'll tell him that. I'll tell him that I lied because I had to. Just like he killed Mom because he had to.

We'll see what he has to say in response to that.

I don't blame him for it. I would have killed her too. I know it's easy for someone to say that, but even in my half-drugged state, I could understand the threat, and I also knew my mom—just like Dad did. If you kicked her down, stood in the way between her and something . . . she'd raise HELL to destroy your life while completing the journey to her goal.

So he did what was needed to be done. But I couldn't have him locked away behind bars. He's too soft for that. There are no birds in prison.

He did what needed to be done, so I did the same.

I measured the side effects, then I made the decision and I lied.

Honestly, Mom would have been proud.

CHAPTER 96

GRANT

Three Weeks Later

We're finally leaving the house where all this took place. Sophie and I have each packed a single suitcase. Her dolls, her books, her furniture, her clothes . . . it's all staying, as is everything else Perla and I collected over the course of our marriage. Sophie has her journal, and I have my bird-watching book. We have our toothbrushes, a few changes of clothes, and enough money in our account to move anywhere in the world we want to live.

Two decades ago, George and Janice started a whole life insurance policy in Perla's name. They paid premiums on it until their death, and the equity continued making payments on the policy after that. I wasn't aware of it, and we don't exactly need the payout, so I put the $3 million into a trust account for Sophie, which will be accessible on her thirtieth birthday.

I quit my job, leaving the team in a bit of a lurch, but I couldn't think about statistical anomalies or database infrastructure, not with everything that had happened.

Today, we're setting out in a thirty-two-foot RV, driving across the US, and seeing what part of the country fits our fancy. By the time we find a place, Perla's apartment complexes and our house will have sold, and all ties to California will be gone.

"Okay, I'm ready." My daughter climbs into the passenger seat and smiles at me. I'm not comfortable with what she did to get me out of jail. But I can't argue with her results. In addition to the bathtub-drowning attempt, she told a few other stories . . . small things, but when combined with Paige's accounts, they all helped to exonerate me and incriminate Perla.

On our way out of town, our first stop will be Lancaster Prison, where we will pick up a package that Leewood left for Sophie. She's very excited by this and has mentioned on several occasions that she wants to write a book about Leewood's story and "what really happened" at the Folcrum Party.

I'm sure it will be a bestseller. A bestseller inked in and paid for by blood. I've tried to talk her out of it, but she got her stubborn streak from Perla.

I'm terrified she got something else. Maybe her mother's love of lies? Maybe her detachment? Her broken moral compass or her need for attention, damn the costs?

It's probably just paranoia, but I'll be watching my daughter very closely. Looking for the clues that I missed in her mother. Working every day to try to show her the importance of honesty, kindness, and humility.

It's not lost on me that I have more in common with Leewood than I ever dreamed possible. I sat across from him for hours, judging him with such contempt—yet I'm not sure how different we really were. He was a single father and a widower, just like me. Both of us loved, and then tried to kill, the same woman. Both acts spurred by a fatherly duty. And we both were locked up as a result. I got free; he did not.

There is a common occurrence in birds when a young bird is killed by its parent or sibling. It generally occurs when resources are scarce, and is a strategy to reduce their competition. Some parents encourage it, while others prevent it. A parent's likelihood to participate in infanticide or encourage siblicide is often based on cost and effect, and can be broken down into an algebraic equation, where the level of parental investment in an entire brood is given an absolute maximum value and could calculate a measure of future reproductive success, based on that value and the cost of reproduction.

We didn't have an entire brood in which to gauge our level of effort and dismissal. Sophie had no competition for our resources. There is no mathematical equation to explain why Perla thought she was expendable, or that the removal of her from our lives would strengthen or improve them in any way.

"Dad." Sophie gestures impatiently for me to put the RV into gear. "We getting this show on the road or what?"

I love her so much it hurts. I would kill for her again and serve a lifetime behind bars if it means keeping her safe. I am a peregrine falcon, claws out, ready to take on any predator and fight to the death to protect my young.

"Yeah." I put my foot on the brake and pull the gearshift into Drive. "Let's get out of here."

Acknowledgments

This section of the novel is where I give thanks to all who helped with this book. Buckle in—this one was a doozy.

First, its creation was in no small part thanks to Megha Parekh, my fearless editor, who has not managed to fire me yet, despite my repeated attempts to stress her out by turning in books that are very different from what I have promised her. I promise, Megha, it's not intentional. I am passionately excited about an idea when I sit down to write . . . the characters just don't always get the same memo. This character, from the very beginning, took my mind and dragged it down a winding path of insanity, one I enjoyed every twist and turn of. Megha, thank you for your continual support, cheerleading, patience, and understanding for the mental gymnastics of my creative process. I sincerely appreciate all that you do for me.

To Maura Kye-Casella, my agent. It's been a wonderful decade, and I look forward to another ten years, another dozen books, and more dinners and experiences together. Fingers crossed I can be back in New York soon.

Occasionally I borrow names from real individuals, and this book finally gave me the opportunity to bring Wally Nall to life on the page. The real Wally Nall is a true southern gentleman and nothing like the gun-toting redneck in this book, but I knew that his sense of humor would embrace this character. Thank you for letting me use your name, and for your friendship and support. A big thanks to Kathy and Mat as well—your characters are coming soon.

Susan Barnes, thank you for squeezing this book into your editorial calendar and giving it an early look. Your insights helped in some powerful ways, and as always, I appreciate your honest feedback and ideas. For anyone looking for a wordsmithing genius, I highly suggest her talents.

To Charlotte Herscher, another extraordinarily talented developmental editor, who has now carried me through *Every Last Secret*, *The Good Lie*, *A Familiar Stranger*, *A Fatal Affair*, AND *The Last Party* . . . thank you for yet another fantastic experience. You understand my voice and my mind so well and provide such fantastic suggestions and ideas—I love working with you and elevating these stories with every single draft. Thank you for your flexibility, dealing with my squishy deadlines, and never being afraid to consider a new direction, ending, or draft.

To Rachel Norfleet, copyeditor; Kellie Osborne, proofreader; and Steve Schul, cold reader: Thank you for taking this manuscript from rough to smooth—you spotted errors I was blind to, smoothed over rough spots in my writing, and kept me from making a fool of myself in so many different places. You are the behind-the-scene magicians, and I really appreciate the care and diligence you used with this novel. To the talented designer Shasti O'Leary Soudant: Thank you for creating a cover with just the right mood for this book. It wasn't an easy task, but you pulled it off to perfection.

To the rest of the Thomas & Mercer team—Gracie, Darci, Sarah, and so many more—thank you for all that you do to promote my books, grow my audience, and support my passion.

To my family and the love of my life, Joe—thank you for all the missed moments when I was tucked away writing or up late editing. Thank you for keeping me fed, hydrated, and sane. Thank you for believing in and supporting my writing and for always celebrating the small and big moments with me.

Lastly (but certainly not least!), thank you, dear reader. Thank you for sticking with this roller coaster of a story. It was dark, one of my darkest yet, and I appreciate you trusting me with your time and journeying into the dark recesses of Perla's mind. I hope you enjoyed the journey and hope that you clean your mental palate with something light and funny or deliciously chocolaty and filled with caffeine.

If you'd like to be notified with my writing (and life) updates, please subscribe to my newsletter at www.alessandratorre.com/newsletter.

If this is your first book of mine and you're looking for something similar, I'd suggest *Every Last Secret* or *The Good Lie*. Both have very interesting female heroines and storylines that will keep you guessing.

Thank you again; I appreciate you.

About the Author

Photo © 2022 Jane Ashley Converse

A. R. Torre is a pseudonym for *New York Times* bestselling author Alessandra Torre. Alessandra resides in Key West, Florida, where she spends her free time on the water, roasting coffee, and doing crossword puzzles. In addition to writing, she is the cocreator of Inkers Con, an educational community for more than thirty thousand authors. Learn more at www.alessandratorre.com.